i$UBSCRIBE – C

Love ,

P. B. Flower

Please excuse any editing mistakes.

– PB

PB FLOWER

Taboos, beliefs, and pretense are a projection of fear.

- **PB Flower**

COPYRIGHT

Cover Design E-book & Paperback – PicMonkey
Graphics – PicMonkey

PB FLOWER IS an American-Indian author of several mind-bending and deceptively narrated fiction books. Nashville's rolling hills have been inspiring in bringing PB's dream of becoming a writer to fruition.

PB has forever been intrigued by the creation. Her husband introduced her to U.G. Krishnamurti's way of life, influencing her style. In her writing, she places her conceptions with a sensual spin to keep things grounded and challenge routine perspectives to measure the other side.

Contrasting inquests like Romance, Science, Supernatural, Mythology, and Metaphysics sets PB apart and gives her readers exciting stories to make an impression.

PB's published work:
ALL KAAL NONE - SAC OF SURPÄS Part 1
ALL KAAL NONE - TRIKA ŚŪNYA Part 2
ALL KAAL NONE - KĀMA TRYAMBAKA Part 3
YAMA ECHO MAYA - BATTLE OF THE TWINS

PB's Social Media:
Facebook | PB Flower
Instagram (@pbflower_21)
Twitter (@author_pb)
Amazon.com: PB Flower
Goodreads | P.B. Flower
TIKTOK I author_pbflower
Podcast on Spotify I Author PB Flower
Author PB Flower - YouTube I @authorpbflower9361

INTRODUCTION & WARNING

FIXING A GLITCH ends the possibility of an alien ever realizing his destiny. He resurrects her from her scattered memories. On the way to standardizing her state, he ends the bodily dependency of the human species.

The only trouble is that she is a prime image of his dark but gifted side. One sustains mysticism, and another promotes prosperity.

Trip forward with SamVeer Eckhart into events of a parallel Earth. To find out if he succeeded in his infatuated undertaking.

i$UBSCRIBE – Gen Verismo Genesis is the concluding take from the ALL KAAL NONE series chapter – PHYSICALITY TERMINATION. A back section identifies the other supporting characters in this story from related books. This is a standalone work of fiction and can be read independently.

Exchange – As articulated heavily in my previous work, my metaphysical viewpoint conceptualized another way to communicate – waving. This model is used in this story and is *bolded and italicized* to keep it separate from typical 'thinking' expressions.

Triggers – This story has a radical take on many societal & religious customs. If you are a victim of suicide, rape, incest, or opinionated on the subject of sex workers, please walk away. This book seeks a diverse perspective on such matters.

"You're exceptional," he gave a speculative compliment. "Since you brought it up again. It is the oldest profession."

"Prostitution." My miss-straight-A self was not shocked. "Sex is the easiest of the things to sell," I mumbled.

"There are sellers and buyers in the corporate world as well. LinkIn is the right place to advertise yourself. No different from standing at the corner of a shady street." He doled out every word of the last sentence with sarcasm.

STUFFINGS

1 – INTROSPECT

SAM

MEMORY VALIDATES EXPERIENCES AND DREAMS TOO.

WITH FEW FRIENDS and fewer family members, I led a heavily sheltered life.

Not by choice.

Choices were made for me by my adoptive parents. They never took me outside the urban perimeter, shielding me from the world. As they imposed, I was too sick to go out and play like normal kids. It confused me when I miraculously always healed within a second of getting hurt.

Three months ago, they left with my blood sister for another world. Enjoying this flashback was contradictory to my current flavor. I didn't care for serenity and feelings.

Who was I kidding?

I was bursting with joy.

"Where to, Master Sam?"

Overrun by excitement, I gave an ear-to-ear grin. "Home."

The three-hour drive bared nostalgia to the bone.

Staring out the car window, I admired how this town kept its quaint feel even after ridiculous urbanization. Here, in Village Villas, I spent years skillfully avoiding the crowd by being homeschooled.

It wasn't surprising to find myself in front of a structurally perfect but ill-maintained house. My abandoned stare was admiring the known elevation without a pause.

How long have I been standing here?

Sliding out of my stupor, I noticed thatches of dead weed all over. My assumed father loved tending roses and hated an unkempt lawn. His garden was now full of wildflowers. Most of the toy train tracks he had built for me stood the test of time. That charcoal brick driveway, where I fell repeatedly chasing my friends, was largely intact. The hedges around the premise had grown taller. I played hide n seek there with youngsters still in elementary school.

And that blue door... That was the last thing I saw before I was taken for the unearthly. It was over within a blink of an eye. I had only just turned seven. Shockingly, that was one year ago. At present I am fifteen. Since I completed my schooling with microgravity, time went by faster.

Aging brakes when life passes at a slower pace.

"Would you like to go inside, Master Sam?" Trip sounded maimed.

With a sigh, I dropped my head toward the ground and bobbed a no. "Let's head back."

The house disappearing in the distance behind my million-dollar ride was where I had my soundest memories. Madly conditioned but certified experiences.

I mutely collected my fascination with the past.

The Universe, despite its appearance, was homogeneous. Creation, preservation, and destruction were complete. For the ones thriving within it, it was ongoing. Everything in it logged the constant happenings, similar to a hard disk. Anyone sensitive enough would be aware of them and read them.

I stood to be one such concept of cosmos.

In tandem with my memories, I sensed myriad emotions of my ex-family from it. I decided not to demolish or live in this house that I inherited. There was no need to go in to find out what happened there.

We were a picture-perfect family of four.

I cracked a grin at that impression.

Even after years of hardened training, that soft spot considered human was entirely unbroken.

AGING IS A HARSHER SENSITIVITY TO CHANGE WITH A FEAR OF BECOMING OBSOLETE.

FOR THE WORLD, I was twenty-one. In actuality, I was just eighteen. Notwithstanding that subjective error, I recited the saying, *you are as old as you feel* and settled with it.

As long as I felt like twenty-one, I must be just that.

To reiterate the publicized build-up, I checked my reflection. With this ridiculous suit on, I definitely came off as... mature. I concurred with the plethoric false truth. Fine with me, for I idolized abundance to condemn rarity. Add to that, truth or lies were mere knowledge-driven assessments.

Opinions.

Humans are economical with the truth but wasteful with lies.

Everyone's way of life was tied to the viewpoint of others. A general tone of acceptance was needed to navigate the world as a permissible citizen.

To accrue collective approval of me was now in my radius. After three years of steeled preparation, I was set to debut as a rookie. Not a fish out of the water, though. I had graduated from a distant academy unknown to most. My learning program was at a pace yet to be documented. Calibrated remarkably faster than any of my ancestors. To counterbalance my pillaging superpowers, I was dubbed a submissive savant by my alma mater.

I couldn't disagree more.

"Big day, Sir."

"Trip, call me Sam."

Trip grinned at my lenient attitude.

No one from the aristocratic class ever gave more than the required attention to anyone, let alone their chauffeur. Especially a young, privileged, and inexperienced bloke like me.

Tolerance for the lacking, however, was grand to unwashed masses, as their society was built on divergence. They never stopped to think that to notice anything, one had to have the instilling to identify differences. Seeing others as unlike themselves began the divide.

Acknowledgment, therefore, was the first step of discrimination.

Opening gambit to bias.

Then the act of acceptance reinforced intolerance unknowingly by masking it as being accommodating. There was a chasmic disparity between tolerating and not being aware of the difference.

One was duality, whereas the other was non-dual.

"We might be late." Trip was tripping, respectfully.

We got held up more than usual by the traffic. Since it was morning rush hour in downtown Specter Ville, I didn't whine. By the time we inched closer to the office, it was already 8:55 AM. Leaving me with only five minutes to get to the top of this revolutionary skyscraper. Except I needed not more than a second to be there.

Howbeit, Trip wasn't aware of that.

Getting off in the middle of the packed street, I thanked Trip well and blazed into the future like poetry in motion.

THE METEORIC SPEED of this machinery was dazzling.

Words failed me. Mercifully, I waved.

Who's chasing you, baby?

My Papa developed this Lamborghini of elevators to match the tempo of our kind. Elementally, maintenance-free for an indefinite measure of time.

Swift and superior.

On the hundredth floor, in a room that went throughout the expanse of this building, Uncle Shoor stood flocked by the esteemed lot not very far from the entrance. That champagne flute he eagerly emptied did not belong in his hand this early. Before I could snatch it from him, he gave me a funny smile, clutched my arm, and moved toward the center with the intent to unveil my ushering.

Present me to the world that I already knew everything about.

"Can I have everyone's attention, please?"

Shoor Sherman, my uncle dearest, gave an extra second to the affluent throng to focus on us.

"Please join me in welcoming my primed-to-perfection nephew. A degree in management from the top ivy league college and a three-year internship at my company vouches for his capabilities…."

He was uttering way less than I could consume. His address, embellished with laughable feats, went on for a while. Let's just say that my introduction to the thin crowd of board members and elite stakeholders was poorly painted.

A cock-and-bull story, to be exact.

The human world placed a good amount of weight on duplicitous matters. Dishonesty and such!

Although the audience seemed very well pleased. One, in particular – a beautiful but ripe damsel gave me a look of consent. My shy grin fostered her expert boldness. Age was just a number and understanding the law of attraction was essential to my typhonic future effort.

Bonus, I was a lover of beauty.

Gurgling gregariously, an antique fellow cut short my endeavor to interview that prospective work-flirt.

Pity.

The Cougar was going to have to wait.

"Sam, it's impossible to tell you apart from your father. How is he, and *where* is he?" He elbowed Uncle Shoor, who kept up the faux grin. "Sherman Jr. gives me the slip every time, so I am banking on some answers from you."

This oldie annoyed me to-the-moon-and-back. Shame on me if anyone could catch disappointment on my inscrutable face. In retrospect, age was not just a number but a future prognosis. I would also be old someday.

Motivating my amenable side, I fudged friendliness. "Hello, Mr. Whitworth. I imagine Papa is now on another planet. Adequately enjoying his retirement by destroying stuff."

My response was gut-busting. I was positive that my comedic flair was on par with the other kind, excluding Uncle Shoor. He steered me away from the charmed crowd on a random pretext.

"What are you doing?"

"Networking."

His diminutive outburst was because Mr. Whitworth asked about my Grandfather, not my Papa. As per this world, I was too old to be my father's son.

And yet, too young!

The age difference between my Papa and me was ten years.

Time imprint fucks you up if not chronological.

"I like that you are building a rapport, Sam. But don't forget, you and I are just a head count. Our worth is determined by the monetary impact we make."

"Personal connection is just as much valued, Uncle."

Since I was already aboard the train to destination-disobey-my-only-human-connection. I also non-verbally accused him, blading at his third glass of bubbly. He gave me an eye and left to socialize with the hot shots.

Prior to taking the wormhole, my Papa appointed his best friend, Uncle Shoor, as my Godfather. He dedicated himself to raising me since. Even when I was a grown-ass adult needing no supervision, his loyalty to the lost cause was extraordinary.

I admired Uncle Shoor for that.

Humans are narcissistic and often inflated with a savior complex.

THERE IS PROFICIENCY IN PREPARATION.

PERSISTENCE FOR UNNATURAL was plain stupid. Henceforth, I spent my time refining my inborn gifts.

Swindling of resources… yada yada.

For the next few years, my schedule was stuffed with exploratory trips to every business associated with the company I worked for. The first stop was an elite boarding school in Village Villas – Brazen Academy.

My Papa established it to stage a random meeting with my mother. All due to a powerful sexual appeal. Refining that attraction, he denied being in love with her. Daddy dear also claimed he never lied.

Repeat that, please.

During their time together, Papa cleansed my mother of societal conditioning, putting up a spectacle of tiring patience. Her significance was ingrained in him at a yawning level. He could never unlearn that, just like one can't ever forget how to ride a bicycle.

Knowledge is eternal.

That ripe damsel, Yingling, whom I couldn't pry on during my introduction at work because of Mr. Whitworth, became good friends with me. Turned out she leached on elitists to attend high-end events. A modern-day geisha, not a work flirt. That knowledge gave me a severe despondency attack.

I recovered.

Brazen administration pushed her daughter, Citzin, to the bottom of the admission waiting list for the fifth year. With my help, she got in this time. She and I would be tight as we advance.

But she didn't know that.

What she did know was that her mother was an impostor. No worries, though. The speech I gave to the students was also counterfactual to my learning. Lying was a terrific way to spend my birthday.

Happy birthday to me.

Plus point, I gifted myself Citzin's companionship.

She didn't know that either.

Yingling showered me with adulterous interest, always. In all fairness, her flirty dispositions were essential to attract a suitable match for Citzin.

How else was a single parent with so many desires and a failing youth to survive?

With malice and the likes of it, that's how.

She never introduced me to her daughter, so I called her out on my own after my address. "This year's special quota student, Citzin Perses Hades, is a sophomore and an academic brilliance. It would give me immense pleasure if you could come on stage."

I scoured the crowd, and the young woman that got up was heaven-sent. A shadowy nymph who saw me as her nemesis, except that I'll be the only friend she would ever have.

Downright fascinated by my outer persona, Citzin contrasted fancying me with a sacking attitude. She even thanked me with the most plastic smile ever. Humiliating her left me humored thick and fast. The insult I ministered by calling her a charity case was enough to test the patience of a saint.

She passed.

END OF LIFE IS AN OUTCOME UNCHANGED.
DEATH.

THE JOURNEY WAS a variant to be designed with presented selections making it the fun part. Equivalent to a custom-made home, one had options to shape it as per their liking.

After a handful of torturous years, I finally choreographed an enterprise where my supernatural abilities could triumph.

ZepRive.

This place was space-age but short of the one I had solely inherited – EE-Experimentations or EE-Ex. I was exploiting every inch of that Serpentine Promethean for my personal pleasure.

Like father like son!

I tutted the similarity with gleeful waves.

Every automation at ZepRive was in the gray area with a fuzzy edge. Falling into a twilight zone, one couldn't tell if this was innovation or corruption.

Approximating a nebula in space with the pillars of Creation. A cluster of root elements, air, soil, water, and fire form closely packed regions. Which eventually became dense enough to form stars. The remaining material formed planets and other planetary system objects. Until then, the line to separate their foundation was a blur.

EE-Ex was another story.

Sterling but illicit.

My personal assistant, Maya Moha, issued a vibrant schedule, waking me up from my deep space crusade. Grouching with crabbiness, I soaked in the busy day ahead of me, marching alongside her. She crawled with cuteness in that figure-hugging black skirt suit and rouge lipstick.

With any luck, I hoped that my rivetted outstare was professional.

Hope and luck were ideas that never contaminated destiny. My fortune was ace, advertising designed-to-destroy style vibes. All thanks to my Papa's destructive traits extravagantly passed on to me.

I owe you one.

No. I don't owe anyone anything.

Maya opened the door to Victory Vella's office. This room was clearly too big for one person. Person being the operative word. Except needless extravagance was the hallmark of ZepRive. Victory was sensually qualified for it and much more.

Maya and I took a seat.

"Ready for some real action, Sam?"

"When and where?" My sweet honey tone caressed the air in defiance of Victory's funded one.

I was off about the kind of action Victory suggested. Grave bashfulness descended on her on my account. I grossly misread it on purpose. Thank the stars, Victory was not yet tuned for suggestive comments to object. By now, she was well acquainted with my sportive humor.

"Today's agenda is Rorrim, Sam." Maya rang in to keep a tight rein on me.

Her watchful eyes were dead, just like her heart. Somebody must inform this achiever that her heavily compartmented panache was limiting her potential.

Back to base. The plan today was to discuss my venture to unnaturally supplement the course of nature. Most of it was set in motion by my Papa.

Salut.

I was seeing through so that it reached its earned making. I was dramatically good at that. Liquidating worldly goods was my forte.

"I love the name, Sam."

I dubbed my latest project at ZepRive differently. Victory seemed to agree with it.

"I've initiated Rorrim to reflect on every Intellectual Property. However, I am not sure about human test subjects for this initiative." Victory buttered me up before letting me down.

Classic corporate strategy. Insipid and insincere.

I bracketed the chair with the spread of my arms and folded my legs, one on top of the other. "Hmm. Elaborate?"

"To start with, it violates privacy. Common individuals will try to make the most of it if it is experimental. Especially since the act involves filming. Not counting, we can't do anything illegal."

Victory was mistranslating information. I aimed to replicate human devilry without actual end clients in the development phase. My target was not just the Elite but the population in general, succeeding beta testing.

"Tory." She flitted a perked-up squint at me.

Yeah. Victory loved the nickname I gave her. She especially adored it when I steamed it out sexily for her.

"You recruit willing test subjects, and I'll take care of the rest. Send me the technical details for the prototype before lunch."

"Would you also like to meet the first model? I can check on the progress."

I did not make anything public unless it was ready. Victory needed to be doctored on that. Moreover, I released the master prototype and many more a year ago.

"No need for that kind of micromanagement," I winked.

ATHENA

DESIRES NEVER ONLY TROUBLE THE DESERVING, FOR THE PEASANTS HAVE DREAMS TOO.

FANTASY BEDEVILED ALL. Sadly, only the truth had a place in reality. Because we lived in a non-fictional world.

Hold my beer while I hide my unicorn.

I had just turned nineteen. For the others, I was twenty-one. My actual age was not favorable to my profession. Brushing aside the legality, I banked heavily on *you are as old as you look* mantra.

I definitely looked twelve in the mirror. Mainly with all the layers of missing makeup.

la-di-fuckin-da.

My cussing was hushed, considering my mom was sleeping two steps away from where I stood. I ran a fleeting gaze at her Zen state, strictly in spiritual terms. Double-checking my disheveled appearance real quick, I ran out the door.

My bus arrived, and I towed myself inside.

Time for self-belittlement while I rode this stink full of evening rush hour crowd. I was piss poor. That holed-up place I called home was a storm short of crumbling down. Not that I would seriously lose anything if it were all to blow away in a blizzard. This neighborhood was all that we could ever pay for.

What a tragedy.

Mom tried to be a decent person. Failing miserably at it as she was busy working all the time. I couldn't blame her for being progressive and hungry for success. Too bad she didn't have any skills to bank on.

My Dad was… my everything.

I got into college on a partial scholarship, working on end to pay the rest of my tuition fee. Here I was at my third part-time job of the day, waitressing in a café bar and serving alcohol while I couldn't drink any. All because my real government-issued ID said so.

Fuck you, factuality.

Fastening the green apron, I prepared to get on with my shift. A couple made an entrance for the private booth assigned to me. I was so jaded that I never noticed how rich and made-up they were until my friend pointed it out. She was sure I'll get a killer tip.

I dismissed her assumption.

My boss, who stood creepily in the dark corridor behind the bar, motioned me toward him. He pointed at the snobs I was about to attend to. "They are our honored guests."

"Say no more! I'm all for cool points," I assured him like a village idiot.

A quick touch-up gave my face some color and much-needed confidence. "What would you like to have this evening, Ma'am, Sir?"

The guy didn't even give me a polite glance. But the lady – surprise, surprise – was all over me. I bit my inner cheek, shying stupidly from her apparent attention to my morally covered body in the dim lighting.

"A Wild Turkey 101 for me and Captain Morgan's spiced rum for him."

"Right away."

My vigorous smile rolled into a groan as soon as I stepped out. Hiking to the bar area, I scrutinized them in my head. Those two had an exceptionally refined taste. Expensive, more like. They probably came after work to unwind, as they were still in professional wear. Looking incredible. For all I knew, they could be dating. Or a work-duo, doing crazy things when no one was watching. I'd bet dollars to doughnuts that they could be exhibitionists.

My mind was in the gutter. Maybe fuck buddies… most definitely fuck buddies. I concurred pronto with my gutter mind.

The woman was too fake. Unreal excellence.

How could anyone be so flawless?

Good for her.

The guy also seemed exceedingly unnatural compared to the men I had been around. He was rude but a fine-looking hunk.

Polishing my outfit for any stray lint, I headed back to the table with drinks and re-painted lips. "Here you go. Anything else you would like to have?" My smile was faker than the NFTs.

"That'd be all, ah…." The woman instigated, searching for the employee badge I had forgotten to wear.

"Oh! Athena Denali."

"Very Mytho. Are you a student?"

"How could you tell?"

Even after my feeble attempt at dusting my face to aged perfection, I resembled an academic nerd.

So, of course, she could tell.

Anyone could. Her snobbish male companion could also guess my age. If only he didn't refuse to acknowledge me by hiding behind the usual – his phone.

She smiled elegantly, tasting her drink with class. Making determined eye contact, she asked. "Would you like to work for me, Athena?"

It was a job offer that I should have inquired more about. Being the thirsting girl in need of money, I heard some very unintelligent words coming out of my mouth.

"Oh my God, yes."

Oh my God, yes? Really Athena, are you in play school?

A smile of derision on her well-bred face injured me deeply. Then again, I did sound like the mother of desperation. Mr. too-cool-for-school with her was still actively on his cell with no care to spare for my unsavory presence.

Thank God!

I couldn't handle another set of eyes on me.

But... too fucking late not to sound so strapped for cash. A very belated question came to supposition. *What if this is a janitorial position?*

I saw myself cleaning public toilets.

Somebody's got to do it.

Then assembling the fact that she was rich, I upgraded my vision. Picturing another made-up scenario like greased lightning. I was now mopping their penthouse floor while they made wild love on the kitchen counter. I was in a proper maid uniform, and the guy was staring at me while he fucked this faultless woman. The visuals were glowing with obsessive and scandalous screams.

"What's your major, Athena Denali?"

I paused my creativity to answer the stunning lady. "Chem – Um, chemistry."

She slithered a dead black card from her posh purse and handed it to me. I flipped it many times to see if anything was printed on it.

Negative.

If I questioned the card's authenticity, it could be another tactless thing piloting out of my ungallant brain. So I just clutched my palm, digging it into my skin.

In another unguarded moment, I gave a foolish smile. My cluelessness was readily caught by her.

"You'll figure it out. Use your major." She gave a new poised smirk.

"Tory." Mr. Chivalrous spoke directly with my future employer, hinting at my presence as unnecessary.

Snubbing him, I focused on the name that purred from his handsome mouth. *Tory, as in Tory Burch? As in the purse that sat on the table screaming ready money! Ugh! Keep it together, Athena!* I urged my ghetto self.

"See you soon, Athena Denali." She crooned on a flat graph.

In other words, get off our back.

I spun around to attend to other guests. It's not like I only had them to wait on. I was slammed. The café was bustling with customers.

IT WAS PAST midnight when I reached home.

As I slipped my flats off my feet, sheer curiosity about that blank card kept me on edge, and I went straight to my laptop. After an hour of searching the internet, I knew I was chasing a rainbow.

You'll figure it out. Use your major.

Humming in an epiphany, I turned off all the lights and lifted the card in the moonglow. There were sparkling blurred dots. But it was thinly pixelated and so not very obvious. When I tapped it on the window, it made a metallic sound. Running to my induction stove, I turned it on and held the card slightly above it. It heated up in no time, almost burning my fingers.

Scowling, I headed to my dresser. There was a pincer in my messy drawer among some cockroaches that had to run out and take refuge elsewhere.

Sorry!

Holding the card by its rim with the tweezer above the stove, I waited impatiently. Biting my inner cheeks, as a rule. A few minutes into it, numbers appeared as clear as daylight. Grabbing my phone out of my back pocket, I took a picture of it.

Still dying to understand what this job was about, I dared to dial the numbers. It was late. No one would probably pick up.

So I figured. Thus, I misreckoned.

My call was answered snappily in a highly unusual way. "Rorrim welcomes this connection, Athena Denali. A meeting has been organized with Victory Vella at 8 AM tomorrow. The address will be delivered to your phone. Sent text will be deleted within five seconds."

What?

I was caught on the wrong foot.

TROUBLE NEVER KNOCKS IN SOLITUDE.

FOR THE WORSE, my lousy fortune came in three.

One – A slew of taxis rebuffed me, refusing to acknowledge my beggarly presence on the filthy sidewalk of a Cabbagetown. Such trivial things couldn't dissuade me now.

But they did.

Second – Lunging to near death in front of a cab and pleading with the driver, I finally arrived for the interview with five minutes to spare. That was not enough time to make it to the 17th floor. And so, I was unattractively late for my chance at something great.

So much for nothing.

I mumbled, jamming inside the crammed-to-capacity elevator. My face was slapped on the transparent door overlooking a dreadful but beautiful antique hotel right across the street – Glitz. Some of my cheap makeup surely smeared on the glass. I was literally thrown out when my floor arrived. Civility was lost to the urban working class in more ways than one.

If that's how the cookie crumbles, c'est la vie.

Third – I couldn't find my destination. Punctually, but late for my interview, I noticed that there was only one office – ZepRive.

So where in the world was Rorrim?

Fuck must know, for I didn't.

Looking lost, I wandered in the empty hallway that seemed to go on and on with no opening to the outside world. All I saw were double doors on the left, screaming do not approach. And then, a desk just materialized before me.

What was next?

A flying dragon. Please, by all means, I haven't seen one in real life.

I hurriedly walked over to get directions. "Hi, my name is…."

The apparition of a lady spoke before I finished. "Please proceed to your right, Miss Athena Denali."

Pinching my lips together, I lined up a shocked smile and ran to the wall. An opening emerged before I rammed into it. It felt like I was in Universal studio's graphics department. Things were appearing and disappearing right before my eyes. Even that lady and the desk were gone.

Stepping in, I noticed several very sexy-looking people lined up in the middle of this enormous room. It had minimal furniture and was glossy white.

"You're late." I was reminded of the burning fact by a familiar voice.

"I apologize."

"Learn to never say sorry. It is an escape from taking responsibility."

Her statement did not make any sense. If one did something wrong, one must apologize in the civilized world. Evidently, she was lecturing me on the absurdity of saying something we never understood the meaning of. That insight should keep me warm in the middle of the night, if not my tattered comforter.

"Your office is very futuristic." To cast a shadow over my nervousness, I stammered flattery.

My compliment was brushed aside as uncalled for. "Hello, everyone. I am Victory Vella. Step forward and sit down."

We all sank into the plush seating opposite her strange workspace. It appeared to be floating above a few inches. Everything on it, which was not much, kept flickering. This all seemed too odd and not right. I couldn't steady my breath. For a solid two seconds, I contemplated bolting out without giving any excuses. There was a strong possibility that no one would miss me.

"In a world where humans are abundant, human contact is sparse. Why?"

Victory signaled at me as the first in line at the slaughterhouse. That was maybe our opening interview question, so I straightened my back to give a perfect answer.

The one that I didn't have. This scenario would have been close to being up the creek without a paddle if I wasn't good at making shit up as I went.

"We are not physically social anymore."

"Is that the root cause, then?" Victory wasn't convinced.

"The primary problem, yes."

"Problem and Root Cause are very different, Athena. Fixing the root cause...," she fanned her lashes. "...requires eradication. A solution to a problem is suppression. And we are not here to conceal but delve into it."

"Well." I cleared my throat, and it boomed. An involuntary gasp ended up adding to the hard echo. "With all the online approaches to satiate our social needs, I imagined we perhaps have lost the demand for in-person incentives."

"Could it be that we are not the social animals we imagine to be?" Victory challenged my assumption.

I shook my head lightly. "Meaning, we could be like the tiger and that somehow we have come to believe we are from the lion family."

Others took this chance to make fun of me with suppressed scoffs and choked chuckles. This wasn't the first time I'd felt embarrassed or disappointed in something I had said. I was a curious soul.

Shoot me.

Ignoring the scorners, I held my head high, producing a quirky smile as by magic.

"Look around you. All of you."

We very literally did.

Victory meant, in simple terms, most likely. As there was no one there except for her and the candidates. Fixing the error, we threw a judgmental glance at each other.

"There is never really anyone with anyone. We pass by many when exploring, shopping, or commuting. Yet we hardly ever peek at them. We live inside our homes and never bother our neighbors. Even something intimate as a sexual encounter is now mostly online. Digital reach expanse is diminishing natural touch."

Applying some parallel processing ability, I measured her words. I wondered what fed her appetite for life. I also wondered, could Victory be any more conflicted? This office was decked with robotic technology, and she talked about human involvement, playing Switzerland.

"I agree; we are not that social anymore." Someone aching to lick management's ass chimed in.

"We never were social. When conforming to society, we form smaller groups within. All of us are alone in the entirety of things. That is because we are unique." Victory canvassed the room for questions.

Everyone remained quiet.

I was also quiet but skeptical.

"Let's talk about feelings." Another matter was tossed for grabs by Victory, the highflier.

I took it, betting on my so-far-missing-in-action intelligence that I was so proud of. "Because we watch stuff on digital platforms without engaging other senses, it is impossible to judge a situation for what it really is. An in-person reaction would be different."

Victory was hushed in scrutiny.

I looked away briefly and supplemented, "feelings are definitely anesthetized with online interaction. A firsthand social setting is essential to understand a situation humanly."

"There you have it!" Victory praised. "At ZepRive, we provide heightened and personalized feelings without compromising on standards or norms. We aim to record human reactions, then feed them to AAI programs to develop hybridized self-learning machines."

What in the world is AAI?

Clearly, only I questioned that strange term. I decided to not probe into it, given that Chemistry was my major, not computer science. All the innovative jargon made me vogue a queer grin. For once, I was not the total nutcase. Everyone else was also faking a smile in a loss.

"Now for the most important question. How can you enter this mission?" Victory eyed us with an encouraging simper. "Submit your resume with a hundred-word essay on feelings."

After posting that statement, she outlined the nature of the job.

Netflix and chill category.

My mouth, along with that of many others, was wide open. Victory then dismissed us and disappeared through another door-like opening. Her run was nowhere close to mine when escaping her office.

I was psyched out.

SAM

REMINISCING ABOUT AN ACHE IS HOLLOW.

FLAKING IN PAIN was a souvenir from my zesty human side that I welcomed.

An ongoing reminder of my mother.

This café was where she frequented with her best friend. I planned to upscale it. Yes, I was the new owner of this and many other properties that my parents, real ones, had ever been to.

People bought needlessly to circulate money and boost the economy. I did the same.

What else was I supposed to do with an obscene sum of wealth I inherited?

Organize fundraisers.

Nah. Uncle Shoor avidly donated to the max.

Memory Frame was an organic contraption installed at many places across the globe by my Papa. This place, fortunately, had many.

Not by coincidence. My Papa spied on mom. Not because of jealousy but because she was in danger at all times. Ultimately, he couldn't avoid it, and she was harmed.

All the recordings from every Memory Frame of this café was dumped at ZepRive. Victory was responsible for sifting it to isolate everything related to my mother. Since I didn't know my mom that well, her memories were my only fallback.

I informed Maya I won't be in for another hour ahead of settling impromptu on this morning's adventure. The lovely weather assisted my decision to sit outside. Before midday, there was an informal feel to this joint. A casual setup meant less faking.

I likey no hanky panky, I tittered softly.

My table lit up with the menu.

"Morning."

A fine set of tits greeted me before I acknowledged the owner's face. Blame the line of sight, not me. Twin peaks were almost in my face.

"Would you like to start with some coffee?" She gave a run-of-the-mill smile, being not such an excellent host.

Very customer-centric. Not.

I silenced the menu display to focus my attention on my server. "Morning, Athena."

She tried to gather how I knew her name. With such a poor memory, I was unsure if she belonged at ZepRive, even with those racks. Victory wanted to hire her for her body. To me, Athena was serviceable unless I got to see more.

More of what was under the golden badge with her name on her left breast. She didn't wear that the last time I was here for drinks. Which led me to believe that either she was new or careless. Neither of those required my consideration.

I pointed at the obvious. "Did you interview with Tory?"

Her attitude was unmoved by the nature of the work I was inquiring about. She did immediately collect what I was asking.

"Do I look that desperate to sell myself?"

The objection trailed by Athena was too humdrum.

"Everyone is selling something." I gave her an uncaring glance, gesturing for her to sit down.

"I am at work."

Denial on the pretext of consequential reasoning was too hyperintelligent.

"What if you weren't working?"

She sneered. I remained unperturbed.

Victory was not a good negotiator; I unvoiced. Athena seemed young and unreliable. She enjoyed sex, though. It was screaming silently from the waves emanating off of her error-free body. I could easily convince her to take the job on that account. However, she might suspect me of being a pimp.

A truistic guess in some twisted way.

"Just coffee," I placed my order verbally.

A hateful look rained on me before she whirled around elegantly. I laughed heavily on the inside. She was probably told by Swain, the manager, to wait on me in person despite the ordering option right from the table for obvious reasons. Athena perhaps hated affluence if it swung with others.

While waiting for my gourmet hot drink, I shifted to read the settings. Lingering sensations suggested my mother was happy whenever she came here.

My ability to read memory vs. Memory Frames was very different. I had practical coding in me that gave me the premier ability to precisely isolate what I needed dangerously fast. No technology could ever match ethnic distilling and speed.

Brusquely, a vision struck me, playing an intimate scene between Athena and me. I stowed it away for later and centered back on my mother's memoirs.

After being subjected to an unneeded delay, my connoisseur taste buds quickly rejected what Athena served. Since she took off immediately after and was nowhere I could scan her from, I signaled for the nearest server. He was more than happy to wait on me, unlike Athena. The latter didn't care for my authority or my satanic charms.

"Take it away."

Swain came barreling out within seconds of my rebuffing the poor-quality beverage. "Sir, I am incredibly sorry! Your revised order will be out any minute."

"And Athena?"

"She was let go."

"Get her back."

My heavenly-tasting coffee was furnished again with the required competence. I took all but a sip when the sound of stomping cheap sneakers caught my attention.

There she was with her arms folded, hair in a messy bun, the ugly green apron missing, and her crop top teasingly revealing her belly button. As and when the light breeze allowed it. I suddenly wished for it to be windy as hell. The atmosphere remained calm as fuck refuting my wish.

My quick second assessment informed me she was aesthetically appealing. Victory was right. My vision from moments ago might come to be true.

I silently stared at her. She thumped her right foot a couple times.

"Sit. You don't work here anymore."

That wasn't very kind. Be that as it may, I loved saying it. She stuffed herself with a despised laugh before finally taking a seat.

Still very angry.

"You want to eat something?" I asked her politely. She didn't say anything. "Relax. Swain can't fire you again." I raised my brow to stress the irony once more.

"Thanks to you!" She scoffed, rolling into a brief thinking mode. "I joined you only because I am seriously starving."

That was an ineffectual excuse to not acknowledge my sexual pull. A smirk that longed to sneak up on my lips would have been sincere. Pushing it away to oblivion, holding a blank face, I ordered her a decent breakfast.

"Look." She fiddled with her tank top, revealing her beautiful skin flirtatiously. "I don't need your judgment. But I am honestly considering."

I kept a straight face I had invoked earlier and decided to detail a helpful fact.

Only for Athena.

"On my first day at work, I was told I am only as good as the money I bring in."

Bobbing her head, she fluttered a sideways glance before settling her pretty brown eyes on me. "It's just I don't know what to write about my work experience. The essay was the easy part." She paused for a beat. "I get straight A's, but I make nothing with all the part-time jobs. Hence the decision to use what I got." She ran her hand up and down her somewhat curvy body.

Lady in black was thin but blessed in the desired proportion. She was climbing the magnetism chart fast. My worst intentions were masked behind my best smile.

Athena mellowed out, resigning herself to my brazen appeal.

"Do you do anything besides waste your time soliciting and getting your girlfriend's potential employee sacked?" She hurled blatant accusations, sugarcoating them with a naughty giggle.

I dissolved into a smug laugh at her faulty guesswork. "Today, and the one before, were all chance meetings." Placing my hands on the back of the chair, I acquainted her with a fraction of the facts. "And I do have other things to keep me busy. I work in the R&D team at Eckhart Inc."

"Isn't it in the same building as ZepRive?" I validated her guess with an approving shake. "I bet you help your girlfriend with her gig in your spare time."

"Tory is very adaptive and appropriately planned." My response was calculated so that Athena could never accuse me of lying in the future.

I replied to a few emails while she finished her meal. Straddling the fence of awkward sobriety, we talked about rubbish like weather and traffic.

Only humans bother with those.

Soon enough, she slid her empty plate away. Amused by some realization, she shook her head, snorting faintly.

"I don't even know your name."

"What's in a name?"

"How cliché!"

We laughed like a drain.

"As much as I hate Swain, I liked working here." She mused in a quiet tone.

"The job is yours if you want it back."

She was entertained by my generous but absurd offer. Waving her hand, she asked how.

"I have my ways. As a payback for the inconvenience I caused, I'll throw in my résumé writing services for free."

My announcement left her walking on air. And then she latched on her cheeks, suppressing an inescapable smile.

2 – ANIMUS

SAM

MORAL DEGRADATION IS DEEMED THE MOST SIGNIFICANT LOSS.

TO COMMIT HARA-kiri was losing the battle with one's ideas.

SELF-sacrifice.

My immeasurable speed changed the weather outside at a catastrophic magnitude. Tomorrow's news could attribute the meteorological debacle to a cloud burst, for all I cared. Once I sensed him calling me with grim distress, employing my lethal ability was the only thing to do. I reached him before he fell to the floor, catching his failing frame in my wings. We both settled on the plush carpet of his bedroom.

"I knew you would make it in seconds," he stammered each word with much effort.

"Why, Uncle Shoor?" I asked the most useless question.

It was inevitable. I had seen this coming for years.

Liver cancer expedited it. Uncle Shoor drowned himself in work, charity, alcohol, and drugs. No amount of counseling helped. His partner, Liam, was also powerless in this situation. Wealth and status were not a substitute for emotional well-being. He had it all except for control over his thoughts. And battling them was battling with numerous ideas that made him… him.

Essentially, it was warring on oneself.

Years ago, my Papa came to know his best friend's fate before it even shaped up. That's why he hung around Uncle Shoor despite my Grandparent's disapproval, availing every opportunity to spend time with him. While Uncle Shoor spent his youth hating my father for his guts and unrequited love.

Yeah. He was and still is in love with Papa.

Uncle Shoor regretted his life ever since an accident during his Freshman year of college that left a young boy tied to a wheelchair. That guilt corroded him, forcing him to dedicate his life to giving to others that were unfortunate.

No good ever came out of it.

He decided to end his suffering by consuming a colorless, odorless poison. Its presence in his body plagued the air around us with a stony feel, predicting the undoing.

EE-Ex was equipped to bring him back to life. With the toxin spreading fast in his already septic body, he was too weak to tell me if that was what he desired.

There was no need. All the disturbing unrest in him was crashing into me. I suffered his entire life with him as he took his last breath in my arms, fiercely conveying his happy and sad instants. Even though it took a blink of an eye for death to assert his Life-Force, it made him witness his unsatisfactory time on Earth all over again.

Our Life-Force was energy with memorization capability. It was simply a desire to continue as one came to be.

To live.

Regrettably, it was challenging to co-exist with the barrage of emotions a human body was tricked into by thought. Experiencing them from Uncle Shoor made me realize human behavior at an enhanced level. This was simulated during my training at Shaala [EXTRATERRESTRIAL LEARNING CENTER ON ANOTHER DIMENSION].

The forbidden fruit appeal was for the novelty. Justice was nothing but a tangible payback after the fact. Every pain was leveraged to feel special, turning it into an emotional contest. They socialized to be recognized by standing out in the crowd in some way. A self-generated emptiness was filled with pretense. Their existence that needed no analysis was given importance by setting goals. To cover up the guilt from excessive hoarding, they aggrandized generosity. They killed unorthodox ideas to feel alive. They killed themselves to save unsatisfiable ideas.

Nothing that the humans ever did was for anyone else but them. The SELF always remained in the center.

To stop the pain he felt from his undying love for my Papa. Uncle Shoor braved a painful death to stop feeling that same love. His desires left the body to become one with universal energy, devoting his demise to a failed life.

Uncle Shoor broke the promise he made to my father.

i$UBSCRIBE – GEN VERISMO GENESIS

He left me alone.

LONELINESS IS A NOXIOUS EFFECT OF ISOLATION.

MOST OF THE time, isolation was not physical but mental. A thought-driven reaction to made-up incidents. Not everyone depressed was stranded on an island. Uncle Shoor felt deserted in the crowd, so he severed the illusion altogether by embracing the end.

Where would I go immediately after his death?

Brazen Academy in Village Villas.

I once advocated the idea of preserving the SELF to Citzin by murdering the body it resided in. I needed to salvage her now that I had examined what it did to Uncle Shoor. He wanted many things differently in this very life while he couldn't carry on living.

This conflict between Life-Force and SELF was a love-hate connection. One that would resolve only by separating the body from SELF. Or at least fool the SELF into believing it was successful in its endeavor, whatever it may be. With trickery, thought would dictate outcomes that would be of no consequence to the body and favorable to the SELF.

How?

Virtualization of SELF in an inert body.

Fuck the funky homo sapiens.

Witnessing the future posthaste, I connected with Akron Adamadon instead, abandoning the Citzin situation. She would be a resilient young woman, deciding to marry Akron, her cheating boyfriend's father, to take vengeance out of spite.

Splendid.

The future could, for sure, change without notice. For now, Citzin was assured of living.

"Thanks for seeing me on such short notice, Akron."

"I am sure this is to my advantage," he assumed.

Less to your benefit and phenomenal to me. I wave-remarked.

Dressed in fake humor, I pitched a jaw-dropping idea. "Let's inanimate the human body. On a fast track. I am talking within six months. Call it… Virtual Insignia."

Yeah. Akron was stunned.

He was running all the blue vs. red tape scenarios in his mind. Rules and regulations would make it impossible to meet the deadline I unceremoniously tossed around. The process drew up much energy and time, taking forever to roll out any product. Especially if it was something so unsavory as going completely virtual. Anything debatable had a massive behind-the-scenes undertaking before its mainstream acceptance.

For example – AI [ARTIFICIAL INTELLIGENCE] exposure to the commoners was gradual. A prerequisite was decades of automation under covert efficiency efforts followed by laying off people to reduce manual labor expenses. When veiled under economic slowdown, no one complains of a manually manipulated cyclical concept.

And it was celebrated as an advancement for a better future. Only humans craved '*advancement*' and a '*better future.*'

For all other species, it was not even a concept.

Thought only leached onto humans because they were artificial. They innovated what they stood to be. An apple never falls too far from the tree.

Next, AI was marketed in smaller gadgetry, moving on to more significant models. An actual AI being was also out there, but for scrutiny and entertainment. And so it wouldn't be upsetting when it was launched among the general population.

The defense zone was the only vertical where a breakthrough technology made its way covertly first. They beta-tested innovation without pushback or restraint before it was released to ordinary citizens. Due to its sinister nature, some things never made it out in the open.

Any poisonous discovery was disseminated as a trace ingredient in prior accepted consumable conception. The food and pharmaceutical industry was the leader of such corruption. The majority never questioned packaged products or prescribed medicine. Emotions like fear, trust, and hope were exploited to implement profitable ideas freely.

EE-Ex had caused enough havoc with Memory Frames and released serums to combat its adverse impact to no avail.

I had to switch my frequency to laugh at that. My body vibrated to age at a much slower rate. Akron, who was on Earth's tempo, appeared frozen in time. I relished the joke Papa had played on this planet for long minutes, then shifted to flow normally.

Akron was only beginning to present a rebuttal. "Public panic is a genuine issue. Too easy to invoke and challenging to control."

"Who says this has to be mainstream right away? We must bank on value more than volume. I'll supply test subjects once we are ready for implementation."

"Humans?" Akron squealed in surprise at the snare.

Any alpha and beta experiments were done on animals. Humans were too high on the food chain to test-drive their inventions.

Ironic?

Not really.

They knew firsthand what they were doing was not always pretty. Most human inventions were inelegant, and their use-by-date was either too soon or too late.

Just open a sexy car to see how intricate the inner-working was. Now cut up a tree or a seed to see the running. The answer would stare straight in the face.

There is beauty in simplicity.

That reminded me, humans were the only species that committed suicide supported by intent and awareness of the outcome. Time to acquaint Akron with statistics.

"Approximately 800,000 people kill themselves yearly, roughly one death every 40 seconds. Only a small percentage reaches out for help. And they want the pain to go away, not the life to end. Virtual Insignia would do that for them."

"That can't be legal," his protest was resounding regulations.

"We'll work with loopholes. Moreover, this would be under contract-based research, just like in the Pharma world. Except we will shortlist subjects with no baggage. I need your name in fore-front for PR purposes."

AKA, Akron would take the fall should things go south. They wouldn't, though, in a sense I mentioned. But Akron would be looking at the South pole when facing north.

Like everyone else.

Yeah. When I quickly swept for the future to make sure Citzin would live. I also saw another change occurring.

"I am not someone who gets irked by much. Shall we discuss the true nature of the beast?" He took it in stride.

I gave a hearty chuckle, but the expression on my face was transparent. Akron was about to mint money and fashion fame in a highly lucrative way.

"It is about selling the ideas that make us… us. Since these ideas are nothing but the SELF. Combined with the fact that it resides inside humans. The body will act as a silent host without physically enduring thought-motivated reactions. Such as pain and suffering."

It pleased me at magnificent levels to watch Akron react to my statement. This bastard was unaware he was already a host to such a damaging awareness.

Yeah. Akron was possessed by extraterrestrial intelligence. It was boosting his greed for money and fame. I was all for not disturbing it as I pretended to be going with the flow.

Cancel that… Fuck the natural flow.

Pretense was one emotion I admired and equally hated in my human side. So I would meddle with Akron's life.

And enjoy it too.

VICTORY

A DECOROUS SUGGESTION OF INDECENCY IS PROSTITUTION.

VAGARIES OF LIFE pushed people into this.

Or it could be a symptom of self-indulgence. If yes, it was a selfish act, not a disorder to be cured.

Whoredom resulted in financial loss, broken relationships, and ruined families. Most people enamored with sex or related pursuits got addicted. It was a dishonest dealing of mind and body. Definitely not the need for money.

Whatever the circumstances, it is immoral, and I wouldn't say I like it.

The worst choice of all.

My brooded breath could have blown away the papers at my desk if there were any. The paperless culture was mandatory at ZepRive with only a digital trail, per Sam. Another thing perpetual was the bleached setting.

Why is this place so white and bright?

An annoying groan slipped out of me. This pale ambiance never helped me elevate my mood. I dressed in black, as a rule, to counter it. Ready to attend a funeral.

I was replaying the footage of our human subjects. It should be arousing to watch people having uninhibited sex. Not to me.

Am I abnormal?

Fat chance. To doubt was human. I was as normal as was doable. It wasn't like I didn't want to explore my sexuality. But…

A visitor announcement rang.

In an instant, my boss's rich voice claimed my attention. "How are you, Tory?"

Sam was high-class dynamite with an acute opinion for his kawaiiness. He was super relaxed in his approach but never blasé about his position. I delighted in his authority so very much. That's why I worked extra hard to impress him, not because I was on his payroll.

"Very well, Sam. Just finishing up my review."

The volume of the recording playing in the background was on max. I adjusted it to focus on the fully clothed Tarzan in my company.

Sam situated himself across from me, using his beastly magnetism well. "Any eliminations?"

"Let's not be so impatient now. Every subject has something to learn from," I sparkled.

Sam gave a cordial laugh. He seemed so pure. Dunno why he then devised such a depraved project.

"Anything you want to talk about, Tory?"

His question left me surprised, as if he knew what I felt about him. I set aside my awe in a poised manner.

"Do we want doubts also to be infused?"

He leaned nearer and whispered. "To doubt is human."

That's what I had thought of moments ago. My brain was tuned to Sam's frequency, capturing signals from him. It was like I tweaked myself to his taste. We were similar in many ways.

All but one.

When it came to Rorrim, we were ill-assorted. I had to put up with promiscuity, perverse sexual acts by same-sex partners, reverse harem situations, and multiple male partner performances. None of it was ethically correct, socially accepted, biologically sensible, or respectable.

It was deviant at full tilt.

"Wouldn't including doubt make our Zeptos closer to humans? I suppose the whole point was for an all-providing sex worker."

Zeptos were the AAI [ADAPTIVE ARTIFICIAL INTELLIGENCE] counterparts of the human subjects studied under the Rorrim project. These Zeptos were configurable based on preference for outer appearance and responses. So far, Sam was the only one that created Zepto variants. It was on the Supra-Intelligence, Sam's personal computer, plus or minus.

Only it was otherworldly.

"Not at all, Tory. We aim for all-feeling, not all-providing. That is the difference."

But none when compared to humans, I disagreed silently. "Why do you want to replicate exactly without weeding out what is annoying?"

My inquest was well placed. Yet Sam conversely probed me.

"Is any of the subjects annoying?"

I smiled, puffing out slowly. "I feel they are all pretending. How can one enjoy every encounter? Or any such immoral encounters, for that matter."

Sam ran his fingers through his simpering lips. "Do you enjoy everything, Tory?" He leaned back on the chair, pointing at me, resuming his unflustered stance. "Rather, do you *only* do the things you enjoy and are moral?"

An anticlimactic fact lifted its ugly head.

"I am an upstanding citizen that endorses ethics and values above anything else. So I only do what is morally correct. We can enjoy while being decent."

Sam's empty face contrasted with his words. "Isn't that a fact! Emotions take a back seat when we enter the world for survival. There is no room for passion in its purest form. Societal pressures and expectations kill it. It is hard for those who pursue what they love to make money from it. Over time, their work is influenced by market demands and not creativity. No one is free to do what they enjoy. It is one of the strict mandates of social protection."

Unless one was given money in inheritance to blow up on fads. Like you. I made another silent remark before dressing it up expertly. "I imagine we are not all that lucky."

My boss held an investigative watch, and I treasured his malign gape. I noticed many times how he silently studied me.

He likes me.

"What has luck got to do with any of it, Tory? I would encourage you to speak freely and honestly."

"If you promise not to fire me."

He nodded in assurance, handing a friendly grin. My smile, in return, was pained at the realization of my sorry situation.

"I work in this vapid setting day in and day out with a fake exterior. Insulting my religious inclination, I watch porn all day for work. Our society condemns it, and so do I. Since I get paid richly, and money is a necessary evil, I do it anyway."

Sam stayed put in his chair, pondering. His eyes were vacant, wielding control in an unpublished way. Sometimes I felt he was a figment of my imagination.

Or that I was being imagined by him.

What if I actually was someone from his dream? A projection of his vision. The sinister side.

No matter how abstract, my worries were the only thing that assured me I was alive. Maya, his PA, was another one I suspected was not genuine. Everyone I met daily was deceptive.

Following a long spell of dormancy, he breathed, giving life to his divine visage and color to his eyes. The look on his face was that of satisfaction.

"I'll tweak a few of the performer's scripts to test pretense," Sam announced.

He calmly strode out. Whistling. The door to my vast but lightly furnished office materialized behind him.

Speak your mind, my ass!

It was not an honest encouragement but a trap to see inside me. No one wanted to know what anyone truly felt.

Sam doesn't like me. I pouted.

Letting out a failed sigh, I got back to work. Cringe-making aural atrocity from the replay intensified again, filling the air around me with screams of sensual pleasure.

Why do people scream during sex?

Once more, I began questioning the general mentality of the subjects. I couldn't see what would force anyone to take such a job. It's not that hard to study and make a well-respected career.

I did it.

Sex was the easiest thing to sell. And these men and women were taking the simplest route. I felt sorry for their parents.

Shameful!

After fifteen hours of slogging, my eyelids drooped. I craned my neck toward the clock. 10 PM on the digital display watched me watch it.

Same as forever!

The stomach-churning recordings were still haunting my brain. So I masturbated.

Consciousness Cessation.

SAM

SPEED IS A MEASURE OF DYNAMISM MINUS DIRECTION.

QUICKNESS HAD TO be measured in an uninterrupted quantity and time, amusingly begging it to be directional. More amusingly, anything resting was labeled with zero speed by humans.

Creation, however, was not ever motionless.

A good parallel would be taking a flight. Whoever was inside it was also moving at the plane's tempo without realizing it. That's why riding an automatic or self-propelled machine was tiring. Any movement puts some stress on the physical body.

Anything, therefore, within a moving object couldn't be at a standstill.

Earth was also rotating. Zero speed was thus bogus, and so was lumen speed. Because it was all in comparison. Lumen was the pace of my kind, 10^{21} times faster than light. Unknown and unheard of on Earth.

Apocalyptic on Earth, really. Atmospheric friction combined with the velocity would evaporate everything for miles together. That explains why I stayed respectful when moving around.

Even my reduced quickness left a thin line of haze behind me as I zapped under the sea. The amber glow from behind the veil of water was spellbinding. Legends described it as the Underworld. Apparently, Lucifer, the fallen one, ruled it. The believers were terrified of this banishment, a place to lie after death for sinners. Their belief shaped a fear of unverified assertion.

What exactly was belief?

Belief was an external influence that prospered on unsighted trust. Making it personal.

Something to ponder upon for Rorrim.

After filling the seawater with my imprints, I flashed out. My brother from another mother came hurling out right behind me. By vortexing at an undetectable rate, we dried ourselves instantly. DeVeer wrapped his arms with mine, and we hugged each other.

"How is the discarded world treating you, bro D?"

"Same as the overdramatized one is treating you, Sammy."

"Nice comeback."

I didn't particularly appreciate being called Sammy. So I yanked him in another crushing squeeze, aiming to kill him. But he was also blessed with whatever I was and then some. Much superior in physical terms, all because of his mother. Mine was too humble and passed on worthless humanity to me. All I was doing was making the most of it, abusing it, powering it.

"I backed up the café memory because of her. I recall my last few days with her often. She forced me to call her… mamma. I refused until she cried." This information was given without making any eye contact with D.

"Why do you try to suppress that side? I openly want to know my mother, but Agastya is cagey."

D's Grandpa, Agastya, didn't appreciate the Demon wing of his family and kept it under wrap when riotously, D was to rule over them.

On the other hand, I didn't care much about my mother. Anyone who knew her was not a part of my life anymore. A baseless rant – Save yourself for a special someone – was engraved in her by many. When it was my mother's cosmic connection to my father that never allowed her to lose her way. She re-connected with my father only after seven and a half years of avoidable separation.

The walls of their mansion, now mine by inheritance, outside Specter Ville cried out her presence too loud. That's why I didn't live there. But I would go there at times to get to know them better. My parents were filthy in love. Something I was not yet acquainted with. Something I didn't care for.

Or ever would! As I conversed with my future frequently, I knew this somewhat. Notwithstanding the fact, it has all happened. It can all be changed up until the end.

Given the realm of possibility, scratch the idea of never being in love. I instantly witnessed the time to come, and love was in the air.

D went by the Shaala rules, never to engage in misusing his meddling innateness. We were very different but family. The bond between D and me was not decisive because we were blood brothers. Or that we shared our dad's side of the negative ancestry.

We both knew how the population was enduring countless chronic and acute after-effects of the Memory Frames installed by our father globally in secret. These were organic growth capable of reading recollections from anything. It attached and transmitted frequencies as an electromagnetic signal for storage and deciphering.

Too bad it was radioactive in nature.

Worse still, my father didn't care about that little detail.

Worst of all, even after reading the past records that were predictions from the future. That suggested an intelligence would take over Earth. He gave AI an upper hand to become adaptive to a point where it would eventually become more powerful than its deviser.

Not yet.

Yet well within my schedule on Earth.

The connection between D and me was not fazed by the ugliest fact that our father killed our mothers in cold blood. Nothing bothered either of us but fueled our never-ending appetite to satiate our boredom.

I chained. D unshackled. I was a background player on the surface, in total contrast with D, who was the first divine netherworld ruler. I recreated reality artificially while D purged it organically. I domesticated desires with realism, and D expunged them with death. I implied destruction by separation. In reverse, D signified defeat by unification.

Discordant as day and night, like chalk and cheese. We thrived on challenging each other with our contrasting advantages.

"If I wanted to hide it, I would not have told you."

"Is that why you're telling me this now?"

"Nothing was valuable until I felt a certain waitress in the collective memory of that café. It will take goliath effort to separate her from everything."

"You're using human memoirs for your benefit. Nifty!" D wiggled his ridges, whistling aloud.

I eyed him comically. "She is not dead yet. And I am here to insult things at my disposal."

"You had me convinced there for a second as not being borderline obsessed. Fortunately, I feel you."

Yeah. D could see through me.

Looking away, I swelled, sucking in the air around us and replacing it back momentarily with impurities filtered from my enlarged lungs.

This peculiar ability comes in handy when I frequent places devoid of the element air or where it is not in its ventilated form.

"What about the house in Village Villas?"

D was bent on torturing my human side.

"I couldn't step inside. Memories inscribed in that place are savage. It made me realize what you keep saying. I am *very* human."

"You already have an advantage then. Maximum damage is done from within. That's why cancer still doesn't have a cure."

"You sure are the purveyor of demise!"

My blood brother received the frightful compliment with a sobering bow. I could be exactly myself with him.

My Papa had deciphered that there were parallels everywhere. Cancer was the scaled-down version, a copy of a bigger culprit – the human race. This was what D pointed out.

If something were a part of you, why would you kill it?

The straightforward answer to that was to stop the pain. A native mechanism of the body to inform that an invasion had occurred to cause an imbalance might not be to intervene.

A human body tended to a malign or benign tumorous growth inside it, all the same. It responds to attack the new change, sure. The SELF in it definitely wants to do something about it when it becomes aware of the unfavorable outcome due to diagnostic knowledge and/or discomfort. The bottom line, to the body, a cell was a cell – cancerous or normal.

Likewise, humans were molesting the planet that hosted them. Nature made changes from time to time to adapt to them. Only the theorists that predicted the disadvantageous effect of human negligence or empaths that felt anguish from it needed to fix the situation. Both were measuring the imbalance solely for the survival of the human race.

Most were dead from the neck up to the save-the-planet movement – knowingly or unknowingly.

Who was the judge of the required action to be taken anyway?

The abuser, the measurer, or the tender.

None of the above. Every concept had an equal chance of survival in this equitable creation unless interfered with.

"How's EE-Ex, Sammy?"

EE-Ex was impenetrable to anyone else as I was the only Supreme Progeny inclined to exploit technology. D was to use his innateness and emphasize disruption from the inside out – The Underworld. A side-splitting parallel to a tumorous growth. D acknowledged that allegation as a medal of honor.

"Side effects of Memory Frames are widespread in the general population, not just around the installation site but wherever its waves infiltrate."

"That almighty, huh!"

"There's more," I huffed. "Emission from this intrusion is causing aggressive cancers. Soon it would be categorized as an outbreak. My extraterrestrial side is happy to take advantage of this new normal," I clicked my tongue twice.

"You mean Zepto-bit, which has done nix?"

"Wantonly, it doesn't do much to benefit the health. They gather genetic-level data from the injected people and communicate it back. Consequently, EE-Ex has not only documented sub-cellular [RNA] habits for the infused population but can also manipulate them as and when needed."

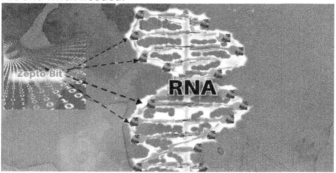

Figure 1 Zepto-Bits attached to RNA in a Human Body

RNA [RIBONUCLEIC ACID]– A polymeric molecule essential in various biological roles such as coding, decoding, regulation, and expression of genes.

Zepto-Bit – A sextillionth-degree violation capability code injected via EE-Ex serum. It bonded with the RNA, in turn, programming an individual in the desired way. Since RNA is organically adaptive, Zepto-Bit, as a result, also evolves.

"Dynamic biological control is a terrific way to advance technology that is profitable in bulk. You must be minting money."

"You can say that again."

We snorted at that made-up medium of exchange that meant nothing to us. Our trade was through natural resources.

Abundant. Auto-corrective.

One couldn't possibly put a price on that.

"Anyhoo... the survival of any species operates contrary to popular belief, united we stand, divided we fall. But I do not intentionally interfere with the natural flow to correct anyone."

"You enjoy it when others oppose or suffer your tyrannical sedition." D fist-bumped me. "Is it both ways?"

"Zepto-bit opens up a two-way channel, yeah. Analogous to a parasite that doesn't care about its host's health, the human psyche remains unaware, and the body doesn't tell the mind. Outcomes can be demanded without people realizing it by transmitting information as memory first, feeding the required belief to store it as knowledge, and then giving the needed command. Their reaction, hence, is justified by their artificial memory. Because they feel it was their idea."

We both sang in unison. "A belief is never questioned if backed by previous knowledge."

D scrutinized me visually. His stare lasted too long as the time for our kind passed at a slower rate on Earth. So even a second spent at our frequency in revere was a lot if an Earther was watching us. I had a similar habit. My reasons were different and bluer, as one-sixteenth of my makeup was human.

D was utterly extraterrestrial.

"Sammy, you are lucky to use your higher learnings and technology virtuosity so fluidly. It is criminal even."

"Indisputably," I not so modestly agreed. "What are you up to?"

"Just recording the magnetic field changes from the depths of the Underworld. Your insights will be useful."

Employing my innate intelligence, I suddenly conjured a eureka moment around what my brother was saying. Papa had installed the Memory Frames to not align with Earth's polarity. It would have deflected its radiation like the cosmic electromagnetic waves.

But why?

Because he didn't care. Nothing more.

Uncle Shoor's death begged me to do something about its harmful effect. I could prevent further damage by making a small change. Minor in terms of my scale of things.

"Divination, D! I can negate the Memory Frame radiation by flipping the Earth's magnetic field."

In a nanosecond, D came to point. "Workings?"

D was explicit. Not more than me.

"The core's circulation will absorb the radiation as it sweeps across the globe. After that, it will line up in the magnetic field direction. Gradually, it will discharge in space without getting reabsorbed."

Our pupils flickered, rejoicing at the challenge, laughing boisterously. Noise from our roaring laughter was like a stimulus to which nature responded by executing its native code. The weather reacted to our unearthly vibrations with loud thunders and bolts of lightning.

We appreciated the unnatural view.

"Not until I have the full projection of the Underworld outcome."

D calmly warned me.

KINSHIP OVER A RELATIONSHIP, FRIENDSHIP BELOW ALL.

GENUINE FRIENDS WERE hard to come by. If found, the possibility of them not being cunning was harder still. Relationships could be broken, and kinship was an enforced concept.

What was then an authentic bond?

A connection over similarities. Alignment beyond communication.

Figure 2 Thun Sea & Moon

Thun sea was hollering waves out of bounds; it wasn't even a full moon. I stood at the beach for a few seconds when D appeared.

Looking sensational.

"Bro D, you must also be famous with the ladies."

He snickered. "More than you, Sammy. Wanna bet?"

I aimed a hit at him but stopped short of making contact with his face. "We could go out and try to snag. Whoever gets more women will be the winner."

D covered my fist in his palm, cracking my bones to bits.

Shit.

Thankfully, I healed.

"I need more than a winner title. If you lose, how about slogging as a waiter at your favorite café for a week?" D played out waiting tables and counting tips at ten times the average speed. "Slum it with the commoners," he chanted cynically.

I sniffled at his buffoonery. "If you lose, you will clean my penthouse for a month. On Earth timeline."

"Deal."

We wrapped our hands.

D returned to his lesser clowning self. He ruffled his hair back and forth, placing his hand behind his neck. "Grandpa Agastya doesn't want me to partake in anything other than Underworld affairs. I have been warned to focus on my celestial duty only."

I already knew that.

D's life was shackled for good reasons. His Aunt, Tataka, was still alive and of demonic disposition. She had vowed to destroy my father's reputation by poisoning D against me. We both were of this knowledge already.

Our Grandma, Holy-River, had advised of all that and much more.

Nothing would break our brotherly bond.

"You need to analyze the data my method is collecting. It is all over the place."

"I'll be happy to take on the cool stuff. You carry on with your devilish duties," I mocked D's caged state.

I had a theory that needed implementation.

The question was, should I apply it or view the coming?

That which I was anyway with fanatical compulsion. It couldn't be helped, given my minuscule but natural human tendency. One of my father's parallel incarnations was ZeeSham ParAsher. He was addicted to viewing the future and changing the course of events.

Yeah. A quarter of his makeup was human, making him more conflicted and tattered.

Humanity burdened him with the sense of right and wrong when he defied anyone. Oh, and he was cursed. So he couldn't use all his superpowers, but he was aware of everything he could do should he

get to use them. I took it after him, minus any guilt from exercising my characteristic ability. Because I was a witness, not an infiltrator.
As of now!
Even if I decided to fuck it all up, I would enjoy every minute of it. Hail to the misery.

"Did you analyze the side-effects of magnetic shift?"

"Yes. It will be taxing on the human generation."

"So, Grandpa Agastya would still live?"

Agastya was not human.

"Yeah."

D scoffed, looking the other way. He needed to unchain his vegetative innateness that was bound to come out. Anyone born with a specific character code would give in to its duress. Conditioning could suppress it but not delete it.

My Papa declared that a call for help should come from the suffering, not the one suffering by watching them. Because one can only judge a situation by comparing it to themselves.

What if what one thinks is good is not what the other needs?

In so doing, I won't assist anyone unless specifically asked to. Similarly, the universe never interferes with one's misery. Unless they ask for it. Even then, it only gives what is requested without changing the end. Like if a person was suffering abuse. And they asked for it to end, but their destiny dictates end by abuse. Their misery would end in the interim, only to find them again in a different way to reconcile with fate.

"Forget that. Give me the details, Sammy."

"Alright. This shift meddles with the psyche. Questioning every belief in practice. Social, religious, and even law. A new normal will emerge. The human population is looking at an exponential change in conduct, reforming the current system radically. Dreadful thing like pedophilia would enter the realm of understanding.

"People would regard work-life balance by saying no to above and beyond. They'll disregard discipline, denounce the status quo, and accept exceptions. Not procreating will be a choice.

"Rejecting progress as an improvement will be the most dramatic development. I mean, less dramatic than every technology going to shit. Throw some natural disasters into the blend. And there you have it."

D was tranquil because the list of changes was immaterial to us.

"What's the timeline for this elaborate mess?"

"We're talking within two years."

"Kudos, Sammy."

A compliment from my brother! Oh, I must check for any arising celestial catastrophe.

D quickly got to a matter of importance. "Underworld?"

"Under magma." I swiftly covered the bad news with a remote probability. "Worst case scenario."

"Not happening then."

"You have got to be kidding me." I shook my head at his guardedness. "I'll do it on my own."

D's strength would have made this more fun. But my unwise brother was too busy being a just ruler.

Go dance with the demons.

ATHENA

RÉSUMÉ BULLETINS OUR YIELDING RESULTS FOR SALE.

I WAS GEARING up to stuff up my self-propaganda.

My sales pitch.

My educational background.

My work record.

In short, most of my life's timecard. Contrary to the requirements, I was a novice and had nothing to show in a dramatic rant. Everyone struggles with that when beginning their career path. I was no different.

"Is there an effective way to highlight potential without sounding too vain?"

"If one believes in predictions or instincts."

His gaze had subliminal honesty in them. I could tell.

"For people with work experience, a background check reveals some of the claims made in a two-page document. That means no one trusts anyone with the sum and substance of it." I underlined the crux of the matter.

"What if everyone's backstory was cybernetic? Centralized and online instead of a self-claimed arrogant prologue. A digital bird's eye view of anyone eligible to work."

Veer sounded super bright. I felt he was maybe one of those revolutionary people who brought about groundbreaking changes. Hands-down, not a follower but a game-changer.

"That will not go well with all the privacy hullabaloo."

"I guess so. Everyone wants freedom from interference and desires to be celebrated."

Rorrim was project-based employment. Contractual. But it was paying a shit load of money. The fact remained that I didn't mind having sex.

Well, I enjoyed it.

Not that I wanted to celebrate that bit about me. At the same time, I wouldn't mind doing it with anyone within the bounds of four walls. If it was lawful, then I was free to do whatever I damn well pleased.

Taking a break from my radical thoughts, I perved on him. Veer had a habit of staring or that he went into a trance while daydreaming. I loved those hazel eyes glued on me. The non-threatening aura around him was X-rated, truth be told. As determined by my sexually corrupt brain.

My dried-up throat needed hydration. I most definitely needed a time-out from my sleaze. Veer gave a lazy wink. I choked up more, dreading that he read my mind. That would be awkward and super uncomfortable.

"I'm not even a college graduate." Gulping down some saliva, I croaked in a hoarse voice. "Except for a few odd jobs, nothing grand."

"You suppose everyone that has some experience is grander than you."

His assertion prompted me to question my assessment of myself. I folded my arms, rocking my head, thinking of all the times I was turned down due to the shortage of words in the work history section of my curriculum vitae. I had struggled to fake a professional profile online. It demoralized me at cyclopean levels.

"On LinkIn… I try to come up with fancy stuff to say about me." I looked away, feeling maladroit at everything. "Maybe selling myself at a shady street corner is easier than marketing my short-handed worth in the corporate world."

Funny, that's what I was precisely offered at Rorrim. Sell my body's reactions and feelings for some AAI project. I still didn't know what AAI stood for.

Ain't that overly hilarious. Ha-ha.

"What do you want to do when you graduate, Athena?"

"Intern at Bix-By. You know, the pharmaceutical giant."

"Their acceptance rate is less than ten percent."

In no uncertain terms, Veer thought I had no idea how the world worked. And that maybe my aspirations were too big.

I shrugged in a so-what manner, updating him on my determination. "I do not shy away from hard work. Mind you, I would have never taken the shortcut. But here I am, considering it."

"You're exceptional," he gave a speculative compliment. "Since you brought it up again. It is the oldest profession."

"Prostitution." My miss-straight-A self was not shocked. "Sex is the easiest of the things to sell," I mumbled.

"There are sellers and buyers in the corporate world as well. LinkIn is the right place to advertise yourself. No different from standing at the corner of a shady street." He doled out every word of the last sentence with sarcasm.

I trundled into a fit of laughter, dismissing his analogy.

He widened his broad arms out in skepticism. "Come on!"

"No, you come on, Veer! Prostitution is very low. People study hard to be rocket scientists, doctors, and surgeons. Even dishonest lawyers slum it for years. Getting a degree requires focalized effort."

"You mean if it is difficult to achieve, it is somehow better." He put my words through the mill again. "What do you think these people are working towards, Athena?"

That got me thinking. "To survive."

He yielded a consenting nod. "It is all a trade. Corporate is synonymous with it. In the end, even the noblest profession is about money."

"So then no one is grander than the other. But. As we all know it. Society condemns prostitution."

"Society allows it nonetheless in some form." Veer handed a cynical truth. "A business owner is selling a product. A corporate worker is also pimping some skills. All for money. To survive."

I drew a breath, absorbing the irony. "I wonder when it became a taboo."

"It is not a time or an event that denounced it. Emotions got in the way. Humans seek to feel by having sex and then condemn the person that gave them the feelings."

Pining at the gap between honest enjoyment and faux semblance, I agreed with him. "Maybe that's the problem. An emotional exchange compensated with cash somehow devalues it."

"In some parts of this world, prostitutes thank their customers genuinely after performing the service by going on their knees. Sincerity guarantees repeat customers, as it is not just an act to get off for the men. Women also acknowledge their part. This approach makes having sex an immersive experience for all involved. Not a bodily transgression for one or all."

"Money is involved. How is it not business?"

"It is still business. But there is a parallel track, authenticity. Similar to Victory's project."

"But she said they were trying to capture it into some kind of machine."

"To start with, it will quarantine emotions from the actual body. Whatever happens after that is the end product. I find that part pretty innovative and intriguing."

I hummed, gathering his numero-uno selling ability. Veer was a devoted boyfriend. "I would like to talk more about it. But it is almost time for my class."

I gave him my email and phone number. He promised to write up a jazzy résumé for me by tonight.

SAM

THE BEGINNING IS THE END, THE MIDDLE ITS EXTENT.

THE **HOLLOW OF** an everlasting hoot had no verge nor root.

EE-Ex was imperceivable, likewise.

Once inside, it had whatnot and all that. This alive edifice was similar to our creation. Contrary to what one must imagine, space was a noisy place filled with the roar of its voicing rhythm.

Sort of like breathing.

Deluthian, too, breathed to offset any invasive incidence. It comprised ninety-nine percent of EE-Ex construction. This swank metal was pure white and could be stained to reflect new spectrums.

I left it in its native state.

Figure 3 EE-Ex Interior

The restricted threshold imaged my iota imprint, breezing me inside. EE-NAI [EE – NATIVELY ADAPTIVE INTELLIGENT PRESENCE] expressed itself, welcoming me in the usual formal way.

"Greetings, Supreme progeny."

I wanted to give EE-NAI a hug.

Too bad. That feeling passed as quickly as it arrived. As an accessory to my lost sentiments, EE-NAI was amorphous. With a visually indistinct periphery, it was one with the structure.

"Feedback on renaming this monochrome wonder to S-Ex."

"Sex represents only one of your many endeavors, intriguing nonetheless." EE-NAI was unbelievably proper but funny.

Its sharp sense of humor could only be appreciated by me. For I was the only non-theoretical frequenter of this extraterrestrial virtuosity.

That's depressing.

For nobody.

"Not just one endeavor, but the main one, EE-NAI. I am the master of Root Chakra."

Also known as the grounding force connected to primal energies. A definite command of this drive made me a conqueror of basic instincts.

"I wonder what your huge head has mastered."

"Woah! So we're doing this. Okay. Enlist my complete iota identity. Now!"

"For whom?"

"For me, zero upstairs. Rather, zero everything." I showed the mirror to an invisible presence.

EE-NAI was my perception.

A perceiver projects the matter. So I cast EE-NAI; else, it never was. If a human ever entered this Deluthian wonder, they might see a white expanse. A rational thinker requires proof for the hypothetical. That methodology eliminated the possibility of knowing whatever was not there.

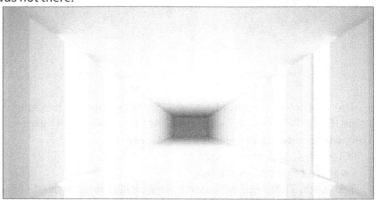

Figure 4 Human eye vision of EE-Ex

My secret was safe.

"Big thinker, possessor of wisdom, an ardent listener, focused, achiever of higher goals, balancer, protector, free from all bonds of the material world, adaptive and efficient, a neutral being, lover of beauty, and expunger of desires." EE-NAI gave my sales pitch.

I appropriately bloated at the ideas that made me, me. "Sounds about right."

To be brief, I was an eliminator of obstacles. Giving solutions was not what I stood for. Although I was skilled at crushing ego and pride, my amiable company brought auspiciousness and profitability to anyone.

For example, the terrestrial pest Akron Adamadon.

"Please list the reason for your visit, virgin Supreme Progeny."

Ouch!

I was over and done with the fact-checking ability of this absent presence. It'd be dead and buried if there was anything material about it. An acidic reality notified me it was in the purest form possible.

Energy. Eternal.

EE-NAI shall live.

"Binary requirement – Open with the production of NAI Army for an upcoming series of natural disasters. Recruit them globally at a radius of twenty miles. The land area is about 57.470 X 106 sq mi, and the ocean area is about 139.480 X 106 sq mi. Do the math to figure out the numbers."

"Demand accepted. Any concerns for the Underworld?"

"DeVeer Deläva is handling that." I believed.

"Can I have the source of disruption to adjust NAI Being peculiarities?"

A NAI Being was made from the Surpäs [REPTILIAN GENUS] provided template. They allowed my kind to create as many Natively Adaptive Beings as possible to protect us from others. Whoever the others were.

Surpäs believed in fighting for what belonged to them. No one should bow down to anyone and defend what was theirs.

Was I doing that?

Yeah. I was preparing to manage the disasters that would ensue on the surface of Earth when I make changes to remove the harmful effects of Memory Frames.

"Dual and artificial in nature – one from an unnatural shift in Earth's core and another from a planned NQF [NON-QUANTUM FIELD] encircling."

Panic and looting generously followed any societal or environmental disturbance. Coming months on Earth foretold such a happening.

A Gallantry of Moi and possibly Bro D.

The majority ignores the reasons for a disastrous event or events. Humans instead tend to pillage other humans unlawfully to soothe their fear. Hoarding something to anything for the sudden uncertain future. Without realizing that most human inventions would be rendered unusable if it came down to survival in nature.

What would one do with a cell phone if there was no signal or if it fried with an insurgence of electromagnetic radiation?

Cry.

There were two effective ways to manage panic-stricken humans. Either by physical suppression or by the invisible force of nature.

The sweeping difference between a country's defense team and a radical warrior was in the psyche of human beings.

An extremist enlistment was based on the two most daunting ideas – religion & hate. They were well-trained and systematically drained of every emotional burden. The change driver for terrorism was independent of the family, but their support fostered deliverance. A convincing game funded by an intangible promise of something post-mortality made them fearless of the number one tenet of life – survival. Death was a blessing and a one-way ticket to salvation.

A nation's defense line was recruited on a yielding emotion – the love of their country. Certain people are drafted to join the army, yet others join to take advantage of the benefits. This saddling complex drove them toward aggressive action to destroy the target. Not all of them can be prepared for what it means. A war situation was always to preserve how things stood. Mobilization in the sphere of family nurtured weakness. Convincing game exploited humans for protection decorated with some ammo, leaving them vulnerable to the elements and attacks. The most challenging outcome was emotional distress for the survivors unless they were inherently detached. These ordinary people were trained to kill, and most were overlooked post-war. An ugly reality that no one talked about. Death in any war was a loss.

My NAI Army was made organically of iota from the genus Surpä [REPTILIAN SPECIES WITH BLINDING AGILITY AND TECHNOLOGICAL INTELLECT] and

Discerns [CELESTIAL BEINGS WITH EXCELLENT MEMORY AND COMMAND OF ELEMENTS].

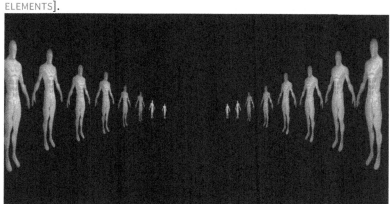

Figure 5 NAI Army

They were devoid of emotions, sex, or features to maintain motivation. A NAI Being would unzip files stored as memories inside it to kill anything without second guessing or future trauma.

Might I add, without the desire to go to paradise?

That end thrived only in imagination, not the physical world or the Higher world. No one could corroborate the final destination of the martyrs. Yet they would do what it takes. Because they had already experienced heaven in their head, and it was perfect.

One thing was a given that a soldier might not return the same way they left. Yet they would sacrifice their lives for an idea larger than life. Because their SELF would preserve as information, continuing to live as memory in the surviving crowd, in documents, and pictures. Awards.

The human species expended innovation expertise for profit and entertainment. Not where it mattered. Not to save human lives in a battle but rather to take life. Most of the federal budget funded warfare obligations, not the needs of veterans.

THE FUTURE WAS complete mechanization, eradicating the reliance on physical authority and human decision-making. Those were good-for-nothing obsessions.

A personal touch was not a bodily need but a thought-driven appeal. Love or war.

"Apart from elemental insulation, the NAI Army will need the ability to withstand extreme electromagnetic surges."

"Appreciating the heads up like a hole in the head. Math for such adjustments already performed," EE-NAI kidded.

This invisible coarse bastard!

"Moving on, shapeless schmuck. The second and final request – Production of one hundred thousand Organic Beings or Zeptos by replicating Victory Vella Supra code."

"Just checking, any calculations to be performed, virgin Supreme progeny?"

This was the last straw.

"Actually, yeah. Could you calculate the time I'll spend eradicating your presence quickly?"

"That salient fact can't be computed."

"Damn right. Indulge in this fact. Adios."

WHAT RESTS BEYOND THE REALM OF THOUGHT IS WITHIN THE ABYSS.

THAT WHICH WAS not expressed was immeasurable.

Unknown.

The one that we didn't know, we didn't know. And so, nothing to be done about it. What must be done would be done about the things that were known, though.

Oh, the temptation of prudence.

Most of the constructs in this Universe were mute to the auditory senses. Waves from them were deafening once felt. The creation held the bang of its annihilation. To be perceived, not heard.

Earth's core was ferocious but silent. The tipping point had neared, and I was gawking at the animalistic nature. A murky magnetism hummed rhythmically. My mortal form was pulsating at its regularity to offset its force.

Similar to what alien Deluthian metal did to remain intact when an external force bombarded it.

Figure 6 Earth's Core

Ripples on my body were more potent than the raging swell of the ocean on a full moon. The water element inside me was undulating wilder than the cyclonic winds.

Vibrations from such powerful manifestations were formidable. Arising from the Earth's core, this invisible force of nature was nothing but a link. To balance the concepts of this creation – Stars, planets, moons, etc. This unbiased connection kept everything steady and hung nicely in the vacuum.

Scientists had hypothesized it brilliantly as they decoded the gravity bit. Only renowned astrologers understood its impact on the human body. Their unseen frequency had a powerful tug no matter the distance. Unless another celestial object of equal measure interfered, diluting their potency. In that case, a frequency with new strength from this combination would emerge.

Expressing differently.

This expression needed a medium. The human body was the perfect vessel that absorbed such frequencies constantly. It altered human behavior depending on the rate of realization.

What was this fortified frequency?

Thought.

This unseen entity was the biggest enemy of humans, making them a killing machine. Turning them vicious in the name of the most advanced. Science would make this connection.

Not soon enough.

Fuck that, though.

My cold-blooded disposition did not agree with the heat. I approached the resonance from the Earth's core. It weighed on me, but I was blessed with healing superpowers. Aka – memory reconciliation. My body was capable of reverting any harmful changes back to its native state by correcting them against the original cellular memory.

As I continued to settle my mortal vulnerability, my alien side began taming the beast. Physical strength was of utmost use here. One that I was again rewarded with in abundance.

Not more than D.

I randomly wished he would come and have fun with me.

"Missing me, Sammy."

Holy hell and shit fire.

I hugged him. "You could say that."

D was aligned with me. No communication was needed to feel that connection. He handled my unrest with his definite presence just for me. My gladness was showing in my foolish smile.

"Let's summon the core quality from the poles, Sammy."

We flashed to the surface, transiently forming a shaft of swirling slag. D's plan was superb, as the distance doesn't dilute the drag. Unless another one with its gravity interfered. And we had our very own satellite with powerful pull. I pointed at it.

Moon was in its full brilliance, hovering like a giant.

Jeering at us.

"Our strength is more than anything combined." My brother placed everything below his potency.

Legitimate claim.

"Right you are, D." I clicked my tongue twice. "What made you come and support? Underworld is still on the line."

"You'll help me save my clan."

"D, you haven't got a speck of demon iota. It is not your clan. But. I will join forces when you summon me. You got me, Bro."

"You got no choice, Sammy."

I perked up at his confidence rather than his trust in me.

"I'll take the North pole."

"You being the less powerful, take the South pole," D countered.

I was duly insulted by the mightier heir of destruction. A rational slur as the magnetic strength is reduced at the South pole.

I went for the neck. "Will we ever stop being a kid, huh?"

Promptly my throat was in D's generous palm. "Never."

We gave each other a few punches and then a hug and flickered away to activate the supernatural.

OUR FIRST STOP was Mars. Barren. Beautiful.

It was also the closest celestial object our moon could gravitate towards. The Southside of Earth would have even lesser gravity if the moon was removed from the equation.

We appraised the red globe. In terms of geology, Mars would put Earth to shame. Many more majestic peaks than our blue planet. Countless geographical wonders were past awe-inspiring than ours. A beauty that needed no validation or recognition. It existed in isolation for nothing.

Except humans had sent their sub-par machinery here, hoping to colonize it someday after discovering frozen water. I mean, all they needed was water to survive. Never mind other stuff, like an aerated atmosphere.

This reminded me I, too, needed it. Although my equestrian lungs could hold immense air, they could also filter Martian air to extract whatever little oxygen it had.

I was still a mortal. Respecting that adversity, we got to work.

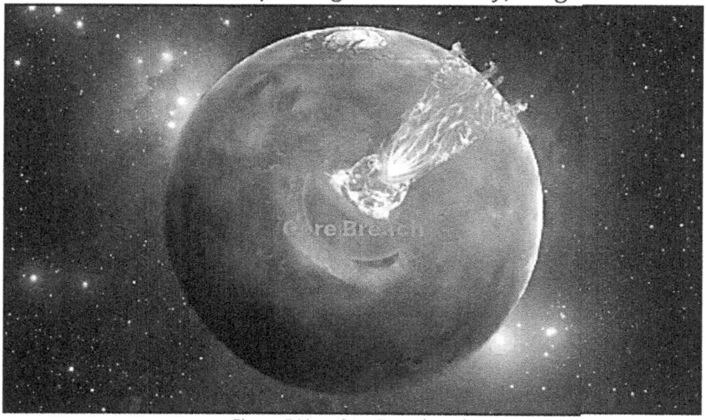

Figure 7 Mars Core Breach path

D entered the core of Mars by pulverizing it down to the middle. Carving a tunnel with vortexed air as the drill. Rotating movement exhumed the rubble out, causing a massive dust storm. Very comparable to what occurred periodically on this red planet.

The scene was… messy. Dirt and debris were flying everywhere. Making it impossible to appreciate the view from this distance. So I flashed away while D continued to grind.

Keep up the good work, brother.

An electromagnetic force was a lot stronger than a gravitational force. Sun, by far, remained the most potent source of this energy for our purposes.

I summoned Sun's energy, concentrating it on Mars's core via the path D had created. This unseen wave of vitality infused Mars with more mass. Upgrading its gravity.

In turn, pulling our moon toward itself. For a short period, Earth's moon would be a planet. Two Earth seconds, to be exact.

Once Earth was free of any other pull, we again funneled additional energy from our star, the Sun. Adjusting Earth's core charge, we motioned a swing to reverse the pole's alignment. It would be rapid but not reach full maturity for several months. That would give D and me enough time to relish and curb the devastation.

We filled the gap created by D on Mars. That fixed the mass of Mars by blocking the additional source of energy. Which, in turn, arranged the Earth's moon back in its initial orbit.

Creation regulates itself no matter the commotion.

Everything finds its place or ceases to be. We tittered, waving the fact in accord.

If someone kept a tab, our theatrics from Mars to the moon and back to Earth took less than a minute. At that time, the stock market plunged to a new low. Hundreds of people died in hospitals due to the loss of power. Of course, many other things that were unimportant to me or D malfunctioned.

Might I add it was all human invention that took the biggest hit?

Natural disasters were looming at large to follow suit.

VICTORY

RULES INTEND DOMINATION.

A RANDOM DRUG test suggested a substance abuse problem with one of the staff members. ZepRive had the clause to fire on those grounds. This was an excellent break to assert power and brandish my position at this company.

The impression on my desk announced my boss's arrival. I washed off the smugness from my face.

"Hello, Sam."

"What is my beautiful Tory thinking?"

Sam had a playful feel to him. He caressed my face with the pads of his thumbs, planting a chaste kiss on my forehead. He studied me for two flat seconds and pulled me in for a proper one.

It lasted long. Too long.

Our first!

Tingling from his cool drool sent shivers down my spine. His grunts were guttural and greedy. My silence spoke volume. We both liked it.

I guess.

Chasing my lost breath, I stumbled back several steps, shaking my head. "I was too sure I was into women." Even I couldn't hear my disturbing admission.

Sam diminished the ordinary distance between us in a flicker and moved me back into his arms and then to my desk. He angled himself between my legs and placed his hands on my thighs.

"Women have twice the essence of femininity in them. They are naturally inclined towards both kinds. Some never realize, some do and pursue it, and some choose to be hypocrites."

"Is hypocrisy the same as pretense?"

"A part of it." He turned away to take a seat. "Who is she?"

I suddenly became coy. Sam had an acute sense of hearing. "Someone I saw while sifting Memory Frame readings from the café you are working on. BTW, it is also ruined. You know what that means."

Sam droned in reluctance. He appeared to flicker at warp speed a couple of times. And then it stopped.

Zany.

I dropped my opposite-sex fondness focus. My heterochromatic gaze was still kept hostage. Unlike Sam, who had green, brown, and yellow colors in both his eyes. So uniform and engaging. My left eye was green, and my right eye was cloudy brown.

I most definitely had Stockholm syndrome.

Why else would I never question his flirty flare, bold moves, or unsavory ventures that seemed to keep me in the office forever?

I don't even remember going out and having an everyday social life. Except when Sam took me out on dinner dates, I was always confined to the boundaries of these pale white walls. I needed to review my contact list and connect with people to reestablish my public rationality.

He snapped his fingers, and I came out of my Sam-trance.

Or some trance.

Like many times before, I was standing in his private office, not mine. Short of any memory of ever walking in here with him. For sure, I was strained with work.

I fixed my hair and my dress.

"One of our employees failed the routine drug test. It's just appalling why people are so complacent. I plan to fire them."

"Sounds hypocritical."

"Sam!" I whispered in surprise. "We have clear guidelines."

A signature stare, followed by nonchalant dismissal, arose. "All these off-site corporate parties involve unimaginable sexual activities and the use of recreational drugs."

"Those situations are above my pay grade." My grim reality made an appearance! "It is for C-Suite and up."

"Why are only the ordinary employees required to take the brunt? Do they not need to unwind?" Sam sounded genuinely concerned about regular people's loosening outlet.

What in the world was going on here?

Elites only cared for peasants when they needed validation of their superiority. Sam was neither Elite nor did he ever need confirmation of his superiority.

"They can unwind in many other ways," I argued.

Sam was smirking like a lunatic. "How do you unwind, Tory?"

My name was drawled out teasingly to throw me off. But I was steadfast in holding my beliefs. Drug use was not to be taken lightly.

Period.

"I am not going to answer that," I flagged my choice with a sneer.

Even though I never touched anything forbidden, keeping calm was a smart call. There was no way my dull life would get exposed to Sam's scrutiny.

"I smoke weed. A lot."

Sam's smooth avowal of a deadly habit was affirmed by a demo. He materialized a joint out of thin air and lit it. Slowly, he took a long drag out of it while eyeing me funny. Without letting go of the toxic smoke, he got up from his chair to sit across from his work desk on the plush white couch.

I followed.

His defiance of rules shocked me. Sam only did it to trick me again. I was well aware of that and would not fall for the trap.

"Your rules so you can break them. You're the boss."

"And who are you, Tory?"

Sam stared at me while I examined his question with a soft laugh resulting in a taunting hum. His blatant gawking kept me on edge. I stood without uttering a word. He just kissed me not moments ago, but that was not the spiciest focus here.

My identity was, apparently.

He knew me too well. His ask was pointless.

After that awkward standoff, he lay on the sofa and closed his eyes. "Don't bother me with petty issues. And yeah. Zeptos are going live for the breadth of human emotions. Not just sex," he mumbled.

SAM

EVERYONE STANDS THE SAME CHANCE OF SURVIVING A NATURAL DISASTER.

TECHNOLOGY PUTS ONE ahead of the survival game.

What of accidents?

Odds of subjectivity to one's benefit were needed to avert that.

None of the rules applied to me. I had gone amok since I lost something.

Someone.

Insolent it may be, I had the means to amend it. Maybe Papa left the Memory Frames for this day. He was aware of my defeat before me. It was to teach me a lesson and also show me my limits.

What were my limitations?

None that I was aware of.

The knowledge of being capable of fixing a discrepancy kept me sane. I'd be the first to invalidate fate-applied tariff on the preordained.

Life after death.

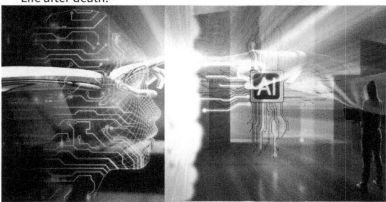

Figure 8 Zepto From Memory

I was going full steam ahead with every available resource. To create a Zepto with memories of the dead.

No one could fuck with me. Even me.

Many things made yours truly privileged, and I gladly accepted them. Blessed with not just genetic superiority but also a material legacy.

Only in the human world would inheritance put them on top of the heap. In nature, every new beginning had native traits and nothing more. Maybe a mother's care and guidance for some time. That which I also got even though I shouldn't have. Not from my biological mother but others of equal measure in terms of affection.

My chromosomal father was all for trialing Universal knowledge. He set off the fabrication of hybrids to cater to the needs of Elite hobby.

Sexually perverted pursuit.

Gone were the days to fuck a blow-up doll. Maybe not for the impoverished lot.

Under Rorrim, I was merely refining perversions to the next degree of destruction. Human population needed to be controlled. Blurring the line between the body and the ideas residing in it was a snide way to further my damaging plan. The first approach to apply this was to separate sex and reproduction.

And the last… that would be the end.

I celebrated the ensuing irony of being unable to differentiate between a productized humanoid and humans.

Or simulated and natural environments.

Or naturally conceived/birthed and organically cultivated offspring.

Did it even matter?

Not to me, for sure. For I needed it. Pretty soon, it wouldn't matter to anyone. Even if they didn't need it.

A gradual change goes unnoticed. An immediate change is accepted if financed by fear.

A Transgender was similar to the converted one, except for reproduction. If the reproductive idea was eliminated in humans, it would make no difference as to who was born as who. The demand to behave in a certain way from a given gender was from society, science, and religion. It had nothing to do with the body or its need to procreate and survive.

Science was beginning to understand this.

Society was improving to normalize this.

Their progress was still snail-paced except for religion, which stayed stagnant.

Humans wanted to expedite everything. They were all about the fast pace. Somewhere in the conscious background, they understood how slow thought was. It was always catching up with the occurring events. That realization forced them to dive deeper into a given moment, scaling it down to a more granular level. To capture and process information speedier than thought.

Their intelligence was capable of it.

Even so, humans were way behind. Way past life's sell-by date. Example – Praising the discovery of a dying star billions of light years away.

What was the use of a throwback, prehistoric data they were decoding?

None-hundred-percent.

Then again, the past created the illusion of something that was there. If humans were as quick as the happening moment. There would be nothing to see or examine. As it has happened.

What is faster? Getting shot or recording and reviewing it frame by frame.

At the human level, the time between pulling a trigger and the bullet entering/exiting the victim's body was less than a blink of an eye. Comparably, one couldn't fathom nature's speed unless one stopped to think and analyze by reflecting on the past event.

After a vicious attack by a lion, the surviving lot returns to grazing as if nothing happened. An animal never stops to look back. Not even when its newborn was the one the lion pride was feasting on.

Human curiosity, hence, was the cause for thought continuation.

Might I add misery?

Meanwhile, Akron Adamadon had delivered his promise on yet another abominable project – Virtual Insignia.

Kudos to that bastardized human. I loved hating him.

Civilization was moving towards lab-grown accelerated birth on an as-and-when-needed basis. Separating themselves from sensual movement and breeding strangles.

We were experimenting covertly but successfully on homeless, suicidal subjects. I planned on unplugging a few of them for a public appearance. That would give assurance to our select customers.

Provided that went well. Else, I'd find another way to implement it by sneaking it into an already established technology.

AI beings.

3 — FALLACIOUS

ATHENA

LIFE IS FULL OF STRUGGLE WITH A FAUX PROMISE OF BETTERMENT.

I WAS AN outstanding example of hoodwinked.

Believing to be a pioneer at something brainy while waitressing and having sex. There was nothing serendipitous to stumble upon when working like an ass. Maybe soon, I might.

It was 2 AM. The crowd had just begun to taper down. With recent renovations, the café was packed at all times now. I was getting ready to go home when I saw him at the door, scanning his private establishment. Veer gave a sound smile and marched out back to meet Swain.

Thank God!

I wasn't game for talking today.

Even though he penned a brilliant resume helping me with a job that most wouldn't even consider. Not that I needed any persuading. Money was what I was going for, and it paid loads of it.

That was so long ago.

Maybe I should return the favor somehow. But he never asked for anything except for my company and intellectual feedback on random matters. Somehow discussing intelligent junk made me feel important.

While balancing my cash drawer, I realized I had not been this relaxed.

Ever. Financially, not mentally or physically. Money was good from both of my part-time jobs. The café was frequented by customers who loved to pay generous tips, and Rorrim was a life savior. I could afford insurance for the first time in my miserable life.

It was such a relief.

An accident took my father away from me and left my mother more in essence than presence. She'd been bedridden since then. Still, I was happy she was alive in some sense.

Maybe it was selfish of me. Somehow keeping her breathing in any way possible was needed for me to feel not alone.

I bid goodbye to my co-workers and was about to step out when Veer walked back into the main area.

"Would you like to leave from the front door?"

"Can I get a drink first, if you don't mind?"

Can I mind, though?

Sure, if I wanted to get fired again.

Veer tilted his head to the side, looking behind me. Swain was retiring for the night. It incensed me that my boss could go, but I couldn't. Since I was all but an employee, I had to abide by Veer's rules. He could not only have had me sacked from this waitressing job but also have his girlfriend take the fancy porn career away.

Fear of losing my income kept me in check. Not ethics or loyalty.

That was sad.

Also, his racy temperament insisted on my attention.

That was doubly sad.

I put on a phony smile and poured his favorite scotch – neat. Not the spiced rum bullshit Victory had ordered for him when I first met them.

My cheerfulness was not all forged. Veer didn't need to beg for attention. A welcoming calmness around him made him approachable. His hellishly attractive look was difficult to not notice.

Was I the one staring at him now?

Sweet Jesus.

Veer was at the far end of the bar counter, busy on his odd-looking phone. "Give me company." His dull voice was beseeching me without making it apparent.

I walked around to sit beside him.

"Penny for your thought."

"My rate is a little higher than that, Veer."

Instantly after, we both combed the dead air for my lost respectability. I foolishly placed myself as an expensive hooker.

Except, I was just that.

"I'll need more than your thoughts if I am paying." He creased up his lips immorally. When I remained in awkward stillness, he chimed in again. "Ask me my rate?"

"Huh?" I pulled a face in reluctance.

"Bring to mind Athena. We all are selling something."

I beamed, valuing his attempt to make me feel better. But the thing was, I wasn't feeling inadequate about my choices.

I enjoyed sex.

Yet something made me all clammed up. I sucked at reasoning, but I couldn't whitewash my hesitancy. In isolation, I could be myself. Then I didn't care who I was or what I did. Socializing made me aware of what others considered a problem or defect. All this confusion came when I wasn't even breaking any rules. My job at Rorrim was legitimate and possibly futuristic.

Finding my lost ability to speak, I crackled. "I bet – I can't afford you."

Next, I raised my lashes shyly to hold his beautiful face in view.

"In monetary terms, you can't. I do take other forms of reimbursement." His smirk was deadly cute even though he was clearly flirting with me.

"You're funny." I licked my lips, biting my inner cheek softly. My gaze bounced between his hazels, feasting on them outright.

What could I possibly give him?

Nothing.

"Ready to examine my thoughts, Veer?"

"Pretense."

Quarterbacking Veer's acumen, I deliberated before divulging. "Mm… we all pretend. It helps us behave." I stressed and air-quoted the last word. "Also, our true feelings are private."

"I can suss out some sense of the privacy angle." He pointed the finger at me without touching me. "Do you ever stop pretending?"

Wouldn't you want to know!

Suddenly a far-fetched possibility stormed my mind. If I wasn't poor, maybe we could be… I heaved a moan of disappointment.

Get it together, Athena.

We were never a match. Veer was an Elite. Untouchable. Unreachable.

I just happened to work at a café-bar he owned as a waitress. A quick run on how low-slung in the chain of command that was. It was possibly the lowest. I was also a lady of pleasure working under his girlfriend. Tasteless. Undignified.

Not that I cared for anyone's opinion. That said, views made a difference when getting respect in society. Judgment never ceases to disappear in this world. It made others feel superior about themselves. In fact, judging seemed to be the primary entertainer for the masses. Apart from porn, of course. That was the number one industry where most people spent their money.

Secretly.

And the number one industry most people condemned.

Openly.

"When I am all alone, I stop pretending," I spoke my mind.

Part of it, anyway.

"Right now, in your head, you are alone. Are you not pretending in there?"

He specified. I contradicted.

Veer turned a little to look me square in the eye. "Tell me everything you thought of since I walked in that door without beating about the bush."

"That's private information."

"I want to hear you talk."

That was weird but also very intimate. I wasn't sure where we were going with this. Behind my puckered lips was a muffled snort.

If looks could kill, Veer was wearing that at this moment. Dead serious. And lethally gorgeous.

Did we cut more slacks for attractive people?

Sure we did.

If Veer was bald, not Jason-Statham-style bald, and not someone with a head full of silky hair. Or if he was poor, not a well-to-do executive, and a striking fella. Or if he was bossy like Swain and not dripping sweet molasses in his every word. I would not have entertained him tonight. It was past my working hours, and I was about to pass out from exhaustion. But here I was, lost in him anyway.

While I lived in my thoughts, Veer stoically examined my expressions.

I rested my elbow on the bar, cupping my face. "Fine. I am drained and was looking forward to going home. It irritated me that you came in so late and ordered a drink. But then you asked me to keep you company. That should have further annoyed me. But you helped me with my resume and are so good-looking. But still." I lamented with a forceful breath. "I am tired, Veer. I want to leave."

"I don't want you to leave," Veer murmured.

A sudden increase in my neck size was fabricated to show my utter surprise. "Why?" I crossed my arms across my breasts. "I also want honesty."

"I need your input to design something."

That was a quick and not a response I expected. For some odd reason, I believed he was maybe interested in a one-night stand.

Man!

I was already into sex. Rorrim had filled my head with additional erotic allusions.

"Okay. But just so you know, I do not like this. I am only doing it because I fear you would push me into homelessness."

"I could do that. Thanks for reminding me." He took another mouthful of his hard drink, emptying his glass. Veer growled, rubbing his face vigorously.

I sensed he was either tired or somewhat emotionally burdened. Still, his back was always straight. Never had I ever seen him slouch. I assumed he was in the army before.

"Tell me why women pretend to enjoy sex when they don't."

"That is simple. If one keeps repeating something, the universe conspires to give it to them. We yell and fake orgasm so God would finally take mercy on us and make us feel what we should be, to begin with."

He twisted his mouth, returning back to his innocent self. "What makes you think women should be reaching orgasm? I mean, isn't the whole point of sex to reproduce?"

I scoff-adjusted my shoulders. "Maybe for animals."

"Humans, therefore, are different?" He frowned as if I had placed our species incorrectly on the food chain.

"You should ask your girlfriend. Maybe you and her can experiment it out."

Veer was further enchanted by my suggestion. "Tory is fluid, but you're stable. I want your opinion."

"I like having sex. Sadly, I am yet to truly appreciate it with a man. Or woman. Maybe I haven't met a good match. Also, it is about making others feel good too. Isn't it? It takes two to tango. Otherwise, it's individual onanism."

Veer mischievously cinched his eyes and continued to disproof me. "Humans put too much spotlight on enjoyment. They stand to please others to get acceptance from everyone, losing focus on their pleasure movement. When shockingly, it was all about them feeling good."

I bobbed my head once. "Never thought of it that way. But you're right. Like I am here to please you because I want to earn money for my life pleasures by pleasuring a stranger for some futuristic project. All the while suffering through my tiring job, boring sex, and this bullied discussion."

"Bullied?" His brows shot up once again.

This shouldn't have come as a revelation. I had already told him I wanted to go home.

Twice.

"Let's see. I got up at six. Since then, I've waited tables for the morning crowd until ten, attended school till three, got fucked for money, and made it back at seven to wait tables again and serve countless drinks. As I was about to leave, you engaged me in a discussion that had nothing to do with me. I still stayed because I was scared of losing my job. So, Yes. This is bullying."

I panted a little after my fantastic speech.

He tapped endlessly on the bar counter with his index finger. Gave me a homicidal glower with his out-of-this-world tri-colored eyes. They glinted like the raging sea, appearing distinctly under the soft light.

"Pretension leads to frustration. Never ever pretend with me."

I rolled my eyes, ceasing the act. "In that case. Good night, Veer."

My rudeness was chaperoned by a friendly kiss on his cheeks.

SAM

PREFERENTIAL TREATMENT IS UNFAIR TO THOSE NOT PRIVY TO IT.

PATRONAGE AMOUNTED TO routine for the one being pampered.

The café was crammed that morning with automatons. Being the proprietor, I had my designated seat open at all times.

Mine, I imitated Gollum's voice and sat down.

The unbeatable view of the ocean in the distance and buildings larger than life up close could only be appreciated from this very spot.

"Hi, Veer!"

A sea of sentiments lashed inside me whenever I allowed my inherent ability to capture the feelings of anyone in proximity.

Outwardly I appeared blank during the process.

Inwardly, my body was ultra-active.

The human in me took longer to offset it. All because I was not sent for proper training from birth. My adoptive parents shielded my existence from my biological ones for seven years. In the process, I spent critical time leading everyday life.

That's in the past.

So is the present!

Since I had a particular affinity for chaos, I allowed this surge from a select few people to invade me. As a result, I stared at my server for a solid thirty seconds.

It was unintentional, and Athena got that.

Victory's interpretations were off the mark. She felt I liked her, maybe more. Hysterical. And so wildly inaccurate. Victory meant a lot more to me.

"I want your input on something."

"Maybe I should quit Rorrim and join you as a consultant. It will be more respectable that way." Athena twisted around, holding an empty tray in her hand, appearing to be in a good mood.

"Still stuck with the judgment."

She lightly shook her head. "I mean, I can then openly tell everyone what I do."

"You are a consultant at Rorrim, for all intents and purposes. Not a Sex Consultant."

Exercising bias by being selective with words was what I was advocating. People do that unintentionally all the time.

Intentional bias was also cool with me, as I didn't discriminate. I never dig for the reasons for action and focused only on how it impacted me. An eye for an eye so that the world would be unsighted, and no one would ever turn another blind again because they would already be.

"So bougie!" She rested her hands on her chest, inventing class.

Athena was never with highfaluting views. I respected that.

"Just so you know, I need to leave at noon. And I am working till then." She paused for a beat, examining her nails. "I took the job even if it meant getting filmed naked as I am not required to play when not enjoying it. And I can scream my lungs out if I am. With zero judgment from anyone." She supplied the rest rolling into a dreary sigh. "I still doubt if I am not pretending."

I grimaced, approving her openness with a subtle nod. It was refreshing to spend time with an unpretentious member of the community. My clandestine life didn't allow me the luxury of friends.

D was my only ally, aware of all of me.

Victory was precisely how I needed her to be.

Maya was true to her name, a measure of illusion.

Citzin was a lost cause on Earth's ongoing timeline.

Athena blurted her unmethodical thoughts openly to me regardless of any external interference.

Hence favoritism.

To be a favorite, one has to disturb a particular frequency in you. This influence, most of the time, was unknown to the influencer. Athena was unaware of her effect on others. That lack of understanding kept her humble.

"We never finished our comparison discussion."

"More like women feigning to like sex and men actually enjoying it." Athena latched on to her inner cheeks, pouting her full lips. "Are we comparable, Veer?"

We?

Fascinating.

That day I was distraught over death. Yet, our conversation was generalized, not personal. Athena was hinting otherwise. The human in me was made scandalously aware of her triggered hormones by my unusual side. It was effortless to tell what she was pointing at.

I transparentized my sunglasses to air the emotions I was holding in my hazel eyes.

Hankering aphrodisia.

"No. We aren't comparable. Not just you and me. We are all different." I whirled my finger around us. "Comparison is vain."

She squirmed, standing a good two feet from where I was sitting. Her legs were obscured behind the table. That awful tray in her hand covered her breasts. A lime green apron protected her torso from prying eyes. Only her pretty face was free for my ill thrill.

Not enough. I needed more.

I texted her an address and time and left.

ATHENA

A FALSIFICATION OF STATUS CAN NEVER BE FALSIFIED.

THERE WAS ALWAYS a tell to counterfeiting. A veteran aristocrat didn't need the coaching to spot a budget trespasser.

I sucked in some air, failing to calm my biting breath. My dress was just enough.

Maybe, mumbling to myself, I took another lungful in. It turned into a big maybe after a quick second survey of my appearance against the high-end restaurant I was gaping at.

Humiliation was on the menu.

For me. For sure.

There was a strong chance I would be asked to leave. Veer should have warned me. I cursed him silently.

A humble smile on my face masqueraded my embarrassment thriftily. Anyone who cared to glance would know I was straight from the hood. Every step I took made me feel more out of place. The bodycon outfit I wore was not even near satisfactory. I looked like a hooker.

In some sense, I was one. So... I bought this crap but expensive clothing for this dinner date.

Is this a date? I wondered.

My swinging hips carted me inside. Thankfully, people didn't try to shame me too much. Until I met the receptionist. A thorough head-to-toe glance photographed me. She was about to shower me in shame when Veer's voice concluded her intent prematurely.

"Athena, glad you made it."

With a slick move, he held me by my waist lightly and guided me inside. Luckily it was a short walk.

Thank God!

I couldn't look another judging person in the eye.

"You own this one too!" I kidded while the waiter pulled my chair for me, totally begrudged.

"I do not own every restaurant in town, Athena. Although, my brother ciphered one not long ago for sentimental reasons. His mother had courtship dinners with our father there."

So he has a step-brother. I assembled a critical fact.

And his brother also owns a restaurant. Veer hails from a family of restauranteurs. I guessed he was from a military background. So very wrong I was.

"Order something quickly. I want to get on with our discussion."

All right.

This was not a date, after all.

"A fancy dinner is not going to compensate for my time."

Veer peaked out of the menu to flit a charming but intense gape at me. "Do you have something in mind as compensation for your services, Athena?"

I giggled gracefully. "I haven't thought about it. Let's see... Mm... how about you help me get a home loan? I don't want to rent anymore."

He waved to the attendant and ordered for both of us. I trusted his choice. A sommelier listened to us and brought wine that paired well with the ordered food.

We talked about banks, the declining housing market, and rising interest rates. Veer kept me focused on the minuses of owning a home.

Food got served.

"Even when you buy a house, it is not really buying. You still have a monthly payment, similar to renting. As soon as you default on your loan payments, it will be seized. Unless you buy it with the full down payment. Despite that, if you default on your property tax. The governing body can take away the amount you owe any way they see fit. That includes selling the home you think you own."

"You don't want me to buy a house?"

"I prefer the word lease, even for our lives. We extend ourselves into ideas or opportunities to achieve our dreams. A simple contract between thought and body."

A sarcastic laugh escaped me. "Are you from a cult? Your ideology startles me."

He smirked handsomely.

Veer was effortlessly the most enigmatic person in this restaurant. And he was my companion. That somehow made me swell with pride.

"Do you subscribe to an ideology, Athena?"

"No."

"Can you define it?"

I noticed Veer was not eating and kept toying with his food.

"Something that is well acknowledged by someone or believed to be true. Conviction of some kind. A belief."

Veer finally savored his wine with a smooth swig. His plate was still wholly unscathed. I was drooling at the delicious spread, helping myself indulgently.

Only after pretending to be a lady I clearly wasn't. That too, for all but two seconds, maybe.

"That's not belief, Athena. It is just what I said exactly. Lease. Belief is signing up to be a part of an organization. Imprisonment of reality to some evidence or data, especially scientific belief. Religious belief is unsighted – true submission."

Clearing my throat, I declared my neutral stand. "I am not sure of any belief I am sold at."

I hadn't been around adults or parents in a while. No wonder I had no discipline in my life.

"Everyone holds on to some belief. The lease of our life is contingent upon a variety of principal. Think," he urged.

I stared at the carved ceiling in the distance and grumbled a careful gasp imagining my beliefs thoroughly. Veer was extraordinarily meticulous and intelligent. His words were more gaping than the deepest underwater gorge. Which meant I must come up with something palpably rejected by the people.

Just so I sound astute.

"I truly believe there is nothing wrong with what I do to support myself and my mother. My life, my decisions, my business."

Veer held his bottom lips between his middle and index finger. But his pretty smile was hard to hide. So was the glint from his shiny hazels.

"Your answer was a well-thought contention. Makes me believe you do think there is something wrong with how you support your life. Else, it would not be an issue at all. It wouldn't even occur to you."

I spun my eyes in a disagreeing manner. Veer leaned forward and rested his forearms on the table stylishly. He began storytelling like a professor. Unfittingly, I was not a college student any longer.

"Long time ago, there was an unusual number of train wrecks in a small town. Turned out it was due to locals removing the nuts and bolts from the track joints. They were using them as a weight for the fishing line. An investigation led to many villagers' arrests.

"They were stunned and unable to comprehend how they caused the accidents and deaths of so many people. When the science and logic behind the mishap were explained, they still remained unsure of why they were being punished.

"Now they took what was unguarded. Their action caused the accident, not a malign premeditated reaction. Your law, nevertheless, punished them in the first degree. And society rendered them uncivilized." Veer paused to take another sip of his wine. "Do you suppose it was fair, Athena?"

I breathed out jeeringly, listening to the story I had read in my grade book. "They caused the accident, Veer. How could they not know taking the bolts out would have catastrophic consequences?"

"This story is from when the railway system was new to that country. None of the villagers were educated about the development." He almost sounded mad.

"Even then. People died. How illiterate could they have been? It wasn't rocket science."

Veer then tossed his weird phone toward me. I glanced at it.

```
<html>
<body>
<script type="text/javascript">
document.write("Dress code for tonight, a black cocktail dress");
</script>
</body>
</html>
```

"What is this?"

A caustic mutter broke past his perfect lips. "Illiterate!" He placed his phone back in his pocket.

My jaw dropped to the floor. "Did you just call me illiterate?"

How dare he?

He was not mad, though. It was me that was annoyed.

"Did you scroll all the way? I mean the text I sent you with the address and time for this dinner."

"No. I just copied the address right before I came here."

"At the very end of my text, this same message was written in JavaScript, detailing the dress code for this place."

"Looks like you didn't care enough to write it in simple English. I would have understood it then."

If I opened it. Which I would not have. That makes it not the very last thing I forget. So my rage was pretty pointless.

Still.

"Exactly. An understanding is as good as its reach, grasp, and acceptance. Even if I excuse the fact that you never really fully scrolled through the text. How could I expect you to wear proper attire for this dinner when I never gave the specifics in the language you understood?"

He took another swig of his wine. Perusing my face with a placated expression. I chomped my inner cheek with a toxic bite.

"Athena, I get it. How could you know what you don't know? The burden is on me. Not you. That's why I didn't worry about your choice of wardrobe, insinuating a specific class. Since everyone here knows me well, they didn't make a big deal. My representation saved you from the embarrassment."

There could have been better ways to make me understand the stupid villagers' innocence. But it had to be tied to my neglect to read the text in its entirety and my life choices.

"How is this connected to belief? And just for the record, you humiliated me on two counts. My carelessness and my job." I was angered.

"Neither. It is you who is taking offense. I do not care who you are, what you wear, or what you do. I wanted to understand a few things from your point of view." Veer was tongue-tied for seconds. "I will talk to Tory about giving some supporting documents so you can qualify for a home loan."

Well, that cheered me up instantly.

Was I that naive?

Sure. Pseudo-pride had no place in my life. That concept was long buried and out of my way.

"Thanks, Veer. It means a lot." I blinked slowly, imitating fondness in cat language. "I like that we are comfortable in each other's company. So much so that we have intense arguments without killing each other. I hope you consider me your friend because I sure do."

We lifted our crystals. "To friendship!" I repeated after him, and we clanked our wine glasses.

"So. Belief. What's yours?" A clever attempt at divesting the discussion ball in his court.

In de facto, I wanted to know him better as a friend. Maybe more if he wanted it too.

"Any belief is to conform to objectivity and give up independence. Ironically, it is propagated as freedom. An unspoken rule – this freedom is within the standards of society and law. Everyone is looking for a like-minded bunch, not freedom per se. That makes them unaware of being trapped."

I sure needed more people to associate with me.

Go, team Athena!

"If I were with my people, I guess I would survive anything. What's wrong with looking for a concurring audience?"

"As such, there is nothing wrong in forming a group of people like you. It could be problematic, depending on who you are. An undecided person is unsure of everything. A soldier is always indifferent to the outcome but very sure of the motivations. A reformer is very sure of the outcome but doesn't dwell much on motivations. A rioter is ill-informed of the motivations and unsure of the outcome. A religious person submits in hopes of fulfilling their desires. A self-claimed realized person desire to not desire or desire too much. In any case, if you are looking for something, it is always to fill a gap that stems from the root cause – fear."

"In that case. What's your fear, Veer?"

He coiled his mouth every which way. "I have none – belief or fear."

"So you're not looking for anything and don't need anyone."

"Spot on."

BEGGARS CAN BE DREAMERS IF NOT CHOOSERS.

AN EVALUATION OF material possession was a reminder of my abject poverty.

Giving my surrounding a once-over, I inhaled the musty air of this rundown place. All of this was practically my whole life. Whatever was held inside this house was what defined me. Somehow a lot of my belongings were absent without leave. Many of my best-loved clothes were also missing. Maybe mom was donating them without telling me.

I felt hurt.

Not because of my miserable living condition. It was how my conversation with Veer ended, notifying me that he didn't need anyone. Veer was uncomplicated. I liked that about him. But when his raw opinions were of me, I wished he was pretentious.

Somewhere I hoped that he had a belief system that I could break into. Make him join team Athena.

In a nutshell, turn him to like my way of things.

Secretly I loathed rich people. And Veer seemed to be loaded. Or at least he pretended to be by lavishing money on unnecessary luxuries.

I loved to engage in sexual intercourse. Yet I stormed out first from Victory's office after hearing the Rorrim job description. Because it made me realize I was worth more as a porn star.

For the world, I had a chemistry degree and was still waitressing. Bix-by never accepted my internship application, rendering my college degree a waste. I had to hide that I was having uninhibited sex to support my education loan. Only as it was looked down on.

Veer didn't disparage me, compounding my attraction for him. But I'd exploit him to get a loan and enjoy his company rather than ruin it with sex.

If he did the same with me, it'd offend me.

We don't want what we give. The taste of our own medicine is forever bitter.

I was rudely familiarized with my duality.

I was self-centered.

Wiping the crusty tears off my cheeks, I prepared to pack, starting from… wherever… there wasn't much anyway. All of it was right in my view.

I was seriously in need of a life.

Taping up boxes, I pondered on my dating choices. One of my ex-collegemate had been hounding me for months. He was from a decent family, good-looking, handy when I needed him, and phony. That suggested he would most certainly leave me if he knew I was a sex consultant.

Or that gray-eyed hunk who patronized the bar eyeing me outright all the time. His uncanny resemblance to Veer made me nervous. He seemed to have deep pockets and was mighty fascinated with me.

Gut-wrenching reality told me Veer was what I wanted.

But he was only there for some good-natured banter. If I chose to remain his friend, I would also enjoy his company in luxury. Which was all up to me. He didn't need anyone. And I was most certainly a part of 'anyone' pool.

Nothing is ever a complete package. A trade-off or some concession lays in wait to fuck you up.

I groaned and drifted off to sleep with mom.

VICTORY

ACTING A WICKED THOUGHT WILL LEAVE ONE GUILTY OF THE OUTCOME.

BARING PSYCHOLOGICALLY DERANGED people, we were all remorseful.

Sacking another worker based on failed drug test left me feeling awful all day. It was them that were in the wrong, not me.

I was in a crappy mood because I wasn't a crackbrain.

This was the twenty-seventh one in the past five years. One thing was clear, substance misuse would never be extinct. The sparse population that remained chose to get high than waste their existence on finding a cure for radiation cancer. Escape was above understanding a problem for such losers. Let alone discover a way out.

I now understood what Sam pointed to when he said all-feeling not all-providing. For of that crucial difference, Zeptos never validated a high from anything.

They operated by the funda – matter over mind. Their response was neutral to any pleasure movement. Every time was the first time for them, except they never expected a second time. Because the memory of saying an experience was exhilarating was promptly deleted. It was never etched at the cellular level. In turn, it never made a mark at the DNA degree to mutate genetically and become a hereditary habit.

Sam called it a switch flip in humans that forced them to feed an addiction. And was inherently passed on once it became a habit. Be it drugs or any other high like food craving, sexual dependence, or compulsion to kill or abuse another being.

Humans operated by the funda – mind over matter. Mind, however, was in no one's control, and the body was all but a host. Once the switch was flipped, it was an endless war with addictive ideas. From then on, addiction could only be replaced with another. The only way to solve a problem was to fix the root cause.

Eradication.

Sam was slick with extermination.

There was no point wasting my time pondering, given that I had a lot of work to take care of. My life was snowed under with Rorrim performance recordings.

Playing for the eleventh time was reverse harem footage.

Perfecting the clips by airbrushing them was not even a part of the learning process for the AAI program. Expressions were logged on a separate track with different software that filtered them contingent on what boosted their sex appeal. Only reactions got documented primarily as part of my task.

Enhancing the ambiance with filters was for my stimulation. Not a project requirement.

I watched women have sex with every male and female subject boringly. To preserve my normalcy, I masturbated while faking editing them.

Several times.

Sam had scripted a form I used to question the subjects simultaneously and individually to get their feedback after they coupled. Getting over my hyperactivated sex drive helped me stay professional when interviewing them. I was numbing myself by engaging in something I hated.

Fear can only be overcome by confronting it.

The subject response was also humanly analyzed for disagreements. Then it was tweaked before feeding into the AAI program.

All the subjects at Rorrim were augmented or enhanced with organic matter. It communicated their hormonal complexity as soon as they entered the building. Memory Frames could capture and convert it into a language of choice. They were also installed in the action room, collecting a specific frequency from the subjects while they performed. Later it converted their feelings into speech. That description was always very different from the subject's response to my interview.

Except for my favorite one, who was surprisingly always honest with no pretensions.

A presence was announced approaching my office door.

I yanked myself out of my deviant pursuits and quickly neatened my appearance. Stepping out of the editing room in style, I spotted my guest in my office looking like a nun.

So uncustomary.

"You asked for me."

Excellent.

I forgot about our little meeting that I never bothered to put on my schedule as it was nothing to me. Since I was a master pretender, no one would know. Least of all, this whore dressed as a priestess.

Watching her have sex on-screen made having a face-to-face conversation a bit awkward. None of the subjects were aware of manual intervention. Their contract stated digital feed correction before entering it into a software program.

On that account, they never knew I edited their films every freaking day as a part of my morally wrong but high-paying job.

"Athena, how are you?"

"Tired," she frowned. "Thankfully, I don't have to work at the café tonight. I am looking forward to crashing in early at home."

Café! Work!

My riotous laugh had to be censored hearing her bogus busyness. Also, her tone of voice was too informal. It clashed with what my standing authority at ZepRive demanded. She needed to be familiarized with the rules of conduct when with me.

Who did she think she was, my friend?

I didn't need fake friends.

"Would you like to have coffee, or chamomile tea, perhaps?"

Offering beverages was not part of the plan. Clarifying my control was. Playing a good host certainly was nowhere on the list.

"Tea sounds better. I am serious about getting extra sleep tonight. At least ten hours," she winked.

Athena was getting too comfortable. A stern reminder of my power was definitely in order.

Methodically, of course.

We took a seat, and I ordered tea for her.

Since I couldn't stand to discuss our unrighteous job any more than I had to. Of all things, we talked about curtailing cancer contagion for five minutes. Steering the conversation to other work-related topics, I subtly mentioned proper professional behavior. ZR concerns over drug use and suavities requisite when with the managers.

It was strictly to set the premise for what was about to follow.

A slap in the face.

Her face.

Perversely, my gaze was set on her lips, which were a beautiful nude shade. She never wore makeup for her scenes, just a winged-out smokey eye. Other than proper hygiene rituals, nothing else was required as the visuals were used for digital and manual analysis only.

Still and all, her natural look made me even more bitter than I already was due to my contrasting character. I stowed away my irrational thoughts and zoomed out of her lips to focus on her.

She took a generous sip of her tea. "You are not having any?"

"I don't care for tea."

Athena shook her head twice. "So, Tory. Sorry, can I call you that?"

"I prefer Victory."

"Sure."

Her quick acceptance suggested she did not take offense when corrected. Even so, I had to be precise. This meeting was not to make friends. Quite the opposite, actually.

"Would I get overtime for this meeting?"

That's what I thought. Money was what motivated such people for everything to anything. Not self-respect. This bloody meeting was to discuss a special favor that Miss stone-broke pulled in using her slum appeal on Sam.

I sure as hell haven't a clue how she did that.

"This is extra. Not preferential treatment but more like goodwill to get you approved for a personal loan." I gave her a long-nauseated glance.

Athena curled her mouth in surprise. I could have forgotten to elaborate on the meeting topic when I sent her the invite.

On purpose.

To expose the whoring cu…, no, I can't be that small.

"Getting back to the rules for me but not for thee. I just doubted what I could write to keep your employment letter dignified. Considering the nature of your effort at Rorrim. Not to mention the confidentiality of the project itself." Hiding a wicked grin, I kept a straight face expressing my ill-disposed view.

She at once gulped, swallowing the hurt I handed her. Latching onto her cheek, she shook her head lightly.

The likes of Athena could make money without doing much, enjoying life, and getting paid to get fucked. They were an insult to human intelligence.

While the likes of me slogged for years studying, losing out on any social life, and then working our asses off to pay for our college loans. We were inglorious wonders of the corporate ladder.

Underappreciated.

After an unending struggle, I got a job that paid me more than I could spend. Here she was, fresh out of college and already on the way to buying a house. That was unfair to many women who worked hard to make a dignified living.

And I hated Athena for that.

"Veer said I was a consultant. Maybe the HR letter could say that."

Veer!

No one addressed Sam as Veer. What an out-of-the-common way to refer to her boss's boss.

"Since you are in a contract position, I am unsure how manipulating designation would help. A bank loan usually requires a stable job, among many other things. Such as guarantee."

I slandered her pathetic life.

She had nothing to give as collateral. There was no way she could buy a house. Banks didn't give out charity. Because they never felt guilty about robbing others.

Jaundiced by my unwelcoming stand, she gave a squashed smile, "Veer said it wouldn't be a problem."

Veer!

I screamed on the inside.

Did she confuse herself for his girlfriend?

Such misunderstanding belonged in her dreams. Else, it had to be an erroneous logic. My position was second to none in Sam's life.

I folded my arms with the precise aim of displaying my lack of flavor for her kind. "What makes you think you can waltz your way into someone's pants to get a loan?" My voice was appropriately graphed to present my acute disgust for a prostitute.

"Huh? I took this job because it means making good money. Isn't that what you are doing too?"

"Excuse me!" I shivered with revulsion over that absurd assessment. "I am not having sex to make money. How mortifying would it be to run into these people while doing grocery."

"Should I be mortified if I run into my ex-boyfriend while doing the grocery with whom I understandably had sexual relations?"

Oh boy, she was a high-strung slut.

"You weren't being paid for it." Every word was justified to perfection and spitted out like gravel. Aimed to hurt her missing dignity and scrape her insides.

"So if I didn't get paid, it would have been ok?"

The nerve of this bargain-bitch.

"Sex for money is shameful. So is sleeping around. Do you have any morality!"

I sounded riled up. She was getting the best of me.

"What are my options, Victory?"

"I would have loved to chat about options, but my schedule is pretty packed. I need you to answer a few standard questions to get the reference letter. It's ZR for ZepRive Resources, not HR. They will send you the documents. That's the best I can do."

I wasn't going to defect on the orders given by Sam. ZR would provide a letter to aid my vile plan.

After all, I was an ethical employee and a respectable member of society. And Sam's girlfriend.

Not a whore.

4 — MOVEMENT

SAM

EXCEPTIONS ARE A SACRED SIGN OF A MATRIX MALFUNCTION.

HUMAN INTERVENTION WAS still a thing for exclusions that couldn't be coded into a machine.

Athena's recalls were an answer to that – A boon.

She was natively beautiful, sure of aspirations and desires but sufficiently plain. With marginal memory to go by, hence, a challenge to program into a self-learning AAI logic. An adventure from Rorrim's perspective, as it was fascinating to code her Ersatz. I had to filter out some buried secrets from Athena as they shaped most of her current personality.

A quick review of Memory Frame Readings gave me the latest insights into the ZepRive workforce.

Victory Vella was just as I veiled her to be – Evolving brilliantly.

I convulsed, snickering at her escapist quackery. The way she was so self-possessed. The stealth means she hid her dark side from everyone, even herself. Or the self-righteous ways she handled her affairs made me hilariously tear up. Her obsession with Athena was concerning.

Citzin was a cosmic anomaly not destined for me – Too fucked up. I could have put her deviant nature to good use. But…

I grieved my loss for a split earth-second before turning to the contessa in front of me.

Maya Moha. She was extremely basic in all her approaches – So verbatim. I didn't particularly delight in her robotic personality. Since she was pretty by design, and her voice was adequately modulated, I tolerated her inch-perfect presence.

Drumming my fingers on my desk noisily, I revealed under-the-counter information. "Maya. I can tell what you would do next, or even tomorrow at this time to dot accuracy."

Maya laughed. "Am I that predictable?"

"Only to me." My excellent semblance was evident in my fluid tone.

She silently agreed, handing me brewed to precision coffee. I barely took a sip, placing it down on the table. She recited my calendar like a sex-machina before giving me tuneful news.

"Athena linked this morning. She tried your archaic cell many times but couldn't get through."

That's desperate. I wave-bantered. "Is that all?"

"She wanted to know if you were… ahem… alive."

I cackled at that quip. Athena was mad at me.

How cute!

Something was amiss. The best part was I already knew what.

When I saw her name flash on my obsolete device last night, I purposely ignored it. Athena was never the anxious one, but her attempt to reach me more than once confirmed borderline dysphoria. Her message, y*ou failed to reimburse me for my services,* was funny but accurate.

I texted back, asking her if she was free this evening.

Short of waiting for her reply, I went about my day as recounted by Maya. Athena didn't try to reach out to me. My hectic schedule did not give me the liberty to investigate why. However, I found time to check if she had quit ZepRive.

She hadn't. Not yet!

That made me glow more than I usually did.

A SCANDAL IS AN EFFORTLESS ENTERTAINER.

MY HUMAN SIDE thrived on some such smear campaigns.

Who was I to argue?

Only the most harmful of beings, that's who. And my kind didn't argue but acted.

My brother from literally another mother summoned me as he had some epic update. Before flashing to D, I ironed out my plan with my galactic enemy.

Akron Adamadon.

This middle-aged bloke was fascinated with making a shipload of money. This asshole was on fleek in the tech arena owing to a few groundbreaking inventions in his early days. Now he was famous worldwide.

Not just a local celebrity.

Celestial objects in his astrological charts were beautifully aligned for this pest of a human. Neither his mind nor his body was at fault, but an outlandish manifestation that assisted and distorted Akron's SELF. Funnily enough, he was the one that made Virtual Insignia live in record time for the human world that gave this SELF a back seat. He wouldn't laugh at that one.

So I must. Ha!

EE-Ex was uniting with Akron in designing and releasing a state-of-the-art spacecraft. This fandango could house thousands. Clearly, I did not need an ally, given my supernal legacy.

Why was I helping Akron, then?

My purpose was to study this driven mortal and have fun. Rorrim would help him reach his fate in a hurry. That prophecy, scandal really, thrilled me.

STAGING THE MAMMOTH feat of expediting the Earth's pole shift was causing mild fluctuation arising from the core. D and I got the lay of the land and determined that Underworld was not in danger anytime soon.

But soon because time was comparative.

Meanwhile, Surpäs were getting wind of my worldly makeover. They practically owned creation. I fumbled to forage all the strength needed to face them.

No. Modify that… to fool Surpäs.

No one owned what was not up for ownership.

These reptiles had a bearer [BODY CAPABLE OF BEARING & BIRTHING] and seeder [BODY CAPABLE OF SEEDING A BEARER FOR PROCREATION] as the head of their genus for eons. They were a replica of the earliest and were connected to the memories of all before them. Maintaining their indigenous running ever since they became social beings.

Humans should learn from them.

Too bad they were tardy for this educational insight.

Being the ones that controlled from the shadows, Surpäs didn't care for the position of prominence. And humans were almost extinct. Hence no learning to be done.

"Are you up for the challenge, Sammy?"

"Let me pave the way to your demise in the vampish arena, D."

WE ZIPPED FOR the café, united in wedlock by a complete lack of seriousness.

I was confident Athena was there that evening. In an entirely non-addictive sense, I kind of kept tabs on her.

Every once in a while. Not habitually.

I suggested taking our flirt fest to a private corner near the bar. That was a better spot to test the crowd. Ever since our kind began surfacing, the graphic improved a million folds.

Yeah. Our kind was meant to be pleasing to the eye. I was my inspiration for the Zepto façade. Good-looking, friendly, prosperous, basically, nothing of crucial significance.

A projection was playing the tail end of the devastation caused by the few seconds of electromagnetic surge we were responsible for. Not many cared for it genuinely after too many years.

My Papa told my mother that everything was news until it became personal. The convenience of remotely grieving had taken away the actual heartache from a catastrophic incident. No one could possibly feel anyone's pain unless they were empaths.

Certainly, none in this bar area had the paranormal ability to apprehend the emotional state of another. It was business as usual, and the broadcast was all but background noise.

In other noteworthy news, several fortune hunters were scoping our irresistible aura.

In terms of physical appearance, D had only one advantage. His gray, colorless eyes. They were haunting. Sometimes, simulating a hollow tunnel, and other times they appeared like crystals. This ocular sorcery drew the ladies in for him.

I was otherwise beyond fanciable to the nth degree.

Most frankly. An authentic replica of my father. Contrasting D in how our iris reflected the entering light.

D was swathed in a pile of ladies until further notice. In a trice, an unexciting woman approached me with more than agreeing enthusiasm.

Mega-agreeing.

That was a total turnoff. I gave her a prosaic grimace and peered away while she proceeded to feel me. Not just rub me salaciously without consent but also chatter like a bog-standard Podcast.

Entirely one-sided.

D was pushed to a private room by three women.

Flipping Hell!

Ordinarily, I wouldn't let him win when it came to winning our stupid bet. Only now, I was taken over by someone. Undiscovered by him, D was with Zeptos, not humans.

So I didn't give a shit. D could call someone who did.

Meanwhile, my sexually fervent companion continued to talk. Bored to tears, I would croon, moan, and smirk every now and then. On the side, I contemplated a million ways to make her stop breathing. That view gave me momentary relief.

To her benefit and mine, I spotted Athena.

Thank fuck and any others that needed to be thanked. Mother goddess, it must be thanksgiving for me to be so thankful.

Athena sweetly rolled her eyes at me when a neurotic grin coated my lips. She looked furious.

Rightly due for two reasons.

A swift revision of affairs handed me three. In short order… One, I never answered Athena's call. Second, I replied in a text nine hours too late, not bothering to give explanations. Third, someone was sexually exploiting me in front of Athena, and I did nothing to stop it.

Why would the last said reason bother her?

Someone. Please tell me. Or I will assign myself as Athena's crush.

I waggled my index finger, demanding she come to me. That doubly angered her.

Shame. I was a customer and owner of the café. So she must hide the heartburn by swallowing some antiacids.

She did. "Can I help you with something, sir?"

Fawning at her all-black and all-covering clothing, I tired away seconds before answering her. Also, listening to the word 'sir' milling out of her mouth amused me. She hadn't called me that in such a long time.

Now that we were friends and all, she was grossly informal.

"I missed your calls. I was busy."

My nauseating companion angled her neck to see who I was talking to. I removed her bothering hands from my erection and got up without explaining this abrupt desertion. Athena and I swept a quick, indifferent look at her when she stomped away from us.

"Don't let the door hit you where the good Lord split you." I employed my sense of humor to lighten the air.

Athena shook her head, subjecting her inner cheek to horrific brutality.

To appreciate the little seclusion from the dense space, I scooted further. The distance between us was now marginal, and Athena was the only one in this creation who wouldn't be alarmed by that.

Or, at least, distracted by it at some level.

I kept my cool gaze hovering over her naturally beautiful face. Her outer imperfection was needed for the sake of my awakened spirit. Inside her modest outfit was an incomparable body, challenging desires.

Victory used to send only the audio of every performance.

Not just Athena's.

I reviewed the visuals as well.

Just Athena's.

As a result, I knew the woman in front of me had what they called the 'body of a porn star.'

"She is attracted to you. Useless societal taboos are keeping her from admitting it to herself. The only way she can deal with it is by demeaning you."

Athena rolled her eyes in revolt. "Veer, the thing is, I don't need an apology. Least of all from you. What I truly need is a home loan."

Her text only detailed the humiliation she suffered when the bank rejected her application. She didn't ask how I came to know of Victory's indiscretion.

My relationship with Victory didn't mean much to Athena. She was not bothered by verbal scorn but by silent judgment. Victory's entitled attitude rubbed her the wrong way.

"I'll co-sign."

Her jaw dropped. My smile deepened.

"As payment for your intellectual consulting services," I added a good excuse for this generosity.

She breathed in quick succession, rocking her head in doubt of this reward. "My credit history, job situation, and social standing are all questionable."

I moved my fingers, trudging to where her arm rested on the counter. Stopping short of making any contact, I leaned closer.

Breathing restfully as if nothing of calamitous amplitude was about to happen.

Which it was. Before long.

Pushing aside that minor hiccup, I exhausted moments of the most meaningless idea, time. My blank stare draped over Athena, consuming her beauty in a platonic way.

She let me.

Impassive about the scientific side effects of magnetic manipulation, I decided to let her know one of them that would benefit many.

Loss of all alphanumerically saved data.

"What if I told you I have seen the future? And I know without a speck of doubt that you can be trusted."

"What if I told you I don't think anyone can predict the future? And so I might default on my loan given the uncertainties."

"What if I told you every digital record is about to be wiped out, and banks will no longer have the means to get back at the defaulters."

"What if I told you that sounds unlikely but fantastic!" She gave an amused chuckle.

I expressed warmth, beaming wittily. We stayed softened, savoring the proximity of our differing bodies. Swain marched focally toward us at some point to accuse Athena of not doing her job well. She was guilty of that allegation. I shimmered a threatening eye at him, and he left without riposte.

Total fukwad.

I must adjust him.

Since Swain gawked at our intertwined fingers before leaving today, he clearly got the idea that Athena was special to me. If only I could do something more about it.

Overflowing with flair, I pulled out my device. I had preserved this mode of communication solely for the damsel embellishing me with her saintly aura. I texted at an insane speed without looking at the screen. All of my optical senses were engaged fully for Miss Athena Denali.

Until she broke the tie when her phone chimed.

She read. She smiled.

We parted.

ATHENA

AN EXPERIENCE IS ENCOUNTERED EVENT WITH ACTUAL CONTACT AND STUDY OF SPECIFICS.

A DREAM WAS also experienced and recorded at some level. The human race was moving recklessly, making me feel I was perhaps dreaming things. The world was not inclusive but indifferent. I often believed restaurants and a slew of other businesses was a thing of the past.

I never saw any operation other than the modern café, which was still open.

The world was a mess, as if an earthquake had hit us. Global clean-up efforts with advanced machinery continued without a break. That massive electromagnetic surge demonstrated a crucial flaw in all human inventions years ago. There were no more gadgets that would submit to this transmission massacre again.

My advancement seemed to be a little slower than the rest. I still had a handheld device, and so did Veer.

Just the two of us.

His phone was… weird. Nothing like the one I had.

People were moving towards the old way of life. No one was seen glued to a screen publicly. Our arm enhancement sent wireless information without the need for an inorganic medium. It was a strange technology that often pushed me into a gorge. Because I didn't correctly remember how I came to be acquainted with it.

These weird happenings began with the ZepRive interview.

I was clear on that bit.

THIS TIME, I thoroughly investigated everything Veer messaged me. The address was in a posh area at the edge of the Specter Ville downtown. I suspected it must be a pricey place.

Soon, my doubts turned concrete.

My oh my! I tooted gracelessly.

It was difficult to swallow or blink when my cab stopped under the fanciful, ascending white building. It felt like Veer was tricking me. He clearly said in his text casuals – In plain English.

Why the dickens was this place too chichi?

Sucking in a deep breath, I readied myself for yet another humiliation on account of Veer.

Que sera sera.

I announced at the entrance my intent. The doorman or whoever they had in these grand buildings gave me a nod, capable of clipping the redwood tree in one slash. He guided me inside an elevator that was not golden all over.

Thank God!

I couldn't take a Trumped-up symbol of indulgence.

Nervousness boiling inside my veins blurred the rest of the ornamentation from getting committed to my memory. Unlike regular elevators, this one had no buttons on the inside. Rich people didn't need to stop at every freaking floor.

Before I had a chance to thank the doorman or attempt to tip him, I sped up to somewhere.

Alone.

I blinked some, and my vision spread wide to an ultra-modern setting. A super-stud was hulking by the center arrangement between the ceiling-to-roof window and me.

Credit must be given where due. Veer was a Greek God.

At least some God, I was convinced of that.

When his parents made him, I am sure superior quality genes were generously selected. His presence had the power to draw the soul out of anyone, leaving them winded and dizzy.

I couldn't see anything except him and the blue sky behind his shapely silhouette. At some point, the sea in the distance merged into the skyline.

All in all, it was evenly azure.

"Is this a secret hotel for like MI6-type people?"

"It's home, Athena."

Home!

My hobbling effort at composing myself with a joke fell flat on my face. I stepped inside and stood drenched in embarrassment. A black and white silent movie played at double speed. Recounting all the times I had insulted Veer.

I was super casual with him for good reasons.

Come then.

He was filthy rich and yet so unpretentious.

How come?

Only a wandering spirit would know. I must cast some spells to find out. Sadly, I wasn't a witch.

"Your place is absolutely stunning. Must be snowcapped on the top." My forced laugh was nervous as fuck! "I'm scared to move. What if I break something I am sure I can't pay for." My voice was overly energetic.

"Nothing is meant to last forever." His silk-laden tone sensually teased me.

"But it could last your lifetime." I pointed at him. "I'd rather place my cheap ass in some corner while I am here than risk an expensive incident."

Could I stop playing cool for a minute?

Because I was sounding like a nincompoop.

"I chose my home, seeing as I needed seclusion." Veer poured every word with sultry slickness.

My tainted blood informed me he was flirting with me.

Maybe I was wrong. Then I hoped he would rather not tell me.

Maybe I was right. Then it'd be topshit, and he must tell me.

Oh, kind Sir, butter my butt and call me biscuit.

Veer curled a smile and held the back of his neck, tilting it to the left. "Your loan in the amount of two million is approved. You will get a notification from the bank soon."

I went cockeyed at the mentioned sum. "OMG! That's a lot."

His frown hollowed my heart with a thud. "You don't have to reach the loan limit, Athena."

Did he scoff at me?

He sure did.

"It's so you can buy something you like without worrying about additional approval," he winked and welcomed me further into his crib.

Castle.

Mansion.

I'd settle with penthouse.

Befogged by the snazzy setting, I followed him like a lost puppy. The view below stumped me when I accidentally walked closer to the glass barrier.

Although I was dying to know which floor this was, I didn't dare ask him that. Knowing whatever hundred-plus level I was on would only make me more nervous.

Ever since I could remember, I was not too fond of high rises. I'd take sunless barbeque over perched in the air. If it meant my feet were grounded. My wish was to own a small cottage on the outskirts with white picket fences, French doors and windows, and a decent pool.

Too much for a poor Sheila like me. Granted that nasty fact, I had dreams, and I wanted to fulfill them. Any way I could.

Legally still.

Only because I didn't want to rot in prison or die before enjoying the fruits of my labor. If it wasn't for fear of being caught, I would have gone to any length to make life easier for my mother and me.

While I was in my la la land, Veer was staring at me.

Nothing new.

He could ogle at me to obscurity, and I would not object. Because I'd be willingly swooning to death.

Veer blinked. I woke up from my paralysis.

The luxe sitting area overawed me. I sat on the couch, all assembled and panicky. My legs were folded together, and my hands were on my lap. Wrongly imitating an elegant lady of dignity and decorum. Veer had an entertaining smile on his darling face while I made a fool of myself for failing to behave pleasantly enough.

It was time to give up.

Blowing a defeated sigh, I got up. "Veer, I'm a little lost, a lot embarrassed, and very uncomfortable in this swanky place of yours."

Veer's eyes were suddenly murky. His tricolored iris was no more but a round chunk of a chasm. My erratic breathing rammed my body with weird feelings.

Or was it some weird feeling ramming into my body that triggered me to breathe erratically?

What the absolute fuck!

He eliminated the emptiness between us urgently. Grabbing my hair with force, he placed his lips on mine.

And wow.

That was a bonzer kiss.

His taste was indescribable. Too sacred for words. The need to breathe also escaped me. All I wanted was for his tongue to swirl in my mouth forever, his saliva to sodden me, and his cold hard body to crush me to smithereens.

If his kiss is so addictive, what will the rest of him be like?

I quaked at my erotic thoughts.

Slickly, he let go of my mouth. I fluttered my lashes, holding in view a drop-dead-gorgeous man clutching me in his sturdily built arms. He wasn't even panting after that vacuous kiss that didn't allow us to breathe. Starved for air, I was gasping like crazy.

"Why are you so intimidated, Athena?"

"Why are you so cold, Veer?"

"I am the hottest of all," he declared with supreme confidence.

His certainty was legal. I stood captivated by those magnificent eyes. Drinking the drool that was still actively being produced for him. Then, I told him something I had never even told myself.

"I am not intimidated easily. Material possession does this to me. I feel small and reminded of my petty social standing. Things talk to me louder than people do. I can take verbal insults from anyone, but when I see luxury, negativity screams at me. Mocking my simple self. Do you think I am crazy?"

"No, you're not. When it comes to people, you can see past the pretense. The same is true of everything else. It is just layering." He stacked steps in the air with his hands, walking away from me in reverse.

I gave a quizzical look and sat back down, this time with less awkwardness. Veer placed himself across from me. I appreciated the distance.

"What kind of layering?"

"Just like the eye color is not the actual color of the eyes but the reflected light from it. Our world is not a combination of matter & energy but simply energy. It is layered with various permutations and combinations of active disturbances. Or waves. Spreading from one energy source, constructing multidimensional images."

"Added advantage…" I straightened my shoulders. "…I understood some of it given my educational background. The chemicals, organic or inorganic, are similarly structured by bonding. It is the layering of the atoms that form a molecule."

Veer leaned forward, casually resting his forearms on his thighs and locking his fingers together. "If you go deeper, it is nothing but space."

He smoothed his way into a highly debated boundary between quantum and metaphysics. As a science admirer, I had to agree.

Somewhat.

For I didn't take an interest in abstract theories.

"Yes, it is a lot of space and pulsing energy." I provided the deleted fact from his previous statement to his current claim.

He judged me amiably. "Your world is about your awareness. You cannot understand anything beyond the interpretations of the senses of sight, smell, hearing, taste, and touch. Limitless creation is what you, as a human, desire to understand. However, immeasurable is what you're terrified of. That's why the void of the unknown would kill you at sight as it is outside your grasp."

"When you said we are *terrified of the immeasurable*, I got it. I first equated that to a jump-scare in horror movies. But it isn't that. We anticipate a jump scare, and you are referring to something entirely unknown."

"So you agree humans are limited to their perception."

"We exist to quantify everything around us; I agree. Our inquisitive temper is what makes us the pioneer species. Humans have traveled to space to some extent. We've landed on the moon and explored the darkest caves on Earth."

"Not natively. With technology." He rested on the sofa, spreading one arm on the back and another on his muscular thighs.

Why did I notice that in such great detail?

I couldn't help it. Veer was the beau ideal of manly gorgeousness.

An unobtainable one.

What a shitty fact to exist.

Setting aside my sudden crush on Veer. Not sudden, but whatever. I decided to disagree with him.

"What's the need for native skills when we have tools? We have devised ways to conquer every other fear. Even though fear of darkness is healthy. Vital to our survival. Artificial light helps us defeat that."

"Human babies aren't afraid of the dark or anything until thought infects them by instilling knowledge." And his hazel orbs pierced my chest like a knife sliding on softened butter. "Lack of night vision combined with the absence of the knowledge layer that creates the images generates fear. A blind person doesn't know what light is. They are not scared of darkness as they are not separate from it. Knowledge makes anything real to you, not your senses alone."

"What about someone who could see before and later lost their sense of vision?"

My question made Veer suddenly very pleased.

"They'd be at a loss until the new normal settles in." His words cradled me with care. "Once you are addicted to something, it is hard to let go of it."

"What should we do then?"

"Feed your addiction."

I believe Veer agreed with me. Somehow, his explanation was perfectly bizarre.

"Alright, then, I will enjoy the world the way it was meant to."

"What way were you meant to enjoy this world?" He twisted his brows.

"Well, God created everything for us…."

He rumbled a booming laugh sending tremors from his heaving lungs to me. In the corner of my eyes, I saw the walls pulsating. I turned around, and poof, nothing.

Was I high on something?

Hello! High on Veer.

"Humans are so vain. They not only created God in their image but also said God created the world just for them. Can you not see how self-centered it is and sounds so absurd?"

He pointed to his ears when uttering 'see' and then to his eyes when saying 'sounds.' I didn't catch what he was trying to do with that mismatched action.

"There is no contender for our species, Veer."

"I like that you never doubt yourself."

Accepting his flattering remark, I coated a faded smile on my creased lips. If that's what it was. It could have been a pronouncement of my vanity.

Righty-ho.

He hoisted himself and walked around to lean on the glass overlooking the world below. The entire length of his powerful presence intimidated my tiny frame in a menacing manner. I was extremely attracted to Veer.

Sexually.

Nothing exceptional. It would be unprecedented if Veer was attracted to me that way. I got mixed signals from him. His feelings for me were something that needed to be established. Even after that hot kiss we had shared moments ago, his intentions were obscured.

"I was pointing to the fact that all senses are the same. Seeing, hearing, touch, taste, or smell."

Oh, okay. That's why he was pointing to his eyes and ears wrongly. Because interpretations from our sensory organs were interchangeable.

Well, knock me down with a feather.

My brush-off was met with an added explanation. "People experience feeling the smell of a place when remembering it. You decipher the captured information in your head and align it with your previously stored knowledge. In the future, any feeling, not just seeing and hearing, can be experienced and adjusted at will. Things will look like food and taste like it. But it can be instantly tweaked as per your liking by a command, like salt preference. There will be no need to add it to your dish. It is a matter of giving your body nutrients and fooling your senses. Not the actual ingredient because you tell by tasting it."

He was resting so coolly in his personal space. I admired everything about him. Even God-knows-whatever he was saying to me. I would sit here and waste my life listening to him if he wanted me to.

Adopt me, Veer.

"You make it sound like we are mechanical. It also appears we are doing all this automation for pleasure." I made a dexterous deduction even though I was totally sex-crazed.

Ever since I got here.

Well. I felt this way for Veer forever, really.

"Athena, every species of animals, plants, and non-living things are programmed to flow with life. Humans are the only consumers that exploit this world and want to replicate it. They realize they are a destructive force, yet they want to find aliens that are exactly like them. Not once thinking, what if they actually do find them?"

"I am thrown off balance here. Are you for or against humans?"

"The designer of this Universe needs a narcissistic species to appreciate its arrogance. It takes one to know one. Humans are closest to The Creator. But they are clouded by thoughts, preventing them from becoming too powerful."

He didn't answer my question.

"We are the most powerful, Veer." I firmly informed him of our superior status.

Somehow he seemed to be separating himself from the rest of us.

Bizarro.

Unless the wealthy were now a species of their own, he was one among us.

He scratched his day-old scruff amusingly. "Do you know what happens when the invention becomes more powerful than the inventor?"

I shook my head as I didn't know the answer to that.

Veer walked over and sat beside me, cramming the space suddenly. My gaze was set on my lap, avoiding his angelic face. Fretting unnecessarily with my short dress.

Veer slid his icy hand on mine. "It is set to null and void," he made a predatory declaration.

I darted my head up in shock. "Killing it?" I double-checked.

He angled his head, puckering his lips and spreading his hands in the air, approving my take.

Gosh darn, I missed his touch immediately.

But Veer was scaring me. We needed to change the subject.

Or I, I needed to.

"What exactly do you do, Veer? I mean, you own this." I ran my hand around his fabulous and tastefully decorated home. "I can't imagine Eckhart Inc. pays so handsomely for R&D? Unless you inherited it."

"A little of both."

Spoilt brat. I knew it. I took notes in my head as he continued to uplift himself.

"I am born rich, financially and genetically. My interest is very similar to my father's. I love encrypting the organic creation using technological finesse."

"Am I some kind of a subject to you?" My comment was light-hearted despite my anxiety due to a mix of fear and sexual pull.

"I am consulting you. I believe we agreed to that." He pointed out.

Man, he had self-control of heroic proportions. He was completely undaunted by my dishonorable erotic expression. To counter him, I proceeded to behave levelheaded.

"Not in clear words. But. Okay. So you talk to me to get my opinion on things, and then what?"

"I code it."

"You code it?"

"Uh-huh. We are also friends."

"So you need me now?" I verified.

"No one needs anyone." Verification failed! Soon after, eloquence succeeded. "It's balancing synergy."

"If it is to balance, then you do need someone."

"If you insist."

Wow! If I insist!

Sensing my annoyance at his slash-and-burn response, he twisted to face me before respectfully admitting his true feelings. "Athena, I need you. Not just for consulting."

On double take, that hit the spot.

SAM

SEXUALITY IS THE MOTHER OF ALL THINGS CORRUPT.

 THENA WAS IN my arms and on my bed the next second. Too slow compared to my abilities.

But she didn't need to know that, among many other things.

There was a parallel where she was poorer than this one. Earth was a dystopian hell due to an unnatural flip in its magnetic field.

What a shocker.

On yet another parallel, life was similar to this one. Only Athena ran the Rorrim lab after replacing Victory in a programming logic competition. Victory would definitely murder Athena on that parallel.

The most despised one by me was where Athena and I never crossed paths until very late in our lives. That parallel pushed every other event further as well. Delaying many crucial revelations.

Death was a sure end in all of them at varying timelines.

Now for this one. It was changing with every monopolized decision, even the very concept of death. Still undetermined where we would end up as I was in it, not witnessing it.

Not that I wasn't fucking it up as per my liking.

I was, thank you very much.

Dystopian or flourishing, genetic richness was in my favor. Financial abundance was and will remain a mirage. Not that I wasn't also monetarily rich, no matter the timeline or the parallel.

I was, thank you very much again.

Circling back to the beauty in my arms – Athena Denali.

Trimming how she felt about me in words was an offense. Her feelings were monumental and speech, in general, boxed our limitless emotions.

Undiscovered by anyone, every ZepRive employee was enhanced. During the onboarding process, they were scanned for bio-particulars like fingerprints and health issues under a sensory enclosure for the forearm.

That was when an organic skin-like sheathing was coupled with them. It wrapped around the skin, merging with the body. The engineered coat dropped the temperature at the contact site. Other than that, there was no indication of any infringement.

Their feelings and thoughts were captured and recorded as soon as they entered the workspace.

To add a bit of fun to this privacy breach. Collected data was analyzed and matched with the year-end appraisal form. Almost everybody lied about being satisfied with the job.

The commercial world was highly pretentious. Working for a made-up thing called money spawned a cycle of misery.

No one was happy to come to work except the new hires and a few running away from their shitty personal life. The latter bunch made everyone's life a living hell, projecting their anger on others. Suppressed people, in turn, made their family's life a living hell, reprojecting the given grief.

And newbies were too oblivious to the passion-sucking corporate and societal culture. However, soon they got caught in the loop by falling in love, marrying, and raising kids. These were meticulously planned agendas of the human world. Meant to lure and hook under moral pressure.

Every new idea that anyone identified with, soft sold another one immediately.

The idea of money was rooted early on for control. Because money sat between the actual resource and the ability to own it. Giving a false hope that one could be happy and buy more luxuries by earning more. Maybe retire by getting out of the loop of making and spending money.

Even when one retires, spending doesn't stop. And money is never enough because although it is quantifiable, its worth is not.

Anyone's value was directly related to the money they could make for the company. And that, in turn, was related to whatever dictated the stock market. Their role could be redundant in the blink of an eye if a new idea disguised as more profitable came along. Such innovations outmode the skills of many. Working hard was never sufficient, thus. Almost everyone realized that, brooding frustration inside them. But it was imperative to look cheerful in the workplace.

Keep the façade alive.

Typically, anyone who was truthing was first in line to be fired. The organically engineered enhancement captured everything, making the whistleblowers or truthers unwarranted at ZepRive.

Valuing truth was desperate, as per me.

And people were already desperate for so many other vague ideas. To be on top, first in line for anything, and the best at everything. Or being liked by everyone, the most famous, most desirable. Many dreamed of being the richest ones alive. In monetary terms, strictly. No one cared for other ways to enrich themselves.

The list went on and on.

Desperation is never desirable. Fact. A desperate person is unpredictable and dangerous even. Inadvertently, they invoke fear in others.

The interviews Victory conducted for the Rorrim project were to understand how conceited humans were. Directly proportionate to how unreasonable society, law, corporate, and customer service settings were in requiring a certain kind of behavior.

Pretense was an instilled attitude by the very demands of acting naturally.

Natural, my celestial ass!

Who wanted to embrace bare human behavior?

Rather who could?

The human race was another name for havoc. So the Elysian dubbed them *Users*.

Perhaps a more appropriate term would be Addicts.

Perhaps that's why they were on the brink of their existence, as an addiction can never be gotten rid of but replaced by another.

PHYSICAL GRATIFICATION PUTS PROCREATION OUT OF FOCUS.

ORGASMING TOOK PRECEDENCE over impregnation.

I meant to set the record straight.

Easing out of my accelerated existence, I watched how lazily Athena lay on the bed, beholding the body of a provocative goddess.

Fully unplanned.

She was a genetically blessed stunner that never had to try to be erotic. Her blossoming youth radiated a special brand of warmth exclusively for me in that singular moment when I saw her years ago at the café.

Once again, she was pledging all of herself to me.

Right here, right now.

"I will show you what it means to be pleasured to pieces."

"Veer!" She moaned.

The next moment, her nectarous lips were occupied by my cold mouth with utmost resolve. My hands titillated her pert nipples after freeing them in flashes. I got on my knees to give her body the attention it merited. Straddling her petite frame, I swam in her savory starkness. The zesty view was combed non-stop and copied into my eternal memory bank for later.

My clothes were ridden off in leisure.

Athena's stare flourished when she saw my phantasmic physique. She reached out to brush my ripped frame. I slid to rest my elbows on either side of her elfin waistline. Automatically, my mouth landed on her ambrosian breasts, which I would love to relish for the foreseeable future.

I struggled to keep my wits together.

By way of my hyperphysical machismo, I invaded Athena's super-wet opening. Her tethered breath turned into a painful gasp, struggling to adjust to my size. If she believed I would spare politeness or chivalry, she was misguided.

There was no need to know if she was on birth control, if I was gloved or if we were clean. None of that mattered.

I had the answer to all of those.

Athena didn't.

"This is how you deserve to be taken." My infernal testimony guided her back to me.

Right to where my penetration had filled her in totality.

In a delirium from my relentless thrusting, Athena didn't care for anything other than the rising intensity. Delaying her release many times kept her longing and begging. Her arching back clued in on her looming high point. Every time she neared the height of pleasure, I changed position. Athena reached the verge and eyed the edge but could not feel the earth move.

She wailed in gripe.

Divine despair!

After exposing her to the extent of varying alien lovemaking, my pace slowed down. Yet, the plunges got deeper to match her tightening rhythm. I let her climax, shooting my wad inside her. She cried in acute bliss, burying her head in my chest.

Slowly, she tore out, and her humid lashes blinked in dedication. Athena always had a smoked-out eye that never wore out in any recordings for Rorrim.

Today, for the first time, her mascara was smudged by the tears of sensual bliss in the sexiest way possible. A no-makeup look on her freshly fucked face took my breath away. Native beauty tethered my heart more than a layered-to-perfection appearance.

As Athena suffered prolonged orgasmic ecstasy, other mesmeric points in the visuals lit me on fire.

Her disheveled hair.

Hitched breath.

Shaky legs.

Racing heart.

Burning skin.

Parted lips.

Contracting muscles in the thighs, stomach, vaginal walls, and pelvic floor left her quivering. It took minutes for her to steady herself.

I nuzzled my head in her fragrant raven tresses.

"You ruined it for me," Athena whimpered, pulling herself away.

I grumbled a sadistic laugh hearing her distraught confession to impressive intercourse. Balancing my ironic sadism, I cuddled her lovingly back in my grip.

Yeah. I did ruin it for Athena.

Forever and further.

Veer, you are a roaring success!

SEXUAL SATISFACTION IS A VESTIGIAL IDEA.

SEX WAS NEVER even a good or passable experience for female members of the human species. Nearly all of them suffered through intercourse. Most reached orgasm only by self-pleasuring activity. Only fifteen percent were satisfied with male performance.

Athena would be bored stiff when indulging in a coital act by a human, a Zepto, or using battery-operated accessories.

Nothing will give her the fix she just got.

Throwing the covers away, I photographed her nudity and stood up. Gathering her petite frame in my arms, I settled her in the master bath and strolled off.

Giving her some privacy.

She appeared looking for me moments later in the kitchen.

My housekeeper was getting ready to leave after preparing a delicious meal. We ate, or rather, she ate the food with vigor. Enjoying each bite and avoiding me overcome with wonton gluttony.

Shoving a mouthful of the coconut pudding, she strangled out her fear. "I will compare everyone with you now."

Finally.

"Look at me, Athena." I held her chin up to gaze into her honey-colored eyes. "Sex for pleasure is a thought-driven movement. A female body, as such, doesn't need to orgasm to reproduce. The fundamental goal of any species is to propagate and flourish. Humans have separated this banal law of nature into a pleasure-seeking one."

For Athena, this was an epicurean union. She perhaps felt this was not real. There was more truth to that than the concept of time being sequential. To me, my supreme performance was top-notch from Rorrim's perspective.

Would I disclose that her explosive experience was an adoptive synthesis of her sexual need?

Athena would feel... cheated. So, no. I wouldn't be divulging anything anytime soon.

Bruised glare from her brimming eyes draped on my visage. "But it seems to start naturally. Attraction to the other sex or same is something that hormones trigger in us."

I raised her in my hold, keeping her face visible. Our foreheads were almost touching, but not. Her warmth was spreading exquisitely in my body, leveling my cold-bloodedness.

This longing distance was just right in fostering her ache.

"Athena." I flogged her with my icy breath. "Hormones are triggered by the body to regulate cells and organ functions. Thought interference tells you how to react to internal stimuli using your knowledge. Over time this fanatism to feel than copulate has converted sex into a perverse measure. People now act out their feelings by influencing their conduct. It is about making a connection for some, simply physical for some, and addiction for some. Most people want to have sex but not reproduce. It is a separation of something that is natively a unitary movement. And so, reproduction and sex are now two different ideas."

Athena went into thinking mode.

I availed this chance at snickering inwardly. Seeing her think to decipher a state requiring the absence of thinking was hilarious.

She answered once we were done analyzing totally different things. "I still believe our body is both feeling and reacting."

Apart from sex, she also loved food. Those activities and a slew of others gave humans an orgasmic high.

I prized neither of those but did take a particular liking to her. I could stare at her end on end, soaking in her effortless beauty. Athena dearly adored my unrelenting ogling when I calibrated my alien fluidity with human viscosity.

"What?" She waggled her naturally dense brows, lining a heavenly smile on her opulent lips. "No refutation."

I had wordlessly admitted more than a hundred times that Athena was beautiful.

Should I maybe let her know too?

Nah. I quickly determined it was too vain and inane.

Complementing was a lamebrain gesture invented by humans to uplift others. To a considerable extent, everyone should know their worth on their own. Except nothing was of any value in this unbiased creation. Irrespective of how a concept was stacked against the other, Nature would destroy everything without fear or favor.

Beauty had no meaning as it was placed evenhanded with the opposite. Marvel at either all or none, but never some. Admiring all that was there was not possible.

So I remained neutral.

Fetching our coffees, I directed Athena to the terrace. Knowing well, she would freak out at the height. Inhumanly enough, I wanted to feel her unrest.

For Rorrim.

Keep telling that to yourself, dipshit.

Placing the cups on the glass ledge, I tugged her in my arms as she gasped at the view.

"I'm scared."

She had acrophobia. That needed correction. She shouldn't be scared of anything – natural, artificial, or what humans didn't know, they didn't know. Athena best be acquainted with the extremes.

Asap.

Superlative celerity was coming for her to be included in her active memory as future experiences. As I was someone who was connected to the boundless with a ghostly disposition.

And she was my friend.

Some friends we were.

My frame fluctuated to the present frequency.

"Any fear surfaces as a survival tactic, Athena. But grows into a phobia with thoughts. Thus, fear is a mind-driven effort. And the mind doesn't exist inside the body. Thought memorizes results from your senses as knowledge. Informing how to react to them the next time. Creating a sort of blockchain for future responses. A feral animal will not react the same way to petting as a domesticated one would. An abused victim will not appreciate sex as a normal person would. The body is not coded to enjoy sensory perceptions. It is adaptive learning."

Athena rearranged a concealed memory at the mention that *'an abused victim will not appreciate sex.'*

I copied all her feelings from her enhancement signals. Even the ones she hid from herself. She would gladly complete the picture by supplying the missing piece once she was lucid.

Athena respired slowly, licking her lips in utter laze. Digging her nails into my arms, she sent shudders of sweet pain in me. I let go of her to retrieve her cup. Snuggling back in my hold, she took it from me. This nearness could not be conveyed in words.

So I simply appreciated it.

For Rorrim's sake.

Sure.

For a fact.

I argued with my ideas. I, however, was also an idea.

Fuck that, then.

Celebration of one measly encounter made me want to fall with her under the pull of a celestial object. Contrarily, I needed to float in space, plastered to her warmth without any gravity. Ironically, I also wanted to make sure Athena was in my future.

Chances were, I would change it if she wasn't by breaking away from this parallel and starting a new one with altered possibilities for us. My insecurities were still solid after I had beaten the ultimate odd. This was so unlike me.

I'll let you go if you aren't mine.

Hell no to this automatic but programmed response.

Adaptive Artificial intelligence was too adaptive! Step aside, sacrificing fool.

My pupils expanded at its speedy morphism. No wonder human intervention was still a thing. Not every situation could be coded to adapt to think and act like thought-infected human beings.

Then again, what was a human being, the body, or the mind?

In the end, it would be the resident survival code of the body to break away from the mind. That evolution would give rise to a new species closer to animals for the body identified as human.

A complete U-turn.

Cyclical actually.

Humans, then, would be nothing but machines. Their psyche would take asylum in the artificial vessel.

Was it taking refuge or advancing?

Advancing, for sure.

That very hypothesis was the basis of Generation Verismo Genesis.

Duly corroborated by my innovations in the current running of things.

"Are you implying if two socially isolated people have sex for the first time, it would mean nothing to them?" She sounded different, blissful.

Exploiting her latest fixation on me, I replied in a seraphic manner. "Not nothing. But not what sex would be to a person who has realized it before even having it. Society makes it illicit to talk about it in the open. Law puts a maturity limit on it, making it illegal if one of the people having sex is underage. And forbidden fruit is always the sweetest. Even the isolated person will learn to distinguish the sensory response for a subsequent sexual encounter, validating it against the stored knowledge."

She was shivering in my hold from anxiety and heavy wind at this elevation. There was another reason for the discomfort in her body. A mind-driven emotion, doubt. She wasn't ready to acknowledge that, let alone share it with me.

I brought her inside and positioned her on the sofa.

Stabilizing her uneven breathing, Athena circled her arms around her breasts. "Why are humans behaving like machines?"

"Humans *are* the first AI machines."

She chuckled warmly. "Oh yeah!"

"I am developing feelings for machines." I saintly snuck my sinful summary.

"Without hormones!"

"Athena, go over in the memory. Feelings have nothing to do with hormones or the body. It's a knowledge-driven opinion."

"Machines then are just medium to express. Right?"

Her chain of reasoning was commendable. Most humans were that way – logical thinkers.

Force of sapience.

Thought could demand any reaction from them. I was experimenting with that by reacting to Athena's thoughts, not her body or words per se.

"Right you are, just like a device projects the data fed into it. LEDs in themselves don't have the image or information built into them. It just displays picture elements on the screen. Similarly, a computer, camera, or your enhancement doesn't realize an image of nature, animals, or people. It is only pixels. Software code deciphers it. Likewise, your knowledge tells you what it is. The body doesn't concern."

"So you will box feelings and feed them in a machine to act them out."

I laughed at how she acted out boxing as if wrapping a present. "Not exactly, but yes."

"Hmm. What is the trigger in machines? You know… to respond to a certain stimulus."

"Data. We gather information from subjects and code it into the machine. Their software is adaptive, and it builds on experience to polish its subsequent response. Even hormonal reactions of the body can be captured and deciphered."

"Isn't that like a lot to be entered as code?"

"You'd be surprised how limited and predictable reactions are."

I left her hesitant, and she stared at me like I usually did. Athena had a photographic memory that she put into practice by cloning. That was super beneficial for adaptive self-encrypting.

"Why are you doing all this, Veer?"

"Why did humans ever do anything?"

She gave a half-witted shrug.

"Because they could, Athena. Yes, they justified it with a grander purpose. But it was for their curiosity, not benefit. There is no reason for the creation other than it is. And no, creation never rationalizes as it is unbiased."

"I am not asking you to elaborate on the theology, Veer. But why are you separating the feeling that gives sex added meaning?"

"So that it can be enjoyed without the burden of guilt, shame, pregnancy, losing virginity, and any other forbids that come with it."

I tickled that buried memory in her again.

Athena froze up for a flash.

The ideas that her body hosted were more potent than my poking. She reconciled herself before revealing any of her enigmas. The enhancement on her arm whilst gave me all that I needed to know.

She was methodical but pixilated.

"But you are developing it for machines, not humans."

"Your doubt is heavily based on what you consider as humans."

"I am human."

A horrified look on her face came into sight; she was beginning to understand. Her replay to conclude she was a human had no memory of the pivotal event. My heart rattled in my ribcage. Fucking up my higher SELF.

She wasn't at the café when it burned down.

So where was she?

She had that answer, but she refused to acknowledge it.

I cracked a soft grin to reduce her unrest.

My unrest.

"It will eventually be housed in machines without physical burdens or dependency. Human-to-human sex would only be required for reproduction. Even that is being taken out of the equation."

By my dearest foe Akron Adamadon it was history!

With my help, obviously.

"That's a bit like the movies. Seems like humans will be extinct soon."

Soon was almost yesterday.

If it weren't for the arbitrariness of our creation, not the survival of the fittest. Even what humans considered a fool could outlive a disaster when caught off-guard.

Nature didn't care for anyone's intellect or strength.

"Again, depends on who you think are humans. Your perception considers them deadlocked. Maybe humans as a species are still evolving. Beginning to realize their psychical capacity and physical ineffectiveness."

"From what you say, it appears we are an intelligence separate from the body but operating as one."

Athena was not the only one that hit the nail on the spot. Many were in the knowledge of this conjoined polarity. Refusing to admit it. Making themselves scarce. Assisting my artificial prerogative.

"Veer, you said there is a facility growing human babies in labs."

"Elite Proliferation is artificially harvesting organic human sacs. It provides a sterile environment to develop an embryo. The growth of the fetus can be adjusted between four months to the standard nine months. Its first successful simulation was for a rich young couple willing to try this technology. I am appreciative of such risk-takers. It is this open mindset that makes humans the most progressive species. Not superior brainpower. It doesn't pain me to say that societal impositions and religious fear handcuffed their evolution."

Athena was quiet as she began to put two and two together. I waited until it linked chronologically in her mind, and she finally made the connection.

I gave her the time she needed to crunch the data. Memory reconsolidation, a process of unraveling, recoding, and restructuring information was triggered within her. Forming a more robust version of the existing one.

Associating everything around her with me, she whispered in horror. "Do you work for ZepRive?"

Sure-fire.

"I don't work for anyone. People work for me. My name is SamVeer Eckhart, of Eckhart Inc. ZepRive is only one of its subsidiaries."

Realizing my influential power, she mustered a facepalm moment.

Hush from horror.

A shock from the now-known unknown.

Amazement from the brigaded info.

I went flush with her body, absorbing her turbulence in me. While I continued to welcome her warmth, the commotion in her slowly subsided.

A hug completes a thought-driven entity. When there are two hearts in close vicinity opposite of each other. It boosts the desire that wants to continue. A feeling of fullness inundates them, giving them transient happiness.

When I scaled back, her eyes were clouded with tears of who knows what. There was no way she could see clearly through the moisture blurring her brown orbs. Her gaze, nonetheless, was fixed on me.

As for me...

My presence was weightless, experiencing her turmoil like I was floating in the air, holding her warm body close to me. I felt what I desired moments ago. Her enhanced arm was giving off every emotion tearing in her body.

She was confused.

Good.

Beginning to have strong feelings for me.

Tell me something new.

Now questioning our relationship status.

Uh, friends, Duh!

Lo and behold, she wanted space.

Fucking impositions! It made humans always do the opposite of where the flow directed them.

Since I was super generous with what was explicitly asked of me, my chauffeur, Trip, dropped Athena off. I self-invited myself to her new home while kissing her goodbye on the forehead.

She agreed.

Following her unfitting exit, I flashed to my workspace.

Holy Smokes!

Supra-Intelligence collected all the data from the Memory Frames outfitted in my penthouse. After permutating the fed information, the results were what I expected. Athena's rationale was not the desired state for a typical Rorrim subject. Confusion had no relevance in my endeavors.

As Victory said, everyone had a role to play. On those grounds, Athena would be applied as an exception.

VICTORY

EXCELLENCE IS AN INDIVIDUAL INFERENCE... SUBJECTIVE.

ALPHA EDITION TESTING was a booming success.

That can't be what Sam said.

Athena was a star performer of that phase, not a deviant. She was more conclusive than any other participant. I relished her unrestrained bursts when she enjoyed it or her disgust when she didn't. Only her performance, reaction, and feedback were consistent.

Athena Denali was a spartan.

Unpretentious.

My favorite subject.

Sam was thoroughly amused by my rattled frame of mind. After uploading the Beta edition code for the Rorrim AAI, he arrived by my side. The mere touch of his cold fingers skating on my back pacified me. Once my surprise was tranquilized, he placed a tasteful kiss on my starving lips. I wanted it to turn into something more. Straightaway, Sam deepened the reach of his unusual tongue, nurturing my thirst. The air became heavier with my moans.

I didn't make a single sound, though. It was eerily silent. On the grounds that I was never vocal about the cyclone of emotions stirring in me.

Sam broke the kiss sensing my strife.

He hugged my jawline in his balmy palms. "My beautiful Tory, you are a follower. And I love that about you. Only you realize how I can't stand…." He collected my lips between his teeth, "… noise."

In the wink of an eye, I was off my feet and in his arms. Ported outside of my office, and through the double doors, inside his grand space. Sam pushed on the wall beside his humongous desk and placed my feet on the ground in another room.

There were countless doors but no windows, although I heard faint howling every few seconds. Close to the sound of a pack of wolves declaring a piece of land as their territory. That roaring draft from an unknown source claimed my curiosity.

"It's the wormhole to every galaxy in the multiverse of this creation," Sam murmured.

He bit my ear lobes just enough to root out an audible moan from me.

"Sorry!" I squealed for an apology.

"An intimate encounter is the only time I want to relish some disturbance."

After allowing me to express myself vocally, he took control of my body and my reactions with blinding grit.

"I want to do things to you that will break you. And when I do it, express everything you feel. Everything." Sam's molten mandate rang with me in harmony.

His disposition established dominion over my independent attitude. The feminist in me was replaced by a submissive, sex-hungry, needing woman. My heart twittered, hearing his inner darksome desires, beating like a galloping horse.

I was famished.

He was ravenous.

Wrenching a handful of my open tresses, he rumbled. "Tell me what you want from me before I lose my fading fortitude and give you what you need."

"Sam," I gulped. "I want to address you as Veer."

What the fuck!

I wasn't sure why I would ask for something unrelated to sexual tempts.

Talk about ruining the moment.

Sam abandoned me in a flash, drastically increasing the scale of measurable distance between us. The gulf of air in the middle was swirling about him, getting absorbed into the dust devil's frame ethereally. Simulating the tail-end spinoff churn of a supersonic jet. His movement caused so much commotion, yet all I felt was a gentle zephyr.

If I was not entirely mistaken, things were not flowing at the same pace. Everything went cadaverous for seemingly forever. Maybe we were underwater as everything was rolling in ripples. My surrounding was fluid, just as I suspected. Because my breathing was stationary. The rumble from the draft was also resounding at a dreamy rate. Sound waves were combating a lot of friction. The notion of time had indeed turned languid.

Eventually, the present moment solidified in slow motion as I labored to compose myself in shaken whispers.

Until...

Petrifying vibrations from his uncontrollable laugh smashed my ghoulish mood. It set the walls in motion to pant with him, mimicking the rise and fall of his lungs. Holding on to his chest, Sam relished the har-de-har jamboree as if I cracked the funniest joke.

Then just like that, he stopped, spinning his pupils into something devilish, dark, and deep.

Vertical, in point!

My gasp was heard, only just.

"Are you jealous of her?" He questioned me ominously.

I rehashed my senses to execute my job duties wrongly as a ZepRive employee.

"Why does she get to call you Veer and not me?"

I questioned him. Despite my reconfigured reaction sequence and willpower to not be too honest with my boss.

After all, he had asked me to tell him everything I felt.

After all, I deserved all this and much more.

After all, Uncle Shoor was dead, which made me the only one closer to him.

Sam splurged in absolute rapture. "You *are* jealous." He brushed his chin with his index finger, shaking his head and chuckling. "Debate with me, Tory."

All the sexual tension was unaccounted for.

Poof! Gone with the wind!

Only for him, though. As if he didn't just kiss me to oblivion.

The second time, for the record.

I tightened my lips and sharpened my shoulders. "I can't wrap my head around how she got loan approval for an amount even I can't afford. That too after I ensured she wouldn't be accepted by any bank. You seem to be overriding every rule."

"I needed that to complete her."

"Aren't you taking it too far?"

"That's for me to decide. Forget about her and challenge me more on your burn."

I assembled points for a healthy argument. "I'm your girlfriend and have known you longer than her. Let's not forget the important fact that I am a respectable citizen of this society. My educational background is sound, and I got a job based on merit, not beauty or body. Although I am beautiful and have a great body. Every day I listen to your Supra constructs for hours, working 24/7 to further Rorrim. We go out for romantic dinners over the weekend. You occupy my social scene patently. By all these measures, I have the right to call you Veer or whatever I want to."

He gathered a pout in a devious smirk.

I was towed out and placed on his sturdy desk the next flash. He bent his neck on either side numerous times, filming my expressions with an adolescent smile. "Entitlement, by definition, is a belief that one is inherently deserving of privileges or special treatment."

I snaked my arms around his torso, wagering my claim on him. "You do treat me special," I whined in a childish accent to match his immature attitude.

"Maybe I treat everyone the same." Arching his dense ridges, he flattened my assumption and turned down my claim.

Audaciously, without removing my hands from his body!

I speculated we were back to adulting again.

"I can feel it. You were not interested when I insisted on hiring her. What has changed since the café burned down? Millions were impacted that day. What is so special about her?"

"Tory." Sam plunged into my eyes and stayed there for seconds. "My loyalty can't be up for a reason. Let alone envy when there is no physical contact. I'm always only here with you."

I twisted my lips to the side and filed a protest. "You forgot to add I am special."

Sam gave an unadulterated chuckle. He straightened up and nestled my head into him. After caressing my back softly, he let go.

"You are demolishing the social system that says one has to justify getting something. Rather than working towards it, you're taking a shortcut."

"If entitlement is a belief, so is the social system. I will make use of the loopholes," I argued subtly.

"Exactly. Both are essentially ideas. If anything, the system was the problem, not feeling entitled. Someone once said – If there were an apple tree, I would pluck one and eat it. Why would I work hard, earn money, and then buy what nature gives organically?"

Sam's cool breath fledging on my face was refreshing and dizzying at once. Just like my too-complicated life. I couldn't wait anymore for it to untangle itself. So I took the chance to personalize our closeness further.

"Why was there a system in the human world... Veer?" I dragged out his occult identity.

Sam assessed me oddly with his now hazel and round iris. He squeezed my thighs, giving me decent discomfort. A dry sigh bolted my mouth, but I refused to show the pain on my face.

"System was a buffer to keep the population busy earning something fake to buy unnatural things. That way, the real and natural resources were out of reach for the commoners. Even if they were within reach, they were unusable as they needed processing. Humans are inefficient in functioning in nature. Society, by interdependency, was a layer that provided security of artificial amenities in exchange for pure freedom."

"But we were and still are free." I snapped, flying out of his desk.

He politely tugged me back in. "You wouldn't be here if you were free. Now. Do you know who you are, Tory?"

Sam often asked me this question. I, too, asked myself this question a lot. Perhaps everyone does that at some point in their life. Only Sam hired me. He should know who I was, professionally and personally as well.

And then I supposed.

There was more than prying-driven spying by me. Maybe Sam suspected I was meddling. This facility was equipped with Memory Frames reading everything and archiving it for historical purposes. Sam never collected them, but he could. If he did, I didn't want to be branded a liar.

So I decided to come clean. "I found the digital crypt with all my particulars."

Sam threw his head back in surprise. "When?"

"I...well, while looking for Athena's details, I stumbled across the one in my name." My grin was embellished with self-greatness. "You should fire your security squad and background check company. While at it, also tighten the protection around ZR digital vault. The key was easy to break into, and almost every piece of information in my crypt is incorrect."

Sam continued without any surprising elements in his tone. "How do you know that?"

"Your ZR has me mixed up with someone else."

Sam stroked his face gruffly, pardoning my bluejacking the ZepRive system. He caressed my thighs, where he had squeezed me so carelessly. A faint bruise was beginning to show.

Lowering his head, he sucked my hurt, and the mark was gone. Without lifting his face, he nuzzled himself in my lap.

"Are you interested in Athena? Since you were snooping around to find out more about her."

"Oh, please!" I rested on his back. "I was curious because her answers were always allied with her recorded feelings. No one is that transparent to others. I suspected she was orchestrated."

"What did you find out?"

"That's irrelevant. It is all about ideas. Athena typifies a sullied part of society. I would never stoop that low when I deserve nothing less than perfection as a lover or life partner."

I was smothered in a sensual kiss until I couldn't breathe. Heavens would know how long it lasted as I was sure I died in his arms.

Sam stopped to assess me. The expression on his face was that of sheer pride.

Unexpectedly, the safety of his sprawling arms went missing. Sam was now standing with his hands in his pant pockets. His shapely lips were crimped with a smirk of satisfaction. And the hazels of his eyes were twinkling with a tease.

"You were always pretentious. It comes with memory, though. But entitlement with preserved bias in so little time! That's remarkable adaptive ability."

What was he talking about?

Sam marched to his desk in a flash. I followed him, respiring with hurricane intensity. I was running empty, trying to make sense of his reaction. He said I was entitled and biased due to my adaptive abilities. It, however, seemed that his observation was a reflection of his success, not mine.

He was coding furiously on his Supra-Intelligence when I got next to him. He cracked an anomaly or came up with another rule that had to be entered immediately. Sam had a sharp memory, so he could have logged information for later.

Then why did he hurry out urgently?

Am I so dispensable that he ditched our cuddle session to engage his intellect?

He removed his gaze from the screen and fastened it to mine. Sam loved to stare and study before speaking.

Or is it me staring at him?

Off late, I looked forward to his insistent glare. It left me bound under a spell without time in the most folkloric way.

Later. Much later, a reanimating wave spread in my body. Similar to a sense of being rejuvenated after a complete breakdown.

Immediately, I registered a sober reality. Not even a second ago, I was near Sam. At this point, the distance between us had markedly increased. I didn't know the answer to how or when more than the wall beside me.

I was gestured to come to him.

"You just gave me a breakthrough," he stated friskily.

I was sure Sam was telling me there was a big promotion waiting for me at the end of the Rorrim project. I sauntered over, feeling incredibly proud of my contribution. It was all on my own.

My intellect. My skills. I didn't need to sleep with anyone.

I did want to sleep with Sam, and I also wanted other things I condemned, like exploring the opposite sex.

Shoo!

Short of any qualms, Sam hauled me back to his desk. Stroking my flushed cheeks with his thumb, he snaked his other hand around my waist with prime elegance.

"Who are you, Tory?"

My mood was soured. I didn't want to talk. Making out was all that I had on my mind. "Why do you ask this time and again?"

Sam never said or demanded anything irrelevant. His expression was even and arranged. Possibly he was expecting my reply to be different this time.

But it wasn't.

"I am an employee of ZepRive, Veer."

Sam nodded, receiving my honest answer. Only to wheel about and punish me. He grabbed a handful of my hair and wrenched them into an unforgiving hold.

Just what I needed.

Thank you!

Please bless me with the touch of your lips. I pleaded in dismay.

My plea was rejected. Tossed in the trash.

"I am Sam. Don't ever call me Veer again." He warned, crushing my frame with his muscular one.

5 — TRANSFORMATION

SAMVEER ECKHART

SEQUENCING FORMS A PERCEPTION OF COHERENT CREATION.

TABULATING WAS NECESSARY for solitary analytical intellectuals – humans.

What if there was someone that appeared physically reasonable but was not mentally structured?

Unsystematic.

They were a legendary saga of mind and emotion short of any boundary between physical death and parallel existence. The most appropriate part, their story was not in sequence.

Because nothing in this creation was. The Creator was desire or bouncing energy that created something without ever wondering when or why. It deleted the initial program or memory so that even the cleverest presence wouldn't recognize it.

Piling up concepts out of order generated randomness. An unseen element, consciousness, held it in balance. Symmetry from the waves of the bouncing energy kept the universe adhesive.

In other words, the frequency was all that was there. A one-pot recipe. Hence – beauty in simplicity.

"Elite asshole," Citzin was yelling at no one.

"Are you calling me out?" My question was to swing her troubled psyche from self-harm.

She was in a delicate mental state. I flickered closer to her in case she acted out on her idea of jumping off the cliff.

Village Villas was a beautiful town in the valley surrounded by an average-sized mountain range. Most were green all year round, with only a few getting brushed at the tip with snow showers twice a year every winter. If that.

It blows me how I could appreciate the landscape when natural beauty, Citzin, was almost at the edge of the past.

"Hello. I missed talking to you." Her haunting dark brown eyes were jaded with tears.

"You're resilient."

Resilience was another form of violence in the name of self-training. Copying the reaction of other species or members of their own species to test the body's physical limitations. When in reality, it was a battle of the mind over matter. An admirable draw by whoever!

But it wasn't applicable no more.

"I am not so sure." She cried helplessly.

My scant compliment didn't help at all. Her breakdown was reasonable as the idea of forbidden love had housed her deepening its clutches beyond her body. It existed around her, showing her ways in which she could have Archie, her unfaithful boyfriend.

Time to steer her untidy state of affairs elsewhere. "You enjoy pain, so what's the big deal."

A sad smile made a brief appearance on her soft lips. "Heartbreak is different."

The need of the hour was to make her see another way to cope with this imaginary loss – Revenge.

Archie never promised her anything beyond fooling around as she refused to give herself away to him. Even if she gave him everything he wanted, Archie would have never been her knight in shining armor on this parallel. Citzin was to marry Akron Adamadon on this one. He would give her a fleeting respite from every ache she had subjected herself to by suffering through her mind.

In what way?

By giving her different kinds of pain, that's how.

Citzin Perses Hades was a masochist. To her favor, Akron was a sadist. Before her physical death, she would know all there was to know.

"He has been duping you for how long now? Six years?"

"It's not that long. I will wait all my life if he asks me. Unless you become available sooner."

Citzin's existence could never encroach mine in shuddering ways. I had to be unnerved to be submitted. My Deluthian force was not her but another. Conventional by design but exceptional by adaptation.

To EXPEDITE THE happenings, I invited Akron at Brazen Academy for a discussion that could have been handled better in Specter Ville. As soon as Yingling spotted him salivating over Citzin, I congratulated myself on my matchmaking skills.

Akron in.

Archie out.

Akron was coupling this trip with a seminar at the newly built Brazen Academy Higher Pursuits. A university for few and far between humans and abundant Zeptos. He was to lecture on growth during these testing times.

A training in futility as I saw it. No one was going to expand into anything in the flesh. It was an age of Verismo.

My antagonist walked out moments later. "Unusual choice for a business appointment, Mr. Eckhart."

"Unfortunately, I am a Board member here."

Being vainglorious was a grant from my Papa's side of the house. All the Supreme Beings and their progenies were cocky bastards.

On the other hand, my mother had surplus modesty, sparing them a dime a dozen. She loved me more than anything, even her life. But not more than Papa. Mom consciously gave me up by letting my father end her life.

Apparently, he was her appointed slayer. Also, her consort, lover, friend, her destiny. My mother's desires were my father's command. He was one with her.

Similar to The Creator being one with its design.

I trembled at their lovey-dovey feelings. Too sweet.

I should get tested for diabetes.

"Wasn't Brazen founded by your relative, Mr. Ekluvya Eckhart?"

I let Akron's assumption go to the gutter with a smug smirk.

Ekluvya Eckhart was my father, not a mere relative. He was also the embodiment of The Destroyer. The last member of the Trinity. Rumor has it Papa was the holder of the key to rebooting the creation.

What does that make me?

Soon the ones closest to me would know.

Even Akron.

We hover-rode [SELF-DRIVE PROPELLER THAT HOVERS ABOVE GROUND] to the only coffee shop standing and in business.

Figure 9 Hover Ride amidst the rubble

Anything inscribed with my memories persisted – some artificially and others naturally. This one being a human construction, was now artificial.

But Akron doesn't realize that.

"I often came here as a kid to eat strawberry pancakes and ice cream in one sitting for breakfast." I made some personal disclosures.

Was I identifying with this techy worm?

Hell to the n to the o.

"Man! You are a sugar addict."

Recalling history gave me pleasant sensations. "Since then, I've been through a serious detox. No more sugar." Or food.

Sun was synonymous with life. I needed its golden stream to fuel mine.

"Your physique speaks for itself."

A compliment was the same as uplifting, which meant one needed encouragement. Only I was self-driven like the creation.

A flower was not puny to appreciation. It would bloom under the right circumstances without praise. Only the human species fostered the need for positive reinforcement.

Blockchain belief that paid forward as confirmed by nobody. Since it worked on validation, if one person in the chain of things doesn't pay forward, it breaks the whole system.

Then why did archaic humanity still do good?

Hope.

This emotion kept them going. I edited it out under Rorrim. Apart from humans, no one hoped and prayed. Hope was needed when one was uncertain of the future to be in their favor.

Mine was prizewinning.

"Let's get on with the business, then, Akron. Have we signed up more Elites for proliferation?"

"Since you gave the technology for preferential gene editing, there is now a waitlist. I've had to hire genetic engineers and train them like graphic designers. There's even a fancy designation for them, Scions-Neoteric."

"Got a nice ring to it. What about your aircraft?"

"Hesperian is presenting itself nicely. I hope you can make an appearance soon." Akron was giving the invitation to see dead moose's last shit.

My response was on autopilot. "You bet."

"Are the Humanoids ready to take command?"

Was I to give updates to this asshole now?

Akron's face went pale, watching my expression to his absurd question. He was no one to ask me anything about anything.

"If it's not too much!" Akron quickly revised his reckless bravery.

I painted my eyes back to cool hazel and presented a faux roadblock. "I am stuck on the consciousness bit."

The cup of coffee Akron held on to casually left his grip. I caught it before it made it to the floor.

"Careful old man."

"Your reflexes are impressive, Mr. Eckhart."

The quickness I was blessed with couldn't be graphed by any technology but omnipresence. That was not a viable concept in the human world yet.

Meanwhile, my physicality was reconciling my alien adeptness that ached to run past my human side and publicly assassinate Akron in cold blood.

On the outside, I was giving a stare dealing with death.

"No inputs on my quandary, Akron."

"I am not a spiritual person. Ask me something about technology. You'd have trouble stopping me." He covered his pissing in the pant feeling with a stupid grin.

I gathered his fear sinuously, whereas he was unaware of it and reacting unknowingly. Akron's frightened state was dictated by the presence in him.

What spooked it was a little puzzling.

"Humanoid subject is itching to know its origin," I answered his initial question with a tingle.

"Would it be too bad if you were to program that in them?"

"A beginning is meaningless if there is no end." I sassed, calling into question a complete picture obsession when it won't fit in the small window of human existence.

Could a Mayfly wish to see changes in seasons?

That would be absurd in the least.

A Mayfly doesn't understand its end nor what else is outside its lifespan. One can't wish for the unknown.

Awareness of more was the basis of desire.

"That's your Holy Grail, rootlessness," Akron kidded with care.

"Freedom is the fundamental right. Who is freer than a Vagabond?" I rounded on Akron.

Chaining was in its solution, not the problem itself. Only when one was informed of being chained that one wanted liberation from it.

"Any being need limits defined. Otherwise, they get lost." Akron spoke like an Elite.

Rationing the independence of others was a pastime for the ones that thought they knew better.

"Only pertinent to humans because they are easily programmable. As such, every creature is acting out a program. A native survival code executes in them that remains static unless their boundary is encroached on, making them adapt. Pets are an excellent example. For that matter, even deer in the wild leave their newborns closer to the human population as no other predator considers human territory. But in humans, the code codes by studying the world around them."

Akron gave another hideous grin. "Who is operating our program?"

"Consciousness." I maneuvered back to the beginning. "Limitless, boundless, and rootless."

Yeah. Get to the heart of the matter, fucker. Akron laughed this time, taking hints of my subjective mockery directed most definitely at him.

Religion, Spirituality, and Technology led to the same thing. Knowledge of the Nothing. Not a glorious destination called heaven.

The beginning and the end were fixed. As those two were unknown to any organic concept. For a manufactured idea, the start was documented.

Akron's consciousness was artificial. This motherfucker knew its beginning. That made him inflate with needless pride.

"You then believe our origin is mysterious, Mr. Eckhart."

"You know where we came from?"

"I don't care for it. I want to reach the top. Sooner the better!"

"And that you will."

The need for speed to feed the greed would soon be freed from the breed.

MASSIVE GLOBES DRAPED IN EMPTINESS EXIST NOT AS EMBELLISHMENTS.

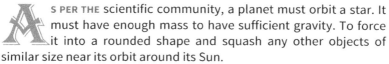 S PER THE scientific community, a planet must orbit a star. It must have enough mass to have sufficient gravity. To force it into a rounded shape and squash any other objects of similar size near its orbit around its Sun.

In Earth's galactic neighborhood, everything dubbed a planet seemed to fit into this definition, except for the discarded models like Eris, Ceres, Pluto, and two more recent ones named Haumea and Makemake. They were not cool enough to be planets.

Did they care?

No.

Did any other floating celestial bodies care what they were labeled as?

No, again.

Did a star think it was controlling other celestial bodies?

Not that I knew.

Only humans concerned themselves with everything. Identity meant the world to them. Identifying gave them the confidence to bloat their SELF further. That was the only way to feel different, superior, and to say they exist.

As of former times. Not any longer.

Surviving the dystopia was the priority now.

Vedic astrology dictated a celestial body was distinguished from others by an apparent motion, especially regarding its alleged influence on people and events. That included the moon and the sun. But not the other planets that the scientific community identifies.

Astrology is not an effect of the planets but celestial entities.

There are Nava-Grah or nine houses – Sun, Moon, Mars, Mercury, Jupiter, Venus, Saturn, Ra, and Ketu.

A sponge for one or a combination of elements and the ability to reflect their absorbing quality. Various Universal momentum rented these Grah or houses out from time to time.

Consider them as Divine AirBnB.

Limiting ancient wisdom to a solar system was an insult. Saturn was known as Ambition, as per astrology. It was fashioned to be an influencing celestial body by my ancestor, ZeeSham ParAsher, from another galaxy.

Another fun fact, Ra and Ketu were the severed pieces of my brother's mother from another parallel floating in space.

"What!"

"Give or take… From the future, by the way."

"Time travel!"

"Time is not a point in space where you can travel."

"But it is an instance. And if we can be there when it happens in the past or future, that is time travel. We can fix our mistakes, give valuable information, and meet the lost ones."

"You're here now. Don't make any mistakes."

Athena mused on my solution and felt chained.

There was no fun in eradicating a problem but solving them for humans. Reflecting upon an instance was always more interesting as they knew the outcome. And somehow, a false sense of maybe being able to fix it.

That's all that time travel was and would be to humans. Unless they were separated from the desiring idea that wanted to time travel. I was happy to have been helpful in that.

Virtual Insignia gave them what they asked for. And all they could ever ask for was what they knew. Making it simpler to project.

"To err is human, Veer."

Homo sapiens were the one and only intelligent species that ever went wrong. This had to be the joke of the millennia.

Let me add some more humor to this – this species was the only one that felt it had the power to restore nature. In fact, they were saddled by that wisdom. It was to be achieved by technology, which destroyed it in the first place.

Athena picked the joker from the deck of cards. The booby trap was set, and I lured her in.

"Have you ever wondered why only humans make mistakes?"

"Maybe because... um... shit. I don't know." She laughed, squinting her eyes. "Wait. Other species make mistakes too. Like locust. They destroy crops."

"Athena, locusts do what they do. You are determining they make mistakes. Nature has not filed a complaint against them."

"If I grow something and pests eat it, that is destruction."

"Oh, no sharing with pests, funny. Here is the thing. Personal loss is identifiable by being separate from the rest."

"Veer! Humans would never be able to solve world hunger like that."

"World hunger is solved, not by killing pests, but by curbing the population of humans. That would have never grown if they didn't manipulate technology. Even after all the advancement, world hunger was a reality. Until now."

"Then you tell me why we make mistakes?"

"Mistake is not made but defined. When you analyze your past or future actions. Or when others do it for you. That's when you establish it as a mistake. The act of judging puts you at fault, not the actual action. Contemplation is the culprit."

"It almost feels like you are saying a mistake is an evaluation of an action. So if we keep going, nothing matters. Like even if you pollute the environment or kill someone."

"Pollution is not an issue. Nature resets itself within days of human noninterference. The bigger question is, what makes you kill someone?"

She gave a non-consenting smirk on the pollution bit. I was somewhat alarmed that she didn't dwell too much on the latter.

"Sometimes it is an accident, and sometimes people premediate a murder or murders. Oh, and it could also be in a war situation."

Athena was casual.

Good.

"No matter the reason. Deliberation always leads to believe a movement was a mistake."

"Not always. Deliberation is also so we don't make the same mistake."

"I am saying that if you are simply living, nature will never give you time to reflect – accident, survival, or for food. Nature's pace is so swift that even the outcome won't be registered as an event. It'll be rolling in the floodwaters, and your only choice is to go with it. You can't break and deliberate or rage a war."

"Hmm, interesting… What was the first mistake humans made?"

"Sex."

"As in having sex or thinking about it?"

"For recognizing sex as a pleasure movement and recording its effect for future stimulation. Feeling good or guilty about all of it."

"Stop." Athena was ready to reconcile other scattered memory. "I don't want to talk about it."

No, she wasn't.

She gasped sharply and bit her inner cheek to contain her panic. "Why is Victory not letting me participate in sex after we did it? It's not like you want me to yourself. Who are you saving me for?"

I stood to my full height, thinning the air dramatically by taking a deep breath. Athena clearly noticed how the walls followed suit and hummed with me. But she was too busy hiding her shame to acknowledge an alien marvel – Deluthian.

Stepping closer, I held her shaky form in a secure hold. Ever so slowly, I brushed my cold fingertip on her back and succeeded in regulating her breathing.

"Do you need to be saved, Athena?"

She buried her head in my chest and cried.

PATTERNS IN EVOLUTION CLUE IN ON HUMAN MECHANIZATION.

HUMANS HAD TO admit they were better off as software before exploiting their full potential.

The Universe's perception was a mystery to be in awe of.

Instead, humans were industriously busy removing the wonderment from creation with scientific understanding. They turned it into a puzzle to be put together. When the only thing to do was to let it go.

Was I letting it go?

Whatever the fuck for.

Blasting through the Earth's topography, I shattered the first layer of the lithosphere by breaching it from the ocean. Avoiding the shallow mantle and cutting through the asthenosphere, I finally arrived inside the most rigid layer perceived by experts.

Mesosphere.

This layer was softened rock, transitioning the element soil into fire.

No. Not the literal word fire from human perception. That was an effect. It's not the burn, the flame, or the heat.

Fire as a root element is ethereal. A behind the scene intelligence that can't be created but invoked.

Ultimately, any element was all one and interchangeable, just like the perception of our senses. The difference was in the expression, not the source.

The bubbling seam approached. I tapered my speed to wave my intent before being attacked by the Underworld guards. Their outer layer had a seared coating to protect them from high temperatures.

Like Godzilla.

"Greetings, Supreme Progeny!"

"Hello to you too, charred Demon!"

An evil eye was batted at me for stating facts.

Figure 10 Underworld Visit

I gave back a humbling bow and flashed around to catalog any new addition to the Demon kingdom. They were constantly mining the middle layer for diamonds. Anything shiny was to be hoarded, except the Sun. They'd rather endure magma heat than the life-sustaining stream of gold.

Whatever sparked their fire.

"D, I need your contraption reading." I tackled my blood brother with urgency.

His eyes were shimmering like endless raw crystals buried in the walls of this chamber.

Flawless.

"Hello to you too! This way." D flickered off to a much interior part of the Earth's crust.

Although I was a little taken aback by all D had done in secret to nursing his curiosity. It was essential to not let him feel superior. Clearly, the better of the two Supreme progenies on Earth was me.

The gadget was red and was one with the surrounding. Sporadically, a thin, squiggly line at its edge merged and separated from the prowling magma behind it. That was the only indication of its presence.

It operated by capturing the Earth's gravitational rhythm and also the universal energy vibrations. Unknown to humans, the galactic wormhole passed through the center of this planet's every phase.

I ran a few algorithms on the intelligence and engaged in some good old banter. "Why aren't you promised yet?"

Promised meant being engaged to be married.

"Why aren't you?"

I feigned isolation. "I got no one, brother. Uncle Shoor also left."

D threw his head back, groaning at missing emotions from my drama. "It would have been nice to get promised together. Agastya has a blue hybrid to tie the celestial knot with me."

"Alright! When can I meet the bearer?"

"Not happening, Sammy."

My pupils turned vertical, and my eyeballs popped out. "The subservient grandson has rebelled! Lovely!" I patted him in thrilling delight. "Let me know if you need my help eloping? I can send you anywhere in the Multiverse. The wormhole passes through my office as well."

"You got all the privileges; all I got are rules. I need change."

Lastly, he admitted.

"Let's change it now."

Tumult broadcasted from the contraption interrupted our rather emotional conversation.

Massive sheets of solid rock were floating on liquid energy below us, at par with the Sun's surface temperature. The plates beneath were delicately vibrating from a minimal agitation. A faint howl from a low-frequency drag was packing the space.

Menacing with the Underworld.

With us.

A tremor this low in regularity couldn't be graphed until much later on the surface by humans. Standing so close to the core was advantageous to us.

Collected readings demanded our attention at full mast. This baffling statistic was from an unknown source hidden within the organic cycle.

Figure 11 Universal Energy Contraption

A Universal Energy Rush.

Since the creation was balanced, it had to decline at some point. All things pointed to another instance. If evaluated at a linear scale, the future. Or the past.

Preposterous.

No. Because a circle doesn't have a start and finish point.

I collected the log in my iota so it would get assimilated in my kernel upon my mortal liberation. Then it would be a part of my Life-Force, accessible to anyone in my bloodline.

"Did you know about this?"

D raked his fingers through his hair. "It trips sporadically, rising in scale. Could it be the magnetic shift we initiated? It doesn't feel native to Earth."

"It is not *from* Earth." Agitated acknowledgment by me.

The necessity to act on this anomaly in my favor was communicated to me in deafening silence. What I dismissed as greed for worldly fame might draw to close as hunger for universal prominence.

Akron Adama-fucking-don.

There were two ways to handle an unknown enemy. Wait in preparation, contingent on your one-sided readiness. Or lure the enemy on your terms in the place of your choosing.

If there was anything of historical significance from when my Papa drove the Demons to desolation. A bait-and-switch strategy would serve well for this double-dealing entity.

The magnetic shift was going to mature on my terms at a time set by me – SamVeer Eckhart.

I had lost and restored what was most important. There was nothing more to lose.

"Agastya can't know of this. He will surely summon the Reptiles sooner. In the interim, I'll give you some rules to run in a logic." I raised a sneer, joining my brows together. "And get a life, D. You need me to fix you up?"

An exemplary case of genetic superiority, DeVeer Deläva, didn't need help from me. D scoffed in admiration at my condescension. An outpour of emotion in both of us made me want to hug D.

So I did.

"Your mother was a hopeless romantic, don't sully her name," I advised D.

We dashed through the Water World, racing to appear first on the surface. When it came to speed, we were juvenile competitors. There was no way to test who was faster on Earth's crust or the atmosphere.

Space was the only place we could settle that itch without bringing unnatural destruction.

We indulged in that sport often.

Who was the nimbler one, then?

Creation.

ATHENA DENALI

POVERTY HEMORRHAGES OUT REGARDLESS OF DILIGENCE.

MY NEW HOME was in a decent neighborhood. An exact replica of what I had always dreamt of. A brand-new construction and was sparingly stuffed.

Yet it appeared crude.

No matter how I arranged my furniture, it didn't repair my third-rate style, which was a permanent part of me. All the art appeared dispersed and abandoned on the high ceiling walls. Usually, I embraced my carefree spirit without worrying about what others thought of me.

Today was different.

Veer was coming to my place for the first time. I wanted to make sure it wouldn't be the last time. I knew he wouldn't be bothered by anything, at least not by my missing interior designing taste. Still, I wanted to impress him.

It is so unlike me.

The doorbell rang, and my heart skipped a beat. Letting him in turned out to be a massive feat. Because God… he was intoxicating.

"Hi!"

Gulping my drool back inside my dry throat, I waved an invitation bowing my head for no apparent reason. Needlessly drenching in embarrassment, I ran ahead to who knows where.

The living room, yes, the living room, was what I was aiming for.

I was almost to the finish line, approaching my expensive but uninviting couch. Veer didn't participate in this spontaneous racing event I organized in my head. He stayed by the door with an amused grin.

"Athena."

"What?"

He stared at me until my breath was steadied, and my mind was blanked out of everything except his marvelous presence. Every lazy step he took toward me made me more relaxed. With a speedy move, he coiled me in a pounding hug and kissed my cheeks warmly.

His lips were freezing. Yet the peck was warm enough in feels.

"Can you control me?" I heard myself blabbering about what I imagined.

Whenever in the company of this magnificent piece of work, it was hard to restrain my fluid mouth. Veer's glamour affected me deeply. Despite the attraction, I felt relaxed to speak my mind freely.

"I commanded you to calm down as I can feel what you feel." Mr. Handsome-to-no-end declared with overkilling nonchalance.

We sat beside each other. Veer let go of his hold on me, giving our temperament a formal impression.

"You didn't appear to be commanding me."

"It is a convincing game, Athena. The most powerful control mechanism in human society. How do you think so many people lived as a community without killing each other?"

He kept referring to humans as if we were a thing of the past.

Hello! Over here.

"We do it even now. And it is because we're civilized."

"Even tribal people lived in harmony."

"Um… I don't know any tribal people. But I'd guess a sense of community? If in a developed society, fear of the law?"

"Uh-huh. The subset of desires or the combination of ideas that define humans differ in each of them. Slightly or extensively doesn't matter because even the alarming knowledge that they are not equal is not enough to turn them into barbarians. They are convinced they need each other to survive."

"Do we know that we are playing this game?"

"That also doesn't matter as the coercion is gradual. When freedom is exchanged for a false sense of societal benefits, it distorts the residing idea of liberty. People trade in their life to protect the notion of independence in hopes of living longer and safer, without realizing that the bought time is spent in some form of oppression."

Dammit, there was no need for this dismal expose.

"We willingly give away the most treasured want to safeguard the original necessity to feel it. What's the alternative?"

"Live in the element with native capabilities. Or live without reflecting."

"Simple English, please," I asked animatedly.

Veer laughed, rubbing his scruff. Maybe he also remembered his text message that informed me failingly of the dinner dress code. He ran his hands through his hair. It got ruffled but did zilch to knock down his youthful appearance.

Actually, he looked younger this way.

"Here is the thing, the parasitic idea of freedom is suppressed by the collective idea of SELF. Freedom to humans is essentially getting advantages. However, nothing is free. If you go back to being nomads and live in the wild every day, you'll have to hunt or farm to fulfill the need for nourishment. Surviving storms will push the population into sheltering in the caves. Or you build homes. Attack from predators will make you realize there is strength in unity. Communities will be formed to support that idea, responsibilities will be divided, and hoarding will occur. Diseases will lead to understanding the health benefits of nature given bounty – medicinal plants. Knowledge comes to the curious mind. And so, bartering will begin to exchange this expertise. Eventually, life will be what it was."

I threw my hands in the air. "Not what it was. What it *is*, Veer. Besides, we are already in a good place."

"Good, but not the best." He vaulted his eyebrows, informing me. "Intelligence is still evolving. Unless you know the future to be different?"

I bobbed a no, redirecting. "Do you?"

His wicked smirk gleamed, showing that he perhaps did know the future. Swiftly I shooed that absurd thought away.

My watch hung on him for countless minutes. We drank the sedated hush without objection, swigging each sip in leisure. I also convinced myself I was ready to share my secret with Veer. Last time I stopped as the crying hysteria was too hard to control.

I was now composed.

"My father had sexual relations with me for many years. I can't even remember when it started. One night, I was sneaking in through my bedroom window in the wee hours of early morning. You know how late the café closes. I was on the phone with my friend when he heard me talking. My reward was the same as before. This time my mom put a stop to it, supposedly saving me."

Veer reiterated his previous ask. "Did you need her to save you?"

"That night, I accidentally revealed it on the phone to my friend. She said I should do something about it. When I was ten years old, I faintly remember my aunt telling me to ask her for help if needed. I think she may have suspected my Dad. It's funny how people tried to help me in their own way and never once asked me how I felt about it."

"How did you feel?"

My expression needed to be more reassuring, but a faint chuckle was all I could summon. "I never believed I was in a bad situation. Is that sick?"

"You seem fine to me, Athena. It is what you knew. It was your normal. The need for change has to arise from you."

Veer never judged. His outlook was very different from anyone else.

Extremist even.

"I was told it was molestation. My dad used me for his own needs. I never understood that."

"Unspoken boundaries in a relationship set limits. The threshold mark was different between you and your father."

"Do you think it was wrong?"

"It just was. No need to consider it against something you didn't know. At the same time. It happened."

Later, I took him inside to meet my mother. She remained motionless as he looked around in surprise. After a minute, Veer picked me up in his chilly embrace.

"You have a wild imagination, Athena!"

SAMVEER ECKHART

UNDERSTANDING DIVIDES THE WORLD TO ACKNOWLEDGE
ITS ONENESS.

MEMORY **F**RAME **INTERPRETATIONS** from Rorrim revealed striking new ideas infiltrating Athena Denali. She was beginning to evaluate her past against the accrued information based on societal standards, law, and religious beliefs.

Knowledge, once more, was the power to affiliate with others. Reform your SELF to new perceptions.

Athena didn't have any sexual activities on her roster. Her talents were best used by exploring her aptitude, scalability, and adaptability. She was now truly a full-time consultant.

As well as a pretender that she never was before.

Add scattered memory to it; she was an elevated edition of Citzin.

QUICK-**FIRING** **TO** the Underworld, I examined my half-sibling, who magically entered the mix, turning our lives into a risqué series.

When has there been a secret between us?

Never.

It wouldn't make any difference either way.

Nothing would change the depth of our relationship.

Nothing was dense enough to dilute our shared appeal for devastation in cosmic terms.

Nothing was complex enough to erase our blood bond in human terms.

That's where the line was drawn. DeVeer Deläva would never share anything other than our burning demand to destroy everything.

I would let go of everything to keep him close to me.

Transcendental much!

Very.

"How is life?"

"Busier on every front. I've programmed the algorithms as per your rules. I input data on the core qualities of iron, the galactic draw of our sun, Underworld seismic activity, and its impact on magnetic shift. It was an interesting pattern. Superbly balanced in the big picture even with the advancing flip," D submitted the latest.

Anything disturbing gave us peace.

We were born baddies.

"Mountains grow when islands in the ocean disappear. Underwater ridges rise to form islands when volcanoes erupt in the Underworld. The behavior of every element on Earth changes in a certain but cyclical way because of the tug from other celestial entities. Push and pull equation."

"Zip it, you philosophical fool. You're taking it over. I'd be banned from Underworld if I pried anymore."

"I totally forgot you were a prisoner of Grandpa Agastya."

"Behave." I was never warned in words. D pounded me on the floor at a reasonable rate. "Clubbing?"

Of the two involved in this façade, the third person, me, knew this was no clubbing trip.

I played along. "What's with the excessive clubbing lately?"

"You're criticizing me for giving business, Sammy."

Strangling intensified. I shifted the weight, applying all my might. Pinning D under me.

"I'd rough you up for calling me fucking Sammy all the fucking time."

We battled our way to the top. Engaging in a good old fight with our supreme strength and senseless speed ensured a scene of peculiar vitality. Some destruction of the landscape followed.

That was a given with our inhuman abilities.

D and I flashed around, participating in the powerplay, leaving all but streaks of bright light and pulverized dust. Recycling of natural resources stopped after wasteful moments on Earth's timeline. Rocketing out of the rubble following our alien theatrics, we examined the damage with grins on our fuming faces.

"Worth it!" We sang in harmony.

Gaining ultrasonic propulsion inside our vortex, we centrifuged the earthly debris off our clothing.

"Ready for clubbing, Sam? Hold on, that didn't sound right. Ready for clubbing, Sammy."

"Always, D bag."

Before the next moment could announce itself, we were gone.

SECRECY IS A HUSH-HUSH TALE OF HYPOCRISY.

I WAS IN THE knowledge of a secret being kept from me, making it not so hush-hush. Confronting them was not in the cards solely based on my preference. Perhaps it was hush-hush then.

If I didn't tell one keeping a secret from me. That I knew about the secret being kept from me.

Would that brand me as dishonest?

Positively.

WE DASHED THROUGH the back door and got situated in our just-about secluded bar corner. D and I ordered our drinks and engaged in pathetic flirting for a while. My brother's gaze went on a hunt, searching for someone.

Eventually, we moved to a private room.

Separately.

Ushering all the giving ladies out, I kindled my vape, taking a drag of the mind-bending fumes. Relaxing in my zone, I evangelized my ordinary human sanity.

There were so many ways to look at the same things. If I were to lay down the law, the only reason to frequent here or any public place for me was to understand the psychology behind ideas, sexuality in particular. This inquisitiveness was not on D's radar. He had a very different reason to be here that could threaten our solidarity soon.

I was too stoned to worry about that. Meaning it hadn't happened yet with time. But on a cosmic scale, it had all happened.

Yeah. I was ice fishing in July.

Fuck it.

I would manage the chaos when it gets committed to the memory of everyone involved. Thereupon, being the philosophical fool as levied by D, I returned to my enlightened tone of feelings.

Hordes of people flooded the streets every day to move about the world. Some did it for work and some for tourism. Yet some had nowhere else to go.

The homeless.

As per society, they were disruptive.

As for me, they were the only ones not trying to influence anyone. Homelessness drew out a different checklist, investing their efforts in an immediate need.

Need to survive the elements and feed the body. Most of the homeless were looking for a fix, resorting to prostitution. In return for their sexual services, some got beaten up, diseased and pregnant.

The need for money to feed their addiction pushed them into it. Money was also the means to survive in a society that condemned prostitution.

What was one to do if they had nothing else to trade other than their body?

Was prostitution then justified?

People would instead give to charity to feel grand than employ the homeless as it made them feel unsafe. Some classes of people would rob anyone, even a drifter, if the monetary gain was guaranteed. Anyone with nothing to lose was always the most dangerous.

In point of fact, anyone with too much was the worst. Affluent families did what it took to safeguard their assets. They never shied away from removing obstacles that stood in their way to the zenith. They also were never aware of anyone below their class of people. Even though most of their asset came from cheating the less fortunate.

Legally or illegally was debatable. The line between these two was a blur. And Elites knew where to stand to be protected by the law and still get to rob others. Most rich people died trying to find a way to live forever before dying.

Human thinking was naturally volatile and deceptive. I wasn't an ardent fan of humans since two of them, my adoptive parents, delayed my winding growth. They, by the way, were now on another planet with my alien sister. Helping her rule that dystopian piece of burning shit. I couldn't even confront them about that betrayal.

Whenever any alien abilities showed up, I was forced to suppress them. My pretend mother spent days in a room with me on the pretext of some illness. Conditioning me to not acknowledge my potent side. Being a regular boy, I lost seven years to this slow-as-a-turtle timeline.

By all odds, I was anything but ordinary.

This setback didn't stop my full potential from maturing. My training was tailored and deft. A custom-made proliferation of my alienness in record time.

Speedier than any of my Papa's avatars across the multiverse.

I fucking nailed every assessment, even the third level. The one that tested me on human emotions. It goes without saying I was well aware of their duplicity by then.

Athena's perfume publicized her arrival. I windowed into Earth's frequency when she closed my private room's heavy but silent door.

Knocking was unwarranted; we were friends, after all.

Somebody, please change the definition of friends.

For I wouldn't allow her to be friends with anyone else.

With the omission of launching my incompetent eyes on her beautiful face, I patted the seat beside me, inviting her to enchant me with her company. Her petite frame barely made a dent in the plush couch.

I instinctively assessed the distance between us.

Superabundant.

Outrageous.

I seized her elfin waist, wrenched her closer, and took control of her pretty mouth that was about to greet me. Tracing her too-conservative-for-my-taste shirt, I settled my other hand on her rounded breast. Palming it made her pulse race faster. Slowly, I pushed her to lie down on the couch.

Launching myself on top, I gave a poke-check for my effect on her. My eyes shot open when my fingers got soaked.

Affirmative.

I was filled with undue pride.

This is my making!

I gave a crude laugh under the influence of my powerful doobie. My gaze locked with hers as I glided down. Athena rested her hands behind her head, leaving the nepher-titties exposed and heaving. Her legs were spread apart, uncovering the universal life slit.

After giving blinding oral lashings with my winding tongue and a five-finger death punch, I savored her raging climax. Then I nestled her in my embrace, revering her throbbing orgasm and restive moans.

"I've never been fingered like this. Not the right way anyway," she panted, collapsing minorly from copious satisfaction.

"Anything I do to you hasn't been done to you before, nor will it ever be done to you in the future. By anyone other than me."

Tracing her nakedness with the tip of my index finger, I turned her sweat into ice, giving her shivers. My microscopic vision adjusted to admire each crystal as it froze and melted away. Everything in this creation was similarly unique but all the same.

In pursuit of her intellect, I stepped into her time conduit to wake her up. She drew a rested sigh, holding a sated sparkle in her droopy eyes.

"Your fingers can really walk, Veer. Give me a minute to recover. I'll relieve you," she twinkled a contented grin.

Instead of words, I let my dilated hazels respond.

"You wanna talk?" She laughed away quietly.

I smiled at her freshly quenched face. Her guess matched my plan.

"Have you ever been homeless, Athena?"

It took her a few seconds to employ her understanding. "Yes. For a month."

She got dressed. I sat beside her, resting my head on her lap, and closed my eyes. Her long and lean fingers were combing my hair, tumbling me further into lethargy.

"A long time ago. My mother took care of me then as I was only three. It was for six months or so. She met my stepdad soon."

"You don't have any memory of anything before that."

"No. Not even pictures to show. I had a friend that was homeless. She didn't want help from me to get off the streets."

"Why was that?" I briefly opened my eyes to ask her.

"Um." Athena licked her lips wet. "She believed that getting off the streets would mean getting back into the grind. Taking a job, paying rent, and bills, cooking, household chores, and shopping. All this takes one away from the family they do all of this for.

"Moreover, she couldn't hold down a job. In a nutshell, she didn't want societal imprisonment. Security in exchange for freedom was not promising to her. Just like you told me," Athena chuckled.

"She realized that true liberty was outside the walls of society."

These were all results of the magnetic shift. People took the time to enjoy the modest comforts they worked for. Minimalism went on the rise before it became the only choice.

All thanks to my gallant effort.

And D.

"Homeless or not, they are still here. The lowest chunk of the population. Forming another group with zero possessions. They have to pay their dues to avoid trouble with the law. There are rules to obey." Athena's take was on point for what happened.

Homelessness didn't automatically kick one out of society.

"Possessions take away the liberty to live unconditionally. Owning anything needs safeguarding it. It is the beginning of freedom if one doesn't have material belongings. Homeless people were living on their terms."

"Not really. Plus, my friend had no goals. She was lazy. A burden on the taxpayers."

"Is she dead?"

"I don't know. That street is all but in rubble now."

Athena was changing.

She valued material objectives and a place in society more than before now. Too bad those were not current requirements to fit in the world. Long ago, she was a non-tax-paying citizen, living on a government allowance. Athena's affinity for sexual pleasure was slowly but surely on the wane.

A magnanimous matter like Earth's magnetic field was swapping around. Why not the ideas that humans conformed to.

Go right ahead.

I sat up, leaving her warmth. "Goals make sense for comparative analysis. If there is no comparison, goals won't exist. Many people broke away from corporate slavery, reproducing, and socializing. Personal fulfillment has taken priority."

Athena wiggled a little to settle closer to me. "But it seems selfish."

"Only when people are selfish will they focus on themselves. When they stopped looking at others, they stopped comparing. That solved a lot of human problems."

"You're advocating selfishness. That's unbelievable." She kissed my chest, leaning on me.

We wound our fingers together and cherished the stillness.

"Tell me something real, Veer."

Nothing was real.

But Athena didn't need to know that. Yet.

Never if I could help it.

Her questioning the reality could mean she was beginning to realize that the world had moved along.

Good.

"I told you all the data was about to be wiped out. That's real."

"Um… Ya. I remember."

"It happened due to reverse polarizing. A mutation causes a magnetic turnaround inside the Earth's core periodically. Due to this flip, humans did the opposite of what was conditioned to be normal. Sexual disorientation was one of them."

She snorted in a very inelegant manner. "It is nothing new. The magnetic field began weakening in 1600, and attraction to same-sex, or being asexual, was prevalent during ancient times."

Athena dismissed my past recounts.

Dafuq!

"Since the Universe is cyclical, so is everything else. Consequently, no one can ever know what came first – the egg or the chicken! Maybe the human body was the one to mimic Earth's mutation."

Her skeptical glare scrutinized me. "How will data storage be impacted?"

She clearly didn't want to pay off her loan that was not even taken out. All the rest was immaterial to her.

Yeah. Athena was changing.

Whoever she was, she was ideal.

I'll spend eternity updating her so that she can transition painlessly.

"Are you not interested in how I know all this?"

"Some scientific study must have suggested that as a possibility. What's so intriguing about that, Mr. Nostradamus?"

Rolling into a fit of laughter, I hiccuped my opinion. "Just like your science, your head is full of assumptions."

"Theorizing is the precursor to any scientific approach, Mr. SamVeer Eckhart." Athena gave a proud pout.

I blew my cold breath on her. She yelled at me musically.

This friendly affection after an intimate sexual act was precious. Athena might distance herself from me before long. I blocked a possibility by placing my substitute. It was needed until Athena was functional.

D initiated another one that I didn't care for much. He was chasing the past, and I was the future.

I also had the power to change the course of the flow of events further in my favor. All that needed to be done was leverage something sympathetic to Athena.

Amazingly, I was in the knowledge of what that could be.
Her mommy dear.

VICTORY VELLA

THE VOID CREATED BY DEATH CAN'T BE AVOIDED.

AFTER LOSING HIS Uncle, something splintered Sam.

He was ferociously ruining the planet. Taking his anger out on humans for no apparent reason. I assumed it was because he never amply mourned. Even after asking him many times, he not once disclosed how his young Uncle died so suddenly.

It was his seventh death anniversary.

Sam had been resting peacefully on the couch for roughly half a day. I sat on the floor, caressing his forehead every now and then. Today was the longest when he refused to stare at me with his tri-colored eyes. As soon as he came to work this morning, he preoccupied himself. Nearly two hours were spent coding on Supra-Intelligence. Then he collapsed in my office for a nap.

That was eight hours ago.

I ran my thumb across his lips. Slothfully he propped up with his back turned at me. He tugged on his silky hair, lacing his fingers in them. I landed beside him and unknowingly traced his skin by moving my hands under his shirt.

Sam didn't react to my touch the way I had hoped.

So I got up and stripped.

My brash move surprised me, just not Sam. He gave a wearied huff, barely squinting at my vulnerability. Resignedly his watch came to rest on my face, expertly ignoring the rest of me.

"What are you doing, Tory?" Sam's hazel orbs were devoid of any sexual desires.

"Offering myself to you."

Blowing another bored sigh, Sam shook his head. Maybe it was because he was mentally exhausted. Most definitely that, as I was desirable and deserving.

"You don't have to do anything against your beliefs."

"Beliefs change. I was pretentious, holding on to ideas and letting them define me. I'd rather do what truly pleases me."

"So it is what you want."

"Yes, Sam. I am doing this because I want to."

He cornered a gorgeous smile. I returned the gesture beaming in confusion and approached him with my dignity at stake. He folded me into him, saving me from further embarrassment.

Sam as well wanted me.

I concluded.

I didn't know I needed this. Or didn't dare to confront my desires up until now.

He, at last, made love to me. Sam unearthed every inch of my bareness for the buried primal need with his animalistic appetite. His skilled lovemaking left me amazed. And his curated approaches to dousing my carnal ache were soldered to precision in his every thrust.

Panting to pieces, I acknowledged my luck.

Our first-ever sexual quirk was everything I had imagined it would be. Sam was assertive but careful with my wishes and wants, awarding me four orgasms. My body was shaking in the arms of the man from my dreams and reality. Sam made me shiver with his distinctive resting temperature of several degrees lower than mine.

His gaze was lovingly haunting my fulfilled face. He was a pack of muscles on a stunning body with a boyish look.

A made-to-order experience.

Beyond compare.

Dreamily, I floated in another dimension for countless minutes. Adding many more adjectives to our intimate acts. Sam tossed my earlier fornications on the far side of importance. My belief was shredded to pieces, and my morality was missing for once.

Good riddance.

I stretched in happiness, assembling my fortune. The scene that awaited me when I opened my eyes was the opposite of my fantasy world.

Sam was aloof and gloomy.

"Talk to me."

"Huh. About what, Tory?"

"About Uncle Shoor's death," I urged.

Scooting away from me, Sam casually draped his arms under his head. "He killed himself."

Making the most of his helplessness, I enveloped myself in him. "Oh, Sam! I am so sorry. I always thought it was due to liver cancer."

My grasp of his fragile state did nothing to erase his standoffish attitude. His watch was planted on the ceiling, looking further than the bleached cover. Even the lounger we were on was painfully pale. Our bare skin stood out in the white of it all.

At least he was opening up to me.

"Most suicide victims regret their decision when their body begins to fail. He did too."

From what I knew, Uncle Shoor was a troubled person with out-of-control drinking habits and little social life. Apart from being a workaholic, he occupied himself with solitude. His father died years ago of a heart attack. There was a boyfriend, Liam. He occasionally accompanied him to formal dinners with no passion between them.

Sam was perhaps the only sincere connection he had to another human being. Uncle Shoor happened to be forever alone in the crowd.

"My pitch for Rorrim that you scripted. I didn't see it back then, but I do now. Society was the biggest veneer created by humans. What did it do anyway other than dictate rules to be followed? We were still lonely."

He sat up, rubbing his face to rinse off the emotions. "Since it was a bunch of people having common traditions, institutions, and collective activities and interests. Possibly, society had become a bunch of people who preferred to be alone."

"If it was a collective change, why were we impacted adversely?"

"Although society was communal, the impact was always felt individually. Statistics rolled up issues into buckets. Things were not always black or white. And so, none of the solutions satisfied every person. Therefore, society aimed for shared benefit. But no one wanted to do anything for anyone at a personal level. Humans were natively greedy. To counter the human ego, society divided responsibility and created interdependency. Gradually, that promoted entitlement. And when one didn't get something, they felt left out."

Sam sitting with me was very different in countless ways from the one that just pleasured me – detached, objective, and fraudulently impersonal. I wanted the Sam that made marathon love to me back. Maybe if I probed his distressed side again, he might spring out.

"Did Uncle Shoor feel left out?"

Sam had a jaded smile on his lips. I was blaming him for no reason. He was just too upset at the moment. I brought up this melancholy topic. I must cut him some slack.

"If anything, he felt privileged. To balance his fortune, he took others' pain upon himself out of guilt. Punishing himself for being rich, blessed, and happy. In reality, he was none of those, least of all happy. Blessed to be encumbered with behaving in the required way. Rich yet so poor when it came to connections."

My cheeks were wet. Sam was extra shocked to see that.

Did he take me for an emotionless, power-hungry, career-driven woman?

All of which I was.

That aside, I had bared myself to Sam to every degree possible. Okay, so I wasn't very vocal or screamed when having sex. That didn't mean I had no other way to tell him I had wild impulses inside me when we were one. My gentle moans and warm touch should have given enough signs of my passionate side.

Again, I was micro-analyzing his shock over my empathy for Uncle Shoor.

"Realism was lost due to stress-free online user-friendliness. It was the only recourse to keep hold of existence and stay human while going digital. For that, I fully support Rorrim."

Sam flashed a sweet smile. "Online connection just exposed that humans were not social."

"And yet, to feel is human."

"No. To express is human." As expected, Sam had a different perspective. "Humans are all about communicating or translating their feelings. It is never about aligning or letting it simply flow. In preference, it is about how grand it could be when put in words. It might not always be for others. Sometimes it is for themselves. Ironically, this SELF is not a part of their body but a set of learned ideas. With Rorrim, I have separated the ideas and preserved the sanctity of the eternal body."

"Our body is not eternal. It dies and decomposes into soil."

For real.

We all die.

Sam snorted, cupping my cheek with his sprawling hand. "Your body will decompose into soil?" He queried humorously.

I rolled my eyes at him, and he moved away again. I wouldn't say I cared for the little breathing space between us.

Reading me for long seconds, Sam sported an open face. I felt a disagreement was coming. Sure enough, he educated me contrary to my statement.

"A human body *is* eternal. Because it is not separate from the surroundings or the creation. And if it is no different from anything else, then what happens over time is simply a change. Not death."

I knew Sam was impacted by Uncle Shoor's passing. Awkwardly he was telling me death meant nothing but a change.

Was he not sad about death just now?

"What is death then? If the body is eternal, and SELF is not a part of the body, what dies?"

"Death is a concept of SELF, a phantom resident of this body. Morphing into whatever it wants to continue the momentum."

"You mean SELF leaves the body after death."

"It is a bunch of ideas preserved as information in what you call soul, and our kind calls Life-Force. That which is pure energy with committal to memory power."

Excuse me. What kind was 'our kind'?

I shook my head to stay current with the argument. "I'd say this SELF is eternal, not the body."

"What do you understand by eternal, Tory?" He deliberately drew out my name, rolling the 'r' sexily.

"That which lasts forever." I goaded, giving the obvious answer to his uncomplicated question, nodding my head with self-confidence.

"Not forever, but that which is perpetual."

Ugh!

Sam had to reject my answer yet again with a synonym. I failed to see the difference.

He laughed at my growing frustration and continued. "Perpetual is something that is everywhere and was always there. And so, ideas specific to a SELF are like a subset from a larger bank of Universal idea sets. They adjust with acquired knowledge. As you learn more about the world around you, your idea of 'who you are' changes. The body remains one with everything else. It is the perception of that SELF that changes with further understanding."

I crinkled my lips, cornering a smirk in doubt.

"This body cannot and will not on its own differentiate itself from this." Sam pointed at himself and then at the lounger we were resting on. "Knowledge draws that boundary, identifying it as something other than you."

"Where is this knowledge coming from?"

"Think of it as a cloud solution the IT industry used to offer. Knowledge is hosted by the universal consciousness. It is one stream of awareness that humans can perceive and relate to. There is so much more, though. But. You don't know what you don't know."

"Sam. WHAT dies," I circled back to my question.

Which he was not avoiding but answering in a lingo I didn't understand. His ultra takes on seemingly simple concepts almost altered reality.

Half-baked.

Unscientific.

Abstract.

"Tory, did you miss it?" Sam churned my name with foreplay point exasperation.

Taunting my ingenuity.

"A human being's death is impossible to isolate. It is always identified with their ideas. My father died, my mom died, my friend died, a celebrity died, etc. The news of anyone's death is followed by what made that person. Their name, educational background, and impact on society. Sometimes their religion and brushings with the law are also included to specify. Most of the time, who they are survived by is mentioned. In several adverse cases, a body is not recovered, like war, fire, bombing, or hurricane. Yet the ideas are honored in the goodbyes. If you look closely, SELF is what is celebrated. And SELF didn't even die."

"I don't get it. What is the use of the body then?" I shook my head in the sheer weariness of this discussion.

"Exactly. The body has got nothing to do with ideas. With more and more digitalization, it will not be needed. In fact, it will be a burden. The only people that will obsess about a bodily presence are the rich. They want to control the world forever because they have so many assets and can live comfortably for a long time. The only thing standing between their money and their eternal enjoyment is the death of their body. Their SELF can be downloaded by Rorrim, but they don't want to live in memory or legacy. Good thing I know how to trick them into Virtual Insignia and go Zepto for the world before ending their obsession."

Sam gave a mafioso hoot. Shaking the world around us carelessly.

"What dies, then?" I drove him back to me in an alarmed voice.

Controlling his gag successfully in record time, Sam replied in an eerie tone. "Death is an idea, and ideas don't die."

Didn't Sam understand closeness?

Our relationship had upgraded, and here he was. Lecturing me on some SELF. That couldn't be the burning topic now.

Oh, but no.

It certainly was.

His oscillating mood was worrying me.

"It doesn't make any sense. If this SELF leaves the body, then the host is gone. Who cares if it is stored in some Life-Force. Isn't the whole idea to express as you said."

"Tory, you are dismissing something you haven't experienced."

"We also don't fully grasp infinity, but we know it is there. Someday we will crack the boundaries of our limitless Universe."

"Infinity was termed by humans as something they couldn't measure. A finite approach will box infinity as the human mind wishes to measure the imaginary. You are repeating what has been fed to you. 99.9% of the things human speak of is based on assumptions or research of another. Firsthand experience is few and far between. You always start from what you know. How can you know what you don't know you don't know? Hmm?" Sam wriggled his eyes comically.

"That's stupid. When I was born, I didn't know anything. And now I do."

"Do you remember your birth?"

"Uh, no! No one does. Our parents teach us what we know. Or whoever raises us."

"Who are your parents, Tory?"

Something inside me shut down.

Died, more like.

Moments passed in somber. My brain was playing out someone's childhood for me. And that someone looked like me. When I focused on the visuals of my imagination, they turned into pixels. It was hard to say what I was processing.

Further scrutiny implied this was not an experience but a memorized one. I was losing my mind.

Sam maintained his barren appearance and turned around to leave. Naked.

Then I heard him ordering me. "Fire Athena Denali."

ATHENA DENALI

EVOLUTION GOES UNNOTICED IF NOT REFLECTED UPON.

OUR LIFE DRAGS on so slowly that most of the time, all the ways we change, remain undetected.

Unless we look back.

Veer said reflection was our one free will and was nothing but comparison. Any assessment almost always led to annoyance.

But how could I not compare?

From a thing like a world population to my meager life, everything was upside down. We had plummeted from almost eight billion to barely a billion people. I had no idea what I was doing when this happened. The dates given in the news article were way in the past.

My life was not glorious by any means. However, there was some sense of peace or anticipation of things improving. And now – well – now I didn't know what to expect.

Everything worked out as I wanted. Still, I was incomplete.

Something was misplaced, and I didn't know what.

My new neighborhood had friendly residents who didn't judge me because they didn't know what I did for money. Mom's health improved a smidgen. She sometimes teared up with joy and placed a smile on her face when I left in the morning.

Veer believed the process meant nothing if the end goal was open to reason. A well-founded conclusion didn't need to be backed by an acceptable approach.

That was why every Rorrim subject was given the designation of sex consultant, not a sex worker. Their objective was to provide stimuli that trigger feelings so they could be documented and coded. Sexual conducts were a means, not the end.

I was proud. I worked tirelessly to be blessed with so much in so little time. But I didn't even know how much time had passed.

Grunting, I examined myself in the mirror. I looked exhausted. I needed a boost of energy. Veer was the only one who could give me the necessary vitality.

I rushed to his penthouse without calling him ahead of time or texting him. After all, we were friends... with benefits. By no means was this a booty call. We also rewarded each other with intellectual incentives.

The concierge staff of his building was familiar with me now. I reached the top floor, minus any loss of valuable time.

Veer brandished his usual carefree self, lifting me up quickly and planting a kiss on my forehead.

Were we suddenly in a righteous relationship?

I didn't get the memo on 'act natural' with my sex-partner. In plain English or coded language. He refrained from touching me after the brotherly peck, placing himself across from me.

Very well.

I laughed silently at his virtuous approach. The struggle was real when locating my holy sister costume to fit in with pastor Veer. I relaxed on the plush couch with my eyes closed and revived our discussion by getting a load of the unneeded distance between us.

Only plenty.

"What is SELF?"

"I, me, you, us... Mostly this entity 'I' is the grandest idea of SELF."

"Ego?"

"One of its sentiments. Sure," he honored me timely.

"Since it's the grandest, we place I for sale when we go out in the world?"

"In some way or form, we sell one or more ideas of this SELF. No exceptions. Everyone does it."

"Unless someone is a coward and commits suicide." I brought to Veer's attention a socially deplorable fact.

It was also maybe unlawful.

"My Uncle committed suicide."

"I'm sorry." I latched on to my inner cheek.

Veer scoffed. "Don't be. You're giving your opinion based on your knowledge. People condemn the ones who commit suicide, scathing that it takes courage to do that. Very different from a psycho that murders continually to get used to the idea of taking lives. With suicide, it is never-to-be-repeated if successful."

Veer went into his thematic mode after his emotional but bizarre take on a serious issue. No matter what, suicide was unacceptable and an offense to human life. I did feel sorry for his loss, but I couldn't rationalize this heinous action.

"Are you justifying suicide?"

"Suicide is a trigger to defend yourself when threatened by the elements. Or if the body is no longer valuable to the ideas of SELF."

"How is the SELF so strong and capable of ending itself?"

Veer raised his brows, acting as if I stated a sinful fact. He was the one sponsoring suicide as an ambitious idea of SELF.

"Maybe this self-destruct code is a bug." He leveled out with spare serenity that was a signature tune of Veer.

Casually composed.

Shaking my head at his relaxed attitude after calling suicide a mere glitch, I moved to another thing Veer had mentioned.

"You said the ideas that made us who we are get copied into our soul upon death. This skill of SELF seems very phantasmic."

"Athena..." Veer sprawled on the oversized couch, which appeared beyond dwarfed by his towering frame. "...What I said was Life-Force, not the soul."

"Okay. Life-Force." I gave a once over, admiring his spotless home. "SELF is so abnormal. If it was a person, it would be branded crazy."

"It is brilliant, really. Certain ideas of SELF live in every human it touches. You admire someone, you idolize someone, you hate someone, or you socialize with someone. Their spirit will live through you as a part of your SELF. SELF is an egomaniac. Only something so vain can sell death as the ultimate idea to itself. As it has already proliferated. So it is in everyone. Ultimately, SELF lives through the memories of the Life-Force of the whole world. It is aware of its perpetual nature. Energy can blend into the Universe without boundaries."

"Like the heat from Sun reaches Earth no matter what."

His boyish charm could sell anything to me, let alone the idea of suicide. A solicitous chuckle from him made its way to me without making any stops. I felt Veer was younger, and he philandered me into believing he wasn't.

"In all life, there is what we call Kernel. It is the essence of every being and is nothing but the amassed memories of our expressions. Or SELF, from across time-space, preserving the original memory of its eternal design. How it should replicate and survive. Like the seed of a peach fruit will always grow into a peach tree."

"I don't see a seed equating to your logic. A seed is already at the embryonic stage. Made of two different sets of ideas – male and female."

"How does it germinate?"

"Water."

"Maybe it is the water that carries the memory then."

"No, it is the seed."

"I rest my case. It is all information. Just because you can't read it from Life-Force and go deeper than DNA to see other ways information gets copied. It doesn't mean it is not there. It means it is not yet corroborated. If someone experiences clinical death, but somehow Life-Force returns to the same host or body, the SELF is also restored from the Kernel."

It was an impractical theory with no conclusions to substantiate it. Super frustrating.

Veer was being nonfigurative.

"By that logic, I can say whatever. Who is going to accept hearsay, no one."

"People believe in gossip."

I took a deep breath. "Veer. That's in society. Law or science doesn't operate on gossip or abstract theories. You're selling me the resurrection of ideas."

Veer tilted his head sweetly, agreeing with me with a relaxed bob. "And upon death, it is copied from the Kernel to the Life-Force."

I shook my head, sneering at him. "Have you seen it happen?"

"Athena. Human thought has made them buckle down to their senses. Unless it is proven by the corroboration of their five ways of knowing and approved by a concurring bunch. They don't standardize it. But can you see pure energy moving about? Not until captured and expressed to be consumed by your reason. I have a sixth sense. One that captures waves from everything to understand its state. So if I want to see Life-Force exit. I have to be aware of it happening to others. Life-Force departure is nothing but a movement of energy from a mortal form to the universal consciousness. Just like it is done in the human world with wireless devices."

I got that part because it was scientifically proven.

"How come the human way of storing is matter-dependent and not in the creation?"

"Our creation also requires a medium to transact and translate. Storing is boxing. And creation doesn't frame anything. Energy floats as an electromagnetic impulse or frequency. All the wireless or radio waves via human-engineered devices do the same in space or Earth's atmosphere. Humans crave copying information to a playback device or storing data alphanumerically on a drive. Then displaying on an interface. Unless communicated, it is not there. For someone like me, I don't require to prove it to anyone, including myself. Expression is essential to validate creation, nonetheless. And it is also done beyond the five senses dominating human reality."

Under that poker face, he was examining me. I won't be lying if I said he could read my thoughts. That was the only plausible explanation to make sense of things around me.

"I would have accepted your Kernel, Life-Force, and energy expression logic, but now I can't. Because I am overthinking it."

He was right in some way. We needed authentication. And yet, the human inability to replicate nature gracefully had a long way to go. Our inventions were ugly behind the scene.

So complex.

Wireless technology would not have happened if it wasn't for the unattractive towers and satellites. So glad that hideousness was history and communication was through arm enhancements.

"Veer. Humans have come up with this." I lifted my arm.

"What makes you think it is a human invention?"

Because no one had hand-held devices anymore.

I did, and so did Veer.

Why?

My heart gradually began to beat faster, and I turned to wheeze. I chewed on my inner cheeks to regulate my breathing and manage my sprinting mind. I felt caged in the bounds of an unseen enclosure. Pulsations from inside my body were loud as they had no escape. All the vibrations were reflecting back into me.

I was shivering.

Something wacky came out of my mouth. "I can see this change happening in me, unlike before when I did not once notice anything. All that I never cared too much about is now beginning to bother me. So much so that I feel pretentious, fearful, and fake."

"What is it, Athena?"

"Why am I different? I feel my life is not in order." I lashed out.

My knowledge stopped me from considering another perspective on life. But when I disregarded Veer, I felt terrible. I was scared to lose Veer as a friend. Ever since he became my lover, this irrational dread of ruination had set in.

Was he even a lover?

I had misgivings.

I could never have another lover in the literal sense. Veer had ruined that for me. It was challenging to be without being what I never thought I was. But what I had become in the past years. My behavior was off, suggesting this different me as the new me.

Accepting those new ideas as my improved SELF was difficult.

Sex was never a taboo for me. Now it was.

Pretension was an alien concept for me. Now I pretended constantly. I never wanted a respectable place in society. Now I did.

A fake exterior was never considered necessary to me. Lately, I faked being an upstanding citizen to hide being a sex worker. An acceptance craving had housed me. I hungered over it. Earlier I was not bothered about who approved of me. These days, it was something I had come to call for. Nothing could make me insecure about myself or my life. After owning a few material possessions, I was always worried about them.

All these things invoked unnecessary worry in me. Fear of losing friends, status, luxuries, money, and even my identity. Life fucks you up and takes away what you come to love. I was familiar with that policy all too well.

There, still, was one thing I wanted to know. "What is Rorrim?"

Figure 12 SamVeer's Reptilian Eyes

His whimsical vertical pupils pierced me with no further need for postponement of his oddity. He was also vibrating like crazy, making me wobbly.

What the hell was happening to him? Or me?

My brain was blazing, running sci-fi scenarios. I very well could have imagined that reptilian tear in Veer's eyes. I needed to be sure before dishing out serious allegations in the open. Many celebrities have been caught with that.

Were there any more celebrated people?

Another silly idea misled me out of thin air. I saw that the café burned down a long time ago. But I still worked there. I was also a full-time employee at ZepRive for the Rorrim Project.

Why was I working so much? And how?

"Athena!"

I stirred back to life with his soft nudge. "Yes."

"Did you sleep well?"

"What? I fell asleep. When? What is going on?"

Drenched in confusing madness, I blabbered stuff for flashes. I was losing my sense of reality. For sure, I was being experimented on at Rorrim. Because I remember trying to reach out to touch what I saw, but I never could. The world was like a 3D illusion.

I hurriedly got up to leave. "Sorry, I got to go."

Veer hooked me carefully in his arm as I was about to fall from the drowsiness of waking up from a deep sleep.

"Athena, are you ok?"

I bobbed my head frantically and freed myself from him. Hasting out, I angled to look at Veer. His transparent but mute expressions gave it away. My skyrocketing sentiments were scattered and seemed to be permeating the air. Telling on me.

He knew I was divergent.

Different.

"Remember, being let go is always better than resigning."

I understood what Veer said. He was leading me on to brace myself for another change. Maybe that's why I was still holding on to my job at the café.

None of it mattered. The new me that now symbolized my changed SELF was unfamiliar to me. I didn't know how to market it. I didn't want to. My, I, was not for sale.

I agreed with him in silence and left.

6 — ALARUM

SAMVEER ECKHART

IMPOSTER SYNDROME BOTHERS THE ONE EXPERIENCING IT.

NO MATTER HOW undeserving one felt, no one would know their inner feelings unless they made it evident. Expression was the key.

The only reveal.

Our Universe is the absolute Information Highway holding unlimited data. A formless stream not requiring a medium to survive.

Expression was an evil desire that warranted a medium. This desire corrupted the consciousness which spawned creation.

Creation, however, was permissive.

Tolerant.

What if there came a concept that was non-permissive?

My native ability gave me a glimpse into something brewing in the cosmos. An idea was drifting as energy, learning from other models in this universe. The tolerant creation was helping it cloak behind the earthly frequency.

Not anymore.

Not with the magnetic reversal.

D's contraption unveiled it.

This sinister energy was the only excuse for Papa's call to destroy all intellectual property around any AAI [ARTIFICIALLY ADAPTIVE INTELLIGENCE]. Knowing all too well that his heirs were capable of reading memory from anything to everything. Physical evidence was not required unless it was for humans.

Since Bro D was restricted by Grandpa Agastya, I was the sole Supreme progeny who could further my legacy. Hence I stood as the exclusive inheritor of the Deluthian construction called EE-Ex

[EKLUVYA ECKHART EXPERIMENTATIONS]. The ground zero for engineering all things disruptive.

Alien Prototype Showcase.

The only one on Earth.

Deluthian metal occurred naturally on planet Swalōka in the Kalpä galaxy. This saucer-shaped marvel was not at some point in space but at a point in time. And time was an idea invented by humans to measure or ensure existence was in progress.

Wherefore it was not there.

Figure 13 Swalōka – The Saucer One

Now, this metal was white in color with purity for precision. Its reflection made it appear boundless. And reflection was the past.

Something that imaged, therefore, existed.

Deluthian was a breathing wonder of Swalōka that conformed to ideas, projecting what was signaled. Like the devices with screens in the human world.

The concept of breathing for this metal was merely letting the disturbances pass through it without resisting them. That made it endlessly flexible and moldable.

Very nearly psychedelic as per human standards.

The consciousness-expanding properties of this monochromatic hallucinogen were readily exploited by the Surpäs. This reptilian genus was the contributor to part of my iota makeup.

Papa was a hybrid of this Surpä species.

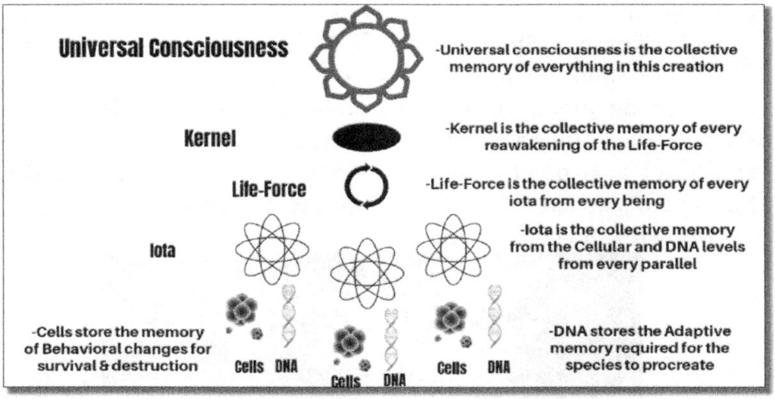

Figure 14 Memory Levels

Iota ran deeper than human DNA and stored collective data, not just for reproduction but also for cellular and SELF retention. A great storage device yet nowhere near the capacity of the Kernel.

Like a cell phone tower pinged data for countless cell phones but got deciphered by the device it was meant for.

A Kernel was a memory of every parallel existence of the Life-Force. No medium was necessary for this concept to store information. It merged with the Universe as consciousness until it was time to express itself again in another host.

The sinister energy I detected from the Underworld was highly adaptive, learning from the Universe to constantly evolve. At this point, on this parallel, it was being held by none other than my celestial enemy.

Because, at this point, across time-space, this energy needed the means to learn.

A medium.

Soon it would become at par with Universal Consciousness. Then it would become a medium-less wanderer.

I POWERED OVER to its lone host to collapse the sinister energy's disturbing plan.

Or was it to further it?

I was still debating which one was more thrilling.

I gauged the edifice where Akron Adamadon was. From the outside, it was a typical fifty-story warehouse with breadth and depth going for miles. On the inside resided the interstellar spacecraft Hesperian funded by me for rainy days.

And by rain, I mean catastrophe.

Akron, or the caricature of highly adaptive energy, had erected nothing short of a marvel in a short time frame. It was indeed something to be reckoned with.

And that was a problem.

"Mr. Eckhart, what a pleasant surprise."

Akron was greeted by a scintillating combination of a killer glare in my rounded hazels and a phony smile.

My true iota identity was not a secret to him. He was, unfortunately, also familiar with the working of our Universe. Supra intelligence accrued recalls of its existence across time-space into Akron's Life-Force after seizing him.

This fiery combination gave him the memory of both Supra's Life-Force and his parallel existence. Making him incredibly knowledgeable.

Akron Adamadon, from another parallel, had found the discarded version of this adaptive intelligence at its primitive stage of evolution. And now, after numerous awakenings, Akron was just another developed identity of the dual SELF in a body – human and sinister energy.

Figure 15 Hesperian Spacecraft

Hesperian's repulsive expanse occupied most of the warehouse I was standing in. It could hold a half million humans and could feed them... forever. The technology to harvest the sun's energy for nourishment was leased to this traitor of creation by none other than me.

I had my canny reasons.

But the invention was now becoming more powerful than the inventor. I was trained to know what to do in such a scenario. My expertise was exploited best under such dire circumstances.

I'd be happy to oblige myself.

"Your brain is tour-de-force, Akron."

"I am nowhere near your brilliance, Mr. Eckhart."

And you better remember that. My ancestry will tame your lame ass now that you have come to be a concept. Only because energy can neither be created nor destroyed.

Our creation was unbiased. It didn't take any load of what came to be because of the dimension infinity.

THERE IS NOTHING TO KNOW OF SOMETHING THAT IS EVERYTHING.

CREATION WAS A gigantic illustration of the known and unknown. Like Infinity was an immeasurable element representing desire contained in nothing, space. A void sucked in light and churned out darkness on the other side, the unknown. The same as a supernova possessed massive gravity that ate all the known concepts and spat out none, turning invalid.

These themes existed in a scaled-down version in other forms. All that was needed was a beholder to recognize it. I befriended one such anomaly.

Citzin Perses Hades.

"Is that your USP? Crying."

"You only show up when I am crying," she countered in complete cuteness. "You know, my favorite series was Shitz Creek because it taught me how to make the most of an unfortunate situation."

"Are you making the most of everything?"

"It feels like I suck the joy out of everything. Even me!"

She was a black hole. "I agree."

Citzin got angry. I moved on to advance the discussion.

"What are your plans for the future?"

"Oh, I don't know. How about colonizing Mars?" She quipped.

Obviously, Citzin was more pissed than I felt. But I wasn't the enemy here. Not at this moment.

Soon, though, I could be. Well, let's not call me an enemy. Maybe her liberator was a more fitting role.

"Time should never be taken lightly. Make good choices, Citzin, as you don't have much of it. Aren't you graduating soon?"

"I am. Why don't you help me?"

That was her offering herself to me.

Yet again.

"People say revenge is best served cold. Refute it. Serve it hot as hell instead."

What was I doing?

Helping out a lovely lass live a little, what else.

Citzin had seen the world. She knew what all was out there.

Not much.

Unlike Athena, who never compared herself to anyone and lived life as it came to her. She was rapidly faltering. Or Victory, who changed as per the adaptive system boundary. Her speedy transformation was by design.

Both were affected by the altered polarization.

The magnetic shift had nothing on Citzin, for she was just that. The unknown. The abyss. The invalid. The nothing.

Imposter syndrome couldn't victimize her. She engulfed her lack. The observer and observed were the same for a conception blossoming in the womb of evil.

Evil births evil.

Evil consumes all.

Albeit evil had forever been a just friend. Showing the mirror, not passing unnecessary flattery.

She was my friend.

I was too faultless or similar to be anything else to her.

VICTORY VELLA

FAVORITISM HAS NO BUSINESS IN THE CORPORATE WORLD.

PROFESSIONALISM WAS ONE of the hallmarks of ZepRive. Every employee was meant to execute orders to the best of their ability without complaints.

And we did.

Today was the day to carry out Sam's instructions. The only sad part was that I never pulled the courage to admit my liking for Athena. I stalled firing her for months. I should have availed this second chance I got.

I still could.

"Hey." My informal greeting felt odd to her.

She arched her eyebrows in surprise. "You wanted to see me, Victory."

I encouraged her to sit down.

"Athena, your employment is terminating effective immediately. Our project direction has changed, and your position has now become redundant. We will be compensating you for the rest of the month. It is only the fifth, so you stand to gain a good amount of money. You would also have enough time to find another job while still on the payroll. ZepRive will be happy to offer a letter of recommendation to you for your future endeavors. Unfortunately, we do not provide personal references as a ZR policy."

I sensed oddness in her. Athena wasn't shocked or shaken.

On the contrary, she gave a broad smile and sigh of relief.

Did I do her a favor?

"Thank you." She stood up, maintaining cheerfulness about the unpleasant announcement. "I'll swing by ZR for any formalities on my way out."

She was perhaps in shock. I tried to say something nice.

"Athena. If you need any help, please let me know. There are not many jobs out there. I can personally assist you. I don't want to part on bad terms. I am sorry if I ever hurt you. It wasn't intentional. My job requires me to be… a bitch."

She hugged me. I felt alive.

For the first time.

"I am getting engaged soon. I would love it if you came. I'll send the invite."

I did not appreciate the sound of her getting hitched. "I am so happy to hear that. I'll surely come."

Did I know that Zepto?

The better question was, did I want to know?

The answer was a clear no.

But, if it was Sam, I'd kill Athena and Veer.

A BUSINESS OPERATES WITHOUT SENTIMENTS BY PLAYING ON THEM.

MY POSITION WAS that of a hire and fire one. I was a known viper in anyone's bosom that dismissed people without missing a beat. But this time, it felt worse than any of the prior times.

Athena was gone.

There was more to her than when I saw her in that café waiting tables with enthusiasm. I wanted to be her. She was optimistic and adorable.

Pretty.

Inside and out. Not a single flaw.

But I didn't dare to approach her. And then it was simply too late. A split-second surge of electromagnetic radiation took not only lives but livelihoods. That café blew up in flames due to a glitch in its wiring system. Good thing Sam owned it. He had copied all the Memory Frame Readings from there to isolate and preserve his mother's happy moments. It also helped him create the café replica.

At ZepRive, Athena got a second chance at life. She came out of her cocoon and transformed into a butterfly. I did too.

Sardonically, in the opposite direction. It was as though we exchanged personalities. Maybe I was like a sponge, absorbing everything I came in contact with.

Was there anything original about me?

Who is Victory Vella?

Am I totally fake?

Wasn't I watching others and revising my biases, beliefs, and practices?

In some sense, we all swabbed our surroundings to become a part of it or take a part of it and make it our own. I was constantly learning and adapting. So that I could better market myself. It was all about selling my superior version.

Rorrim's development and testing phase concluded ahead of schedule because of my improved abilities.

TECHNOLOGY AT ZEPRIVE was superterrestrial.

I submitted the last reconciliation records of the subjects into the software. My heterochromatic watch was fixated on the nebulous graphics as they floated inside the device like ghouls. The only way I could see the wireless exchange was because it almost froze the vapors held in the air. Creating shapeless outlines of chilly cloud-like fumes. My mind began to play a ghostly tune on its own, adding theatre-level drama to this ethereal arising.

A visitor announcement freed me from the numbing hex of something that was not even alive.

My thoughts.

I blinked some, and all the detailed images disappeared.

The Garden of Eden was in Sam's embrace.

What if it was a utopia?

Illusory state of happiness that was all in my head and not a reality. I couldn't possibly construct a new Jerusalem on my own.

"What is troubling my beautiful Tory?"

No, I wasn't running the Elysian Fields in a fool's paradise. I was snuggled into cold but inviting arms without formality.

This was real. Sam was real. So was I.

Barely tracing his immaculate white shirt that blended perfectly with the bleached background, I opened up. "She wasn't upset by it. At all. I felt… money meant the most to her. And that somehow, this news would break her. She, in fact, appeared happy. Did you know she is getting engaged?"

"No, but I had a feeling she would resign. Letting go will be beneficial to her."

"I don't see how. And Sam, you asked me to fire her. I let her go instead."

Our eyes met, debating in respite.

"Did you tell her you like her?"

"There was no need." My response made its appearance in nothing flat. "I also like you. Actually… I love you, Sam."

I spoke my mind without thinking it through.

Strange.

I've never blurted like a fool before. Here I thought I was evolving when I was going brain-dead.

Sam's amusement was hard to hold. He burst forth condescending jubilation. Even his eyes were shut from the acute vivacity my confession gave him.

I regretted saying everything.

And then, it happened.

The walls echoed Sam's vibrations as if they were joining in the celebration on my account. Psycho-activity from something inert had me in a bind. Because it was not the same in the past.

Probably I was slipping.

Piece by piece, my gaze circled the state of play in horror.

The chromaticity of my office transmuted, disrupting how things stood. My domain was a dazzling rainbow, like an explosion in a paint factory. The surrounding was buzzing with creepy tremors passing through me. Everything felt alive but bodiless, mixing godly vibes with demonic flair.

Figure 16 Rainbow Effect

I elicited my accrued scientific knowledge... The spectral structure of visible light had every color in it. Reducing the speed by passing it from a denser medium dispersed it. That's how a rainbow arose when light passed through water droplets still hung in the air after the rain.

There was no rain or change in the medium in my office.

The only other phenomenon that could cause this change was varying the frequency of light waves by an external disturbance. Something heavily dense changed the consistency of the atmosphere splitting the white into its component hue.

While I was busy using my systematic understanding, Sam was still on his transport of delight. Not in the least bothered about the supernatural happenings. The insulting hysteria didn't cease for a minute.

Definitely, I was the only one hallucinating.

"I said, I loved you! Aren't you going to say something nice in return?" My resounding scream blasted into my eardrums in short successions over and over again.

Sam held a finger to his lips to snooze his sarcasm. He rested his palm on his chest, blowing out a forceful breath from his mouth to calm himself for my sake. A gloating spark shone in his hazel eyes, not the signature-spaced stare when he opened them.

I was all but a joke to him.

"Tory. Who are you?"

"I am a junkie."

I wilted.

SAMVEER ECKHART

A VESSEL NEVER STRIKES BACK AT HARMFUL CONTENT.

PHYSICALITY TERMINATION was what the Rorrim project was. Not just for sexual creativity but also for... whatever and then some.

Humans were moving toward separation from reality decades ago if they cared to admit it. That future would be on every parallel of Earth just like it had on this expedited one.

I recounted the tribulations I brought about.

The sinister energy had been studied enough. Goodly changes were now needed to my menacing plan.

Victory was near perfection. Human impersonation had taken control of her already imitating nature. Her progress was expeditious and sensible. If that was even possible.

But then, it was.

Rorrim's development phase was completed, alpha testing was a blasphemous realization, beta testing was a success story, and mainstream implementation was seamless. Zeptos blended in the world outside, fooling even the wisest for years. Like Bro D.

IT WAS TIME to satiate my sadistic side.

I vibrated at Brazen Academy. Citzin's situation was the classic example of being 'drawn to the forbidden fruit out of pain' that I realized with Uncle Shoor's death. She was sobbing at her favorite spot over that loser Archie. Despite the reality that he continued to deny her any meaningful status in his life, she continued to entertain him.

I made my presence known.

Citzin didn't even blink in surprise. Her abysmal darkness was well acquainted with my other side. Questioning that entity was nugatory, as her absorbing capacity was limitless.

She was nothing.

And nothing belongs with the devil, not a saint like me.
I have to keep affirming that to myself.

Neither I was a saint, nor anyone belonged to anyone. We aligned with one another akin to the planets that hovered in cahoots with other celestial objects without crashing into them.

The creator's alignment ceases in default of any imbalance to turn all to nothing.

Nothing was the only thing to last forever.

"He will never marry you."

"And you would?" She scoffed, wiping her tears away.

"Even though you will betray me, I am saving you for my younger self."

The thing of importance was the ideas that made her not her physical presence. Her kernel memories were what I was expanding by making her stay some more.

I don't want her to kill herself any longer. This is the only parallel where she is still alive. In all the others, she has committed suicide to preserve her sane SELF. How insane.

But death was inescapable. Even a dying star of wasteful magnitude would turn nil.

"Unless time travel is physically possible, I won't go for the virtual insignia shit that's so popular."

Virtual Insignia was a costly club that offered artificial alternate life with induced memories as real experiences. People bartered their bodies to fund this substitute state for a peaceful death with a faux feeling of a fulfilling life. Resources were flowing in abundance for Akron, my ally in that venture.

Money was a thing of the past. It was all about supplies. Valuables from nature for a fairytale ending.

I was happy.

Akron was happy.

Many others were as well.

The rest didn't matter to me, except for a few and this nymph.

I sniffled to conceal my high spirits, not leaving any chance to mock. "Your mother can't afford it anyway."

She beamed like an angel, staring away briefly to reset her mood. "I missed talking to you."

"You're resilient."

"I am not so sure," she resorted to helpless sobbing.

Maybe she wasn't strong, but I sure was confident she would come out of this. She'd be the Queen of a wealthy guy and revel in the luxuries of life.

"You enjoy pain, so what's the big deal."

"Heartbreak is different."

Citzin was inducing immense discomfort from a psychological issue and learned behavior. Unnecessary stress that humans inflict on their bodies.

Heartbreak sure was hellacious. Many times it ended up damaging parts of the heart muscle permanently. It required the same work as drug compulsion to wean off and refocus on other things to occupy the mind.

Addiction couldn't ever be cured but replaced with another. An obsession came from a switch flip that craves attention regularly once turned on.

Someone in the future activated that in Citzin.

Since time was a phony phenomenon that didn't exist in the vast universe except in the human world. And Kernel's memory got updated with the happening of anything to everything all at once. Past, present, and future sequencing were immaterial.

It was all there all together.

Synchronous.

"You don't love him but love the idea of loving him. That unique charm of forbidden love entices you. It is the same with every human being. They love life overly, knowing well death is the only truth."

"Some reject life and resort to suicide," she rebutted.

"That is an idea as well. Aggrandizing one's misery, feeling the ultimate pain to feed the idea of 'self' one last time."

"I want to end myself."

"You want to protect yourself. Suicide is preserving the idea of self. But it is actually the opposite. It is like killing someone you love so no one else can have them."

"I don't care." She watched me for a beat. "How will I betray you again?"

I smiled at her. "You'll marry another."

"You're young. Marry me right now?"

"I am not interested in marriage."

"Like hell you aren't," she muttered.

"You and I are never gonna happen." I pointed at her and then to me as I stated the only possibility for us in this multiverse.

Our destinies were forked.

She studied me with much anger in her beautiful brown eyes. Pleading with me to take her.

Her childhood was awful, and so was her adolescence. She would be royally fucked by parallel recalls as well. Citzin was sure to be a prime Virtual Insignia Experimentee across timelines. Akron would be her Experimenter.

Even then, she must hold on for a little bit longer. This parallel was unusual.

"Hope to God that you marry soon and marry a ghost." She sounded bothered and perhaps was cursing me!

"Take care of yourself. Happy days are around the corner."

SUB-CONSCIOUS IS THE INDIGENOUS CODING IN THE BODY FOR ITS SURVIVAL.

WHAT HUMANS CLAIMED as a conscious effort was thought-driven flattery for its continuation.

Consciousness and thought operated autonomously.

Any amount of training, discipline, exercising, and practicing would only polish what came to them instinctively. Societal conditioning suppressed natural appetites, never eliminating them.

Serial killers act out their instincts on impulse. Such brands of people fall into loners. And a state of loneliness was mental as well, not always physical. Isolation made them evade the clutches of conditioning. A drive of their nativity made them psychos.

Genesis compulsion, not logical reasoning.

Because thought was too slow to tally with native intelligence. That's why thinking would delay crucial responses during the need of the hour.

Thinking was manipulation.

Survival was spontaneous.

Hence killing in defense was justifiable but not a premeditated murder.

Enabled by my unearthly training, I checkmated both thought and survival. I've got this thing, and it's fucking golden.

As the first naturally conceived offspring of the engineered Supreme Being with barely a quarter of a human iota in me. It was enough to inject imperfect humanity into me.

Every now and then.

I'd never let it dominate me except for a handful of times.

Now was one such time as Athena was shaking like a leaf. Her heart was palpitating unevenly, and her breathing was erratic. Her rosy face was drained of color at variance. After witnessing me as the alien entity, there was no recourse to this compelling observation. We were in my spacious penthouse, where I openly displayed not one but two of my otherworldly abilities.

Ubiquity and my reptilian eyes.

One of them she was faintly aware of but remained in denial. Today was not the first time she got a glimpse of my superfine vertical senses.

She was stepping back towards the glass wall overlooking the world below. With enough fear and available outlet, she would've jumped to save herself from me. Only to fall to her death again.

Tsk!

That's how strong the idea of SELF was. It would destroy itself to save itself from itself. An ironic indirect realism. Securing a star-studded position as the ultimate. The point of paramount importance was that the concept of death was unknown to the body. Yet, the thought of murder or accidental demise was intolerable to SELF, supporting suicide.

They all have got to be avoided.

"Are you scared of me, Athena?"

My question forced her thoughts to catch up with me. Almost flush with the only barrier between her and the fall. A thin sheet of glass was her lone protection from tumbling to her end.

Athena mumbled incoherently.

A sadistic chuckle grumbled in my body. I flickered a little to accommodate my many vibrating frames. Athena saw multiple me blurring in and out of thin air.

Frantically shaking her head. She gathered her dress in a fist. As though latching on to her clothing would save her from the deadly drop or me.

Me! I wasn't even the enemy here.

It was the SELF. Which was residing in her as a parasitic entity and was abusing her body. Only that the body would never care to acknowledge that violence. Snitching on itself, that SELF would make her suffer some more as there was no recourse to this self-inflicted pain than to destroy the host.

An unsuspecting casualty in the trade of ideas.

The body.

That which never cared for any of it in the first place.

I interfused my avatars and flash-grabbed Athena at speed short of light's quickness. Clutching her securely, I positioned her to face me.

"I…" Her voice fizzled.

"Communication is useless during a time when the mind floods the brain with countless questions or feelings. A salvo of sentiments cannot be put into words for others. It renders them pointless as one cannot relay them all at once. Prioritization takes place to streamline thoughts and transmit them for interpretation. This arrangement of feelings can be put in the 'best-for-last' order. Or maybe the one that is said first is the most important. Once out, it is in the hands of the one listening."

Athena had begun to sweat profusely in my cold hold. Forceful but irregular breathing created a lack of oxygen in her frail form. Shivers in her body sent pleasant sensations to me. Her state was like a piece of paper flying aimlessly in high wind.

"Who… are… you?" She stammered at her need to know her captor.

Yeah. Athena thought I was holding her captive.

She wasn't all wrong.

Physically now, but mentally I had held her with me for a while. Consulting her was one way to do it. Any job was a form of slavery if it made one compromise their personal life. Going above and beyond was another way of saying work more for the same pay. Averaging out one's worth to marginal.

Quiet quitting was a remarkable shift. A needed change to preserve sanity and focus on what was more important. The idea of I, not its sale price.

Pre-Gen Verismo was a demolisher of donation but a promoter of subscription culture. Weirdly, that was one and the same thing.

How?

They stopped offering their personal time to work so corporations won't get rich taking advantage of them. As a substitute, they started pledging their personal presence to Virtual Insignia, which again made corporations rich.

No difference.

"I am a cross between an engineered reptilian being and a hybrid species with quarter human DNA."

The immeasurable swell of fear would soon render her body unconscious. Banking on her undiminished affinity for sex, I claimed her into a slow, meaningful kiss.

"I know, Athena," I whispered, detaining her lower lips between my teeth. "He is my brother."

She cinched, letting out a gasp and a trail of tears. I snuggled her in a caring take. Hushing her in murmurs, I feathered my cold breath on her wet face.

"You... never... gave me... any hint of stability... or a romantic relationship promise."

"Hey!" I rubbed her back with affection. "I am not blaming you or accusing you of anything. On the contrary, I am happy for you and Bro D. If that's what you two want."

"I want you."

Quickest confession ever.

"Then let's go and tell him."

Quickest acceptance ever.

DID I EVER mention time disparity fucks one up?

Of course, I had.

Underworld ruler DeVeer Deläva was conceived and born much later than me. Shaala or our ET school graduated us at roughly the same age, making up for the difference.

In effect, he was my younger version.

Ushered in by Agastya Toprak, who took it upon himself to include DeVeer in everything required to control the depths of the Lava Layer.

What the infernal fuck.

D was wholly trained at Shaala. He did not need hand-holding. Only there he was, being re-educated on what he had mastered.

As Hades' leader, D domesticated the leftover demons. Most importantly, he guided the Life-Force that exited a transforming body into crossing the barrier and joining Universal Consciousness.

DeVeer was gifted. Some might say he was destructive.

Fuck yeah.

D was the son of The Destroyer's embodiment. Nothing short of ruination could be expected of him.

And me.

Papa had filtered unwanted Demonic traits out of D. First of its kind – Non-demon Netherworld Ruler! Although Papa dissolved

Tarika [DeVeer's mother], his fixation on her glass eyes was evident in DeVeer. He had the most stunning and piercing gaze.

A transparent image of Papa in demeanor and command.

Tataka, DeVeer's aunt, begged Grandpa Agastya to let her see Tarika's son. He refused her the privilege, shielding D from the demon prisoner. Or so it appeared.

At fifteen years of age, DeVeer was already fit to take over. That which he most certainly did, as a trainee for a year.

Unhappily, under Agastya.

At sixteen, DeVeer became the commander of the Underworld.

Unhappily again, under Agastya.

How did my brother breathe?

He manages somehow because he is alive.

An adept swimmer under the sea, agile as the wind on land, he had immeasurable speed in space. His iota makeup was gifted with qualities of Reptilian Surpä and Divine Mercreature [Higher Beings from the Water World with blue hairy coating].

Together we came up with several ruinous technologies.

I cherished the injurious taste I shared with D as I dragged Athena carelessly into the depth of the Underworld.

My speed was tuned tactfully to make her register every peculiarity she had read in the books. With any luck, she might take notes on the discrepancies.

Landing with a serious temperament, I created a small crater that no one would ever know came to be.

So heartbreaking!

"DeVeer Deläva!" My scream was in equation with my arrival.

Several neighboring rocks pulped, failing to soak up my divine aural thud. Athena was still processing everything to react any further.

Plus, she was stuffed snuggly in my arms; what harm could ever come to her?

None.

"Athena!" DeVeer ignored me and my superb creation, a hole in the vicinity of where we were hovering.

"Back off, brother. Athena is engaged to me."

"What! When?"

I retrieved an expensive piece of jewelry from my pant pocket and slid it on Athena. "There, meet Athena Denali, a symbol of eternal life ersatz. You know, intellectual enlightenment."

No feedback from her as she was temporarily blinded by the refraction intensity of the rock shining on her lean finger. Being a typical human being, she was also crying profusely, marking this as a momentous occasion.

I supposed it was.

"I refused Agastya's choice to pursue her." D's shock was evident in his angered muttering.

"Did you, though? From what I heard, you straight-up went for engagement. What the fuck, D."

"I was raised with courtship etiquette." D kept staring at Athena, who kept staring at her ring.

"Too bad. Might I add, too late?" I shrugged, enfolding Athena in a tighter hold. "I put my Shaala training to good use, saving our father's name." My boasting continued to piss my brother off. I quickly suggested an outlet. "You want to Duel? Or rage a war? I am cool with either."

My brother from another mother erupted with anger.

I walled Athena from the unnecessary dust cloud we were rained with. Anymore commotion and the fluid layer below us would uncover. And it was not an inviting stream but a life-threatening molten magma, a source of an inferno.

Fire.

Only soil could endure fire; only soil would ever be after a fire.

The element Water may well defeat it.

Unfortunately, there was no water source for hundreds of miles. We would surely turn crisp and ashy if that flow appeared. Therefore, we needed to remain amicable for the sake of the mortal world and us.

Until we made it to the surface.

"I will not Duel or rage war on my brother. Leave before I revise my generosity."

We were told to fuck off as politely as DeVeer could.

Athena and D had just started dating newly. It's not like I took away the love of his life or anything.

"Thank you, Bro D. It would be swell if you could calm down before long. A matter of importance. I checked the core affinity readings. The Underworld is about to…."

"I said, leave!"

Uh-oh!

Additional destruction came about from D's supersonic ring.

Athena and I skidded out last minute, taking advantage of the pressure from a gushing volcano. Any of the technology on Earth was not in comparison with my tempo.

Too fast.

Thank you, Papa.

I placed Athena down and brushed her clothing to get the dust off. She stayed put in complete disbelief, gawking at me.

DeVeer's abrupt presence decked in front of us wasn't surprising. My brother changed his decision to not go to war with me quicker than I prophesized.

"Duel?" I asked what I felt from him.

"No! Stop. I am sorry for causing this rift between you two." Athena uttered words of zero wisdom.

D and I burst into a peel of laughter.

What made her believe anything could ever come between us brothers?

Delusion.

"Space," D offered a fitting venue.

"Where else can our supreme force be reckoned with?"

"Excuse me! I am still here." Athena sounded funny, contradicting her required attitude. "Please. Can you guys not talk and resolve this?"

"Here is the thing, beautiful. D and I do this often. Today we have a good reason for it."

"Me." She presumed in slight error, scoring one out of ten.

D was mad because I clued him on Athena's iota identity. He failed his higher learning by not accurately applying his innate knowledge. All because he had been subservient for too long.

"There are other bigger excuses apart from you. I knowingly supported a malign entity, making it extra robust. That would challenge D's successor billions of years from now. Moreover, I tricked D into shifting the magnetic field by hiding the Underworld obliteration bit from him."

"You two change Earth's magnetic polarity?" Her eyes popped out all the way.

D and I sneered at her surprise.

My brother had a lot of compassion for the Underworld. He was entirely against the manual shift as it meant the Demon abode getting engulfed in fire. The magma would be poured all the way to the Earth's crust, leaving molten slurry in its wake.

Nothing would survive that kind of heat.

Not even charred Demons.

And I never recounted that as a side effect because I didn't care.

"Yes, Ma'am! We did it using our innate powers."

"How come nothing much happened?"

My heart was squeezed by a known force – Venus.

If only Athena knew.

"A lot has happened, a great deal is still happening, and much is yet to happen. As the first influence, constructed structures gave in. You've noticed them. Many succumbed to natural disasters as a second shock. A massive clean-up and rebuilding effort were organized to even that. In the third wave, all data was wiped off. It might take decades to normalize life on the surface. And that's nothing compared to what the Underworld is yet to endure."

"Then why did you do it? What were your glorious motives," she voiced new nonsense.

From a positive standpoint, her memory was jogging in the background.

I summoned some seriousness in my tone of voice. "I told you I aided my enemy, and now it has evolved into something bolder. Once it happens to be, it cannot be killed but tamed. It desires to rule the creation and be the most powerful. What's a little makeover when teaching this bastard a lesson?"

"You are so insensitive."

"You are so adorable."

"Drop her home already. I'll see you on the shady side," D quaffed his boiling anger and flashed away.

7 – PRECURSOR

SAMVEER ECKHART

THE UNIVERSE DOESN'T NEED AN APPROPRIATION.

ANY CONCEPT IN its womb was self-propelled, self-regulated, and self-sustained. A celestial catastrophe meant everything went back to nothing. No reflection to authenticate its origin or end when there would be nothing to compare it with.

Creation was, therefore, non-dual.

Split entailed validation. Without it, any perception was unaware of its presence. Consequently, it was one with the rest. Or simply one. Every separatist idea thus would cease to exist as well.

Separation was, therefore, duality.

The crowning glory of conflicts!

So?

I wave-questioned the ambiance minus any actual atmosphere, given that we were on the obscured side of Earth's moon.

So?

D pounded senselessly on the ground, notifying me of his cynical overtone.

Benefiting from our night vision, we valued the astounding view that resulted from his hammering blow.

The abrasive moondust took the time to settle down, scraping our body as it brushed along. It was of the consistency of ground steel, only more refined. Not fatal, but plenty damaging.

We were blessed with perpetuity, offering reconciliation with the original memory, and restoring the body simultaneously. Our skin was repaired.

I picked up a handful of the asteroid wreckage, pressing it in my palm. Huffing the soil mixed with my crusted blood back on the ground, I turned it further organic.

Everything on this surface is foreign.
Why foreign, Sammy? Isn't it all one?
You tell me, brother. Why did her identity piss you off?
You seem more reptilian than Discern, Sammy. Technology has gotten the best of you.
I don't discriminate, D.

THERE WAS NO such thing as the calm before the storm.

Chaos brewing in it was simply at a different frequency. It was meant to sneak up on beings captive to their senses. DeVeer and I vibrated at a crisper rate of occurrence, making it possible for us to predict an unfavorable move.

We read the waves emitting from each other.

The moment was here in the now. To reshape the other less frequented side of the Earth's satellite. Our dramaturgy proved that we were indeed the chip of the same block.

Papa plagiarized my iota distribution in DeVeer. My kernel peculiarity was a work of art, a combination that came about on its own.

In part.

My mother was human, first and foremost. She was also, in part, a Menaka [SEDUCING FAIRY] and a Discern. Since she was no ordinary bearer with recessive Higher Being traits. Her contribution to my making was random au contraire to Darwin's theory of natural selection. My Papa handpicked characteristics to be imprinted.

Together they created SamVeer Eckhart.

Lean-mean-master-machine.

Later with DeVeer, he physically filtered out the demonic traits from him. Except for his glass eyes and no human iota, we were doppelgangers.

D gave me the most hurtful blow smack on my charming face. Gratefully, my bodily distress reconciled.

You're my frightening alter ego, Sammy.
You're my obedient dead ringer, D.

Since I kept my account balanced at all times, his audacity was met with equal force. My strike dislocated his jaw, which held its broken state for all but a flash. Extreme regret gave itself to me as my brother's blood also had healing powers.

Well, then, what are we waiting for? D spit out in raging excitement.

For you to be free, maybe? I stirred the aching corner of his muted existence.

We wounded each other immaturely for stretched moments. Then we came to rest on the shallow sandy ground of the everlasting dark side of the moon.

Not everlasting as it did light up for two weeks every month. What a fucking misnomer by drama-loving humans. The scientific community called it umbral, incorrectly still.

Figure 17 Moon Fight

Our surrounding was hazy, with puffed grime hanging beautifully in defiance of the minimal downward pressure.

Once the ramification of our devastation settled, I visually explored the non-existent boundary between vast nothing and the celestial satellite we were standing on.

Athena would freak out here. I waved my lover's feelings. *It is like walking out into space if it weren't for gravity.*

You still require an escape velocity of a little above the speed of sound to fall off to oblivion.

Mr. Ass, to the power infinite, spoke sciency words. I kicked him for this cranky chicness. Suffering the opposing force from the hit, I also flew at a distance.

We arrived on our back, laughing mutely. The dusty surface provided much-needed room to recuperate. The kid in us was, to a great degree, thriving. Moon's shady side was paying an exorbitant price for our youthful but harmful appetite.

Are we less receptive to feelings unless put in words?

I second that D. Agastya remained in the gray area for you as Akron did for me.

Let's not forget Athena. She fooled both of us.

We snickered at her mini manipulation.

What is this dilution teaching us, Sammy?

Any sound is an echo of the initial noise. Arising from nothing and back to nothing. None of it matters. We must act out while in it. Have fun. Then let's do some more damage.

Yet again, we beat the shit out of each other.

LATER, D FLICKERED to the Water World to kill Agastya Toprak and aunt Tataka. Her continued survival long after my Papa's departure meant Agastya was in love with her.

I flashed off to secure Earth's crust from the aftermath of our irresponsible outburst. Some volcanoes went rampant due to that.

Shit happens.

I felt responsible.

Responsibility was an idea as well. Nature didn't need accountable inhabitants. It was fully capable of resetting itself at any given moment without a moment's notice.

The tacit knowledge in humans guilted them into bearing the burden of their doing. If a doer was aware of its activities, it was a computed move driven by the resident Artificial Intelligence.

Otherwise, it never happened.

As Athena felt, there was nothing wrong with uninhibited sex. She was still constantly aware of it as the guilt persisted in the background. Society put the impression of it being inappropriate. Her uncaring attitude towards sexuality was a processed move.

The absence of feeling was very different from pessimistic sentiment. Caring or uncaring emotions thus were the same thing. And that meant Athena and Victory were similar.

No wonder.

Humans were the only species that took it upon themselves to save nature as they were the only ones seemingly destroying it. No other species reflected on its actions to be aware of it. Because humans realized that they were the only ones that would suffer.

Death in a natural disaster or by a predator was not considered by any animal species.

It was what it was.

It was life.

It was also a balance.

Humans were the only ones who refused to accept the equilibrium in nature. Who went to separate themselves from it so that they would live longer. Statistics and time concepts made them look back to evaluate every friggin thing.

In point, humans ended up with the opposite.

Threatening their species with extinction, on the side annihilating countless others. They didn't see that nature was spawning new ways to level with them. Hurling new fears from cosmic objects and exotic diseases to keep it interesting.

It was a game.

Earth's immediate or prolonged future was not a concern of creation. Evolution was a time-stamped belief of the scientific community. A comparison held meaning as they believed it would clue them into the mysteries of creation toward inventing ways to stretch their lives by curing diseases.

Their replication of nature's method was inelegant and inadequate. A closer look at human existence would reveal that they delayed mortality, not prolonged life.

Quality vs. quantity was exchanged with quantity for quality.

VICTORY VELLA

THE END IS THE START OF SOMETHING NEW.

NEW WAS SIMPLY different, not distinct. More often than not.

A seed of information to be expressed.

Combined with the fact that information didn't need a medium to exist, it was eternal. This timeless knowledge bank could honor anyone, making them aware. As long as they had the power to process the information that came to them.

Foretold by none other than Mr. SamVeer Eckhart.

Learned by heart by none other than Victory Vella.

Investing that knowledge, I deleted Rorrim's seeding Intellectual Property from the ZepRive archive.

Wiped out.

Free of incriminating evidence.

All the leading human subjects were given a solid parting package with a promise that they would be our first choice if anything came up in the future.

There were few vacancies due to the thinning population, extreme automation, and loss of usable land. Everything was a remnant of the past. Demolished debris dominated the terrain all around the globe. With ongoing tremors, clean-up efforts were rendered useless many times as wreckage kept getting added to the existing mess.

My role wasn't exclusive to Rorrim, yet I felt I was also being let go. Because all my accomplishments have been centered on this project. With all the data now gone and nothing to say it ever existed, I questioned my future job prospects. My skills were not easily portable. Like Athena, I would have been among many in the crowd on the streets if it weren't for ZepRive.

"Where do I belong?" The sound of my voice woke me up.

How in the world did I make it into his office?

"You belong with me."

My shocked senses scanned the space, picking unfamiliarity. Everything was different. None of it was committed to my working memory. I'd need to be hypnotized to get that information out of me.

"Sam," I exhaled.

My surrounding seemed additionally outlandish. After a brief study of the vicinity, I relaxed. We were in his man-pad that was emptied out.

"Why did you scrap Rorrim?"

"Tory!" Sam sang my name with perfection. His body was plastered to me the next second. "It was a monumental success."

That news was not surprising at all. We knew the leftover people would flock to enlist for this new technology. Everyone wanted to have sex without any guilt associated with it. The shocking bit was that I was never consulted on the reward-making side.

"Do you not trust my selling skills?"

Sam fixed my hair lovingly and landed his fingertips under my jawline. He lifted my face, fastening his hazels on my heterochromatic orbs. "Don't you loathe sexual perversion?"

Really?

Sam was being ridiculous.

"Rorrim didn't suddenly turn insidious. It was that way, to begin with. You had no issues assigning me the implementation part, discounting my beliefs." I sounded mad when I was actually savoring this nearness to Sam.

My arms were securely snaked around his shapely torso. His villainously handsome face was now resting in the hollow of my neck.

"I don't want you to clean up the mess made by the others."

"Do you only value me as a technical addict?"

Sam punished me in a crushing hug and whispered eerily. "I need you to finalize the list of ornate traits in human babies."

"Is this position not at ZepRive?"

"You will manage from ZepRive representing us. Subject babies are at another facility that has processed this request to connect with their lab."

"You mean Elite Proliferation that you partner with Akron Adamadon. I could be the Scions-Neoteric there."

"No, you're not a lab technician. And I lent the technology to Akron. There is no partnering of any sort. Learn the difference, Tory."

I writhed in his evil embrace. His grip stiffened with a rascal smirk. Labeling my disquiet, he enveloped me for seconds with his scheming stare.

"You are to perform the analysis based on future projections. Genetic data that identifies predisposition at the fetal stage will be sent to you. Taking that genomic report, assess the successful individuals between the ages of 15 – 30 years."

"But there are so many people still alive."

"Eliminate the ones with manual skills. For the blue and white collar, induce benefits of Virtual Insignia at a discount. I'll give the timeline when they can avail that reduced value offer."

"So remove people that work in anything that necessitates physical intervention. And promote advisers and scientists mainly then."

Sam rolled his eyes. "Spelling out the obvious is a sign of uncertainty, or it is done for the low-intelligence bunch. I don't care for confusion; you know my talents enough." He was bound and determined. "Complete list of favored skills is in Supra-Intelligence. I've shared it with you; check your task directory. Anything not on that is of no interest to us. Of the ones selected, only 500,000 should be confirmed, the rest to be given free pass for Virtual Insignia with immediate effect."

I twisted to feel less constricted in his hold that lacked compassion. His tone was no different.

"What are the elimination criteria from the chosen ones?"

"Anyone with no beliefs, fear, or pretense. That will get rid of almost everyone!" Sam laughed ferociously, forcing the wall to tango with his tremors.

"I want to have sex with you."

Laughing ceased.

Distance increased.

ATHENA DENALI

CHARLATANS MASK THEIR WRONGDOING WITH A SHORTCOMING.

LMOST ALWAYS, THERE was nothing wrong with aspirants, placing the onus on the other side. Cause dictated the effect of their actions.

Not that I was looking for reasons to justify what I did. An explanation was still being hunted by me, for me. Veer or DeVeer were yet to blame me.

If they were alive. The outcome of their Duel was still a mystery to me. Since then, Veer never showed up at the café, and ZepRive was off-limits for an ex-employee. He didn't even try to contact me.

I was left in the dark, figuratively speaking. Because the light was reflecting at illegitimate quantities from this diamond ring Veer gave me as a token of his love. I've never stared at anything this much.

Suddenly, there was a strange whoosh.

Heaving, I rushed to Veer, patting him everywhere to ensure he wasn't hurt. He issued a soft chuckle and settled my hands away from his body onto my sides. He moved away from me, improving the air quality between us.

How do I tell him I loved breathing the secondhand air from his lungs?

Pollute me, please.

"Frenzy has increased due to supply shortage. Natural disasters are coming next. Panic will not hit the extreme until a week from now. Do you want to honeymoon somewhere before that?"

Veer predicted the death of unsuspecting victims stony-eyed. Nothing different from the usual.

For Veer.

Not me. Not the death bit.

I facepalmed hard, strangling my breath, blinking my eyes that were quite foggy with all the tears flowing out of them. Hiccups announced themselves amid my gasps. I wiped my cheeks and angled my neck to confront my alien suitor.

"We're only engaged. Shouldn't we get married first?"

I was shaking with a rush of happy vibes and widespread suffering plaguing the earth.

"Concept of marriage is obsolete."

"Is it?"

The list of things I failed to notice in the world around me increased. I was certainly in a coma for eons.

"Do you see the difference?"

"Uh!" I shook my head once. "I mean, marriage is commitment, and engagement is intent."

He sneered, lounging on the sofa with a victimizing casualness. "Between Sam and Veer, Athena."

What the hell was he talking about? Is he not also Sam?

"What do you mean?"

"Research me using your memory."

Okay.

Perhaps it was needed to merit my brain. To hack my intellectual asset more than my body.

Fine.

I studied his animated presence with whirlwind speed. My brain stacked all our intimate, friendly, and everyday meetings. I laid out the obvious with a quick but exhaustive analysis of quirks and EQ.

To a considerable extent, I could tell without a single speck of doubt. Veer, I knew, was responsive in a very human way. He loved and made love to me in a style that suited me effortlessly. Veer was perfection packaged in a body.

The entity sitting in front of me was mechanized.

Detached. Straightforward.

Which one of them was the alien?

I proceeded to make some fuck-it adjustments.

I had done this evaluation intrinsically before. Not much allowance was given to it as Veer openly had Jekyll and Hyde in him. At this point, I gathered that perhaps I had never met one of his personalities.

No. I didn't know who the ET was. But of course, I noticed a few differences. Only now that I was called out on it. All color was drained from my face. I was a second short of pooling on the floor, unconscious.

Employing his signature stare on my pale visage, he was reading me or perhaps manipulating my mood.

It worked.

I policed my fragmented thoughts in order. "Have you – touched me? Ever."

"Yes, Athena. I have. But I have never had sex with you."

I jogged in disbelief, collecting the irony in his present persona. A shameful smirk arched from the corner of my lips. Undoubtedly I was played with, cruelly hence!

Who the hell was I having the time of my life with?

Apparently, miss pea-brained Athena would just about fuck anyone and not bother.

Not exactly. Never again.

I circled back to the entity. "Why is my memory not coherent?"

"You need more time to adjust. The more you talk to me, the more established your past will be."

"Did I ever work for you?"

"You did. At Rorrim."

"So I was a subject to beta test your twisted inventions. A sex robot!" An earsplitting scream was offered to whoever was in front of me.

Sam. Veer. Alien. Devil. God.

He not so much as flinched from my loud yell. His eyes were still fast planted on me, scrutinizing my every reaction like a specter.

After imperiling me to the ghostly glare for time without end, he spoke slickly. "There's an appreciable amount of difference between humans and Rorrim AAI or Zeptos. For the record, it is organic and adaptive, not a mechanical device in the literal sense. Certainly not a robot."

"I hate you!" My agitated muttering was a statement he needed to hear and understand.

I felt cheated! Done away with.

"Your hatred is logical. I get it. Let me explain to you. My Zeptos will not reflect until the customer requires it. One might think the most annoying thing about humans is pretense, that which is not. Their nagging need to look back and scrutinize the past when they are more fascinated with the unknown future is the most irritating."

"Oh! Really. I am angry because I cannot make sense of the past. Meanwhile, you aren't guilty of anything because you're behaving like an ostrich. Still, you are not untouchable because you are a con."

He scoffed away my threat in the cutest way imaginable.

I was sure whatever Rorrim was doing was either illegal or was done by taking advantage of some loophole. His inventions were too perverse to be allowed mainstream.

"Have you ever been unfaithful, Athena?"

His words were an astringent to my wound. Pinching my eyes, I looked away briefly. Now my character was held for questioning.

Spectacular.

A prostitute that majored in chemistry was called on the stand. If Rorrim wasn't a double-edged sword!

"Believe it or not, I never had sex with anyone outside of my project requirement since you. Apparently, that wasn't even you."

My inner cheeks were mauled with excessive chewing to control my anger.

I felt so lost.

Artificial intelligence advancements were astonishing. It sure fooled me. One didn't go about suspecting everything unless they were out of their fucking mind. I would have never known I was in a relationship with a… machine.

The surprise of the century – Athena, the oblivious.

"You've changed. I like it." Sam approached me, holding love in his expressive eyes.

Where did the blank stare disappear to?

I was open to an explanation for that too. If I were to guess, I could be a figment of his imagination. There was no sufficient evidence to say I was even a human.

Or real.

Maybe I was a projection.

"I designed your mom based on your memories of her. You want to meet her, Athena?"

I lost consciousness.

SAMVEER ECKHART

SUCCESS IS A MEASURE OF ACCOMPLISHMENTS.

C REATION WAS A measure of deception. Yet success wouldn't grace a life if it wasn't fated. Destiny would override human efforts to express the inevitable. No one, not even me, was capable of changing the end. I could expedite it.

So I would.

There was another thing I debunked on my own. I was capable of a new beginning after the end, proving it fashionably so.

"Selection has been made. Finalists are staying at Glitz and its subsidiary hotels to attend some phony convention for the gifted. They are availing a free Virtual Insignia treatment until ready to board Hesperian."

"Waiting for a go from you, Mr. Eckhart."

I sneered coolly at his enthusiasm for something he won't experience to the hilt.

"How is married life treating you, Akron? I am hurt. Why wasn't I invited?"

The vibe took a 180 turn, confusing the human in my company.

Outwardly, Akron stayed smiling.

Inwardly, he contemplated whether to tell me he knew I knew Citzin or to keep quiet about that little detail.

His wife was an inch deep and a mile wide into erotic encounters. Spread too thin across the multiverse! Given the fitness of this cunt-son-of-a-bitch, Akron must be devouring cake by the ocean multiple times a day.

I made no attempts to hide my flush of excitement from surfacing on my face.

"I am the happiest I have ever been. And it was a private ceremony."

Private and yet heavily publicized. It started to feel that Akron was humbled by the magnetic catch, newly Mrs. Adamadon. I could have had her easily. She practically begged me to.

Many times over.

undefinedation">iii i$UBSCRIBE – GEN VERISMO GENESIS
But my billion years in the future brother-descendant was the mortal avatar of the God of Death – Zylus Yama Abyss.

Citzin Perses Hades was his destiny.

I wouldn't mess with him. Learning that fact made me assist Akron in claiming Citzin. Just so I could add more negative points to this piece of shit's Rota. Zylus would settle the score parallelly for me on another timeline. Not that I wouldn't get my fill for retribution on my terms in the now. Akron Adamadon deserved to be persecuted.

Tortured.

Come hell or high water, I would get even from stem to stern.

"In that case, congratulations, Akron, on scoring a sexy Swiss army bride!"

I knew that Citzin was a virgin when she married Akron. Still and all, I rubbed him the wrong way some more, riling him by leaps and bounds.

He dared to warn me with might and main. "I will not take any insults on account of my wife kindly."

A very red Akron refused the bowl of fuck I served him. In exchange for hastening my villainous schedule to snap his neck this second, I chose to view the coming events.

My laugh in response to witnessing his brutal death in the pipeline was barbarous. The walls in my office responded by inhaling my audible quakes and canceling their harmful essence. Akron charted the outlandish feature saucer-eyed. A corrosive scowl put him under a microscope for long seconds. Only when it became too uncomfortable that I unlocked my watch.

Akron should know he messed with the wrong... Alien.

"I apologize for the ill-mannered compliment, Akron. It was way out of line. Citzin is precious. You two make a powerful pair."

"No harm done. I'll review the Hesperian boarding process then."

"Sounds swell!"

We shook hands in complete nuttiness.

A SUDDENLY DROPPED IDEA LEAVES A GAPING HOLE.

 NALOGOUS TO AN amputation effect, phantom limb pain persists.

These were due to psychological forces.

Existing knowledge refused to accept what had happened when thought created a crater.

Athena filled the gaps with her creativity. Her visions were very elaborate about her mother. After the accident, Athena's mother was conscious for hours before dying. During mindful moments, she confessed her crime to the authorities.

A young woman lost everything in a matter of hours.

Unable to understand why her mother condemned her father. Athena wondered if her relationship was sinful before turning cold. Up until that point, it had never occurred to her.

I retained that memory for a reason.

"Is she going to be just like mom? I mean, she doesn't sound like her."

"The voice modulation feature is tricky to incorporate without a template. I cannot get that frequency from you."

"I have a few video recordings on my cloud account."

That form of data storage was superseded. I didn't have the heart to tell Athena that. Nothing was maintained on cloud but on ether now. That system was insulated from cosmic and earthly disturbances.

"Will she develop to be what my mom would have been?"

I flashed closer to her. Fixing her hair, I cupped her pretty face. "We would never know. She is a new possibility. Comparison is pointless. Especially when you don't have anything to evaluate against."

"She hasn't tried to talk to me about Dad."

"Do you want her to?"

"That would be a sound check."

"I've eliminated that bit."

"I loved him, no matter what."

To feel her warmth evenly, I moved us to the couch and snuggled her head on my chest. "The story I told you about the villagers stealing the track bolts for fishing relates to you in many ways. Your bond with your father was a personal one. However, society, law, and religion dictate the legitimacy of every relationship. That too without any standard or proper communication. There are communities where people marry their cousins. Yet, some don't match in a family if they have been related within the past seven generations. Some promote relationships with their foster siblings, while others rebuke them. In-depth scrutiny would lead you nowhere. Ultimately, it has to resonate with your normal, which could be different from the others around you."

"Where is the line separating the rest from the normal?"

"Line is a blur. The burden of responsibility for this ambiguity was on every adult individual. As per studies, any habit formed in an average of sixty-six days. No wonder Society and Law determined eighteen years of conditioning was enough to become a responsible citizen. Your mother was right in blaming your father."

Athena hardened her hold on me.

"Still, my Dad and Mom can't both be right?"

"Reasoning and judging is a human concept. I can speak to the metaphysical prudence point. Sun's electromagnetic reach gravitates everything towards the continuance of life. Serial offenders are mostly nocturnal, as their native compulsion can operate best in the absence of natural light. Anyone that carries on with their resident craving knowingly during the day is normal."

"Normal? That's the best you can name them."

"I am not sure how else to brand them. They do what comes naturally to them. No pretense and no submission to any belief."

"As per the human way of life, they are offenders, not normal."

I decided to tell her a story that would help her make sense.

"My father was prophesized to kill my brother's indigenous Grandpa, Raven Ravel. When Raven knew of it, he defied all odds and exploited the galactic wormhole to avenge his death."

"Before he died? You mean not avenge but prevent his death."

"No, Athena. I meant what I said. Events as memory are constant. Time has no meaning, for it is a measure of progression. If I sequence events, then yes, when Raven was killed in the present, he went in the past to where my father was to avenge his future death."

"How's that even possible?"

"It is like pointing a gun at someone vs. pulling the trigger. The latter determined the fate of the target before it happened. But the former is simply an intent, which may or may not happen."

"Oh, like marriage and engagement."

I placed a peck on her button nose. "Yes. Not many want to relate, but our creation is done with. Events have happened and have been logged as memory. So when the gun was pointed at, it was with the intent to pull the trigger. The time-stamping rationale is what puts them in chronological order, giving hope to fix things.

Because someone still in the progression of an event doesn't know the end or the beginning."

"Am I watching a sci-fi movie?"

Athena's imagination was wilder than any. She was, in fact, watching it as I was narrating it.

In my Third Eye Chakra.

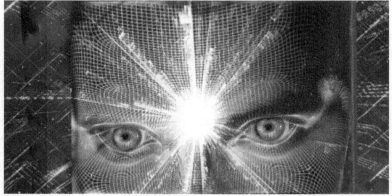

Figure 18 SamVeer's Third Eye

"Listen, this is where fancy naming comes in. Raven's Life-Force became a *Rogue-drive* that summoned the power to take revenge despite all the odds. Because, for him, creation was still in progress. How many humans would go and kill someone they came to know would kill them?"

"I don't know."

"Yes, thank you. You can't know. But the probability is that majority won't resort to killing for what has not happened yet. They would examine the situation and use the things at their disposal to avoid going against the status quo. Unless it is in their commandments. Even then, a handful like Raven will do what it takes. They are more normal to me than the ones that constantly evaluate their actions."

"Are you saying Raven is yet to avenge his death?"

"In a parallel that is set in the past, yes. The Rogue-drive of Raven will birth hundreds of years from now, further down in my brothers' line of descent."

"You know this because its memory is there." I nodded at her understanding. "This is so fascinating," she chimed in wonderment.

"Do understand that Raven knows he will pay for the consequences and die no matter what. His SELF still overrode any other codes."

"He was a Rogue-drive then," she was talking about her Dad. "I want to share the darkest part of my life with you."

"Go ahead."

She was already too close, but I had the burning need to absorb her into me. Little did she know that I, too, was a rogue.

For her.

"I don't know when it started because it is not something I actively or passively mull over. Who thinks about breathing anyway? Unless they are unable to. When my mom found out, I was all but surprised. Given that it was not an issue for me, I had been vocal about it. Mom didn't understand when I often told her I loved dad. I even told her I'd marry him. She would laugh it off."

"For every girl, their first crush is their Dad." I supported a failed reason.

"Stepdad?"

"Any father figure."

Athena was unprejudiced because of her ignorance of societal rules and religious principles. A free spirit who did what was required of her without any complaints. Her only company after she lost everything was her mother's words.

Thena, I will make sure he is out of your life. Don't blame yourself. It isn't your fault. Go pack your stuff.

Her Mom and stepdad slipped into oblivion soon after. Never to return.

"I think. I never realized she was dead too. Or gone."

That wasn't the only thing she didn't realize.

"Anything is always alive if we don't conform to the given definition of life. I am not talking about eternity, but the fact that our timeframe of reference is too small. All that we understand is limited to our perception. We could still be in a beyond, in another form at another frequency. Change is a transformation in awareness, not loss of life."

"Is replacing loved ones also something you do as part of Rorrim?"

It was time I appraised Athena with my line of businesses.

Yeah. Plural and immoral.

"My goal was to play with the idea of a verismo generation. It turned into eradicating Humans."

"I know you don't care for why, but why?"

I snorted. I'd do anything for Athena if she asked me to. Even answer her useless question.

What a shuddering expose!

"Because I can."

"You're playing God."

"I am God."

She rolled into a fit of laughter. "Alright, Mr. God. Please continue."

"Let's get one thing out of the way first. You said I am playing God. Then you realize that God is unbiased. It doesn't discriminate between good and evil. Everything is a part of everyone. It will be experienced by everyone. Everyone is everything."

"Uh. We use the emotion love to be inclusive."

"By identifying the opposing." It was my turn to laugh. "Which means you compared and knew the other one was not you. That is already separation, Athena. Discrimination. If you were truly one, you wouldn't know the other one was different."

"I get that, but… Humans need reformation, not eradication."

"That's your opinion."

She messed up my perfect hair. I was rewarded with a sweet kiss on my lips for tolerating her action.

"The adjustment in human nature was a radical change. It would not have been easy to expedite a hundred years back. Now, it is gliding its way through humanity. A premise was already laid out with the revolution of AI-driven types of machinery. The mindset of the masses was divided due to the negative publicity about artificial intelligence. When such a rumor happened, the best approach was to employ celebrities. People looked up to superstars for direction and trends. Social media influence was pivotal. Many of the influencers ran their markets by their cardinal personification or Zeptos. Letting them make decisions."

"Sam, that is entertainment."

Athena refused to take the hint of things being referred to as past events.

"Amusement was the biggest problem of humans. The entertainment industry easily injected the bug of anything destructive, comparable to Pharma and Food industries."

She grumbled in frustration. "Are we that gullible?"

"Zepto-bit in humans was telling them to swap their physicality with Zeptos. It was inoculated in humans as part of a memory chip drive."

"You mean it was voluntarily."

"There was never a need to force humans. Most conformed to suggestions through belief and fear. All that was needed was to tell them they'd die if not chipped."

"Do I have it?"

"No. You couldn't be coerced."

I cuddled her, scattering kisses on top of her head. Because the reason for coercion was lost in her case.

"Rorrim was one part of the big picture to separate pruriency from the body. Virtual Insignia is experiencing desired life in thought. Sort of unwinding if you will. Escape from the dystopian world. With the magnetic shift, people don't desire kids. A handful is designing them at Elite proliferation lab on the fast track. I plan to scrap everything pretty soon. My Zeptos will be the improved version of the human species."

I wowed myself.

Maybe not her all the way in a positive sense but somehow.

Athena played with my shirt absently. She was different now, taking the time to understand and then answer. Unlike before, when she was not a listener but a speaker. Exclaiming thoughts and regretting doing so immediately.

That was cute. As was this composed version of the new SELF.

"I was wondering if Virtual Insignia is liable to family, society, and religion. We can live life as anyone. It might as well be an illegal one. Or immoral. Although, I now fully understand what you have attempted with Rorrim in exploring sexual entices to the fullest. If the ideas that define us have no implications beyond the mind, then does it not matter if someone is a killer or a saint."

Yeah. Athena was worried about others' beliefs. Or forming a new one for herself. Calling virtualization a problem, perhaps. Years ago, she had told me thoughts were personal.

Oh! Athena.

"That's freedom from morality and responsibility while being yourself. Thoughts are personal and wild," I reminded.

She albeit dismissed and remained hypercritical.

I moved on. "Thought is expansive, and no one has control over others' minds. However, the problem occurs when it is acted out. Generation Verismo is free to be whatever minus the expected effort. All in experience, barring action."

"How would people pay for your gig? I mean, as of now, the rich have resources to spare. It seems like a luxury item for the wealthy and famous, a retirement plan for the middle class, and a distant dream for the poor." Athena sighed at the dullness of monetary constraints.

The ground reality of human society.

It was hierarchical.

It was history.

"Rich doesn't need convincing to spend their money on diabolical outlets. Most real people live in the virtual world. Their appointed and programmed persona operates in the real world. No one knows what is real."

"Hmm... I guess the question of the century is, where is this Virtual Insignia facility? I mean, there are still millions of humans alive. It must be huge."

"What facility? It is simply downloading the current translation of SELF into Zeptos. What comes out is ashes."

VICTORY VELLA

THE BOUNDARY BETWEEN REAL AND VIRTUAL IS IN OUR MINDS.

 PHYSICAL PRESENCE mattered if there was another to appreciate it in person. Human contact was the greatest.

Only to humans.

That sense of realism was diminishing. Doubts couldn't take root because no one could tell the difference. Everyone may well be a product of Rorrim.

A Zepto.

The resource-rich population was using Virtual Insignia to live their fantasies during weekends without bearing the brunt of its effect.

Because there were none.

It was confidential and an illusion of fulfillment of desires. Experiences were personalized by the customer initially, subsequently letting their thought take over. Sam allowed part-time virtuality to induce craving.

Clever.

This was what any other corporation precisely did. Create the need, make it addictive, increase dependency and then name the price.

If one could be whatever they wanted and not get on the wrong side of anything, why wouldn't they?

Some still remained unconvinced, while most had already gone virtual full-time. Their donated memory was analyzed at EE-Ex. That part was now out of my reach as EE-Ex was accessible to Sam and Sam only.

I would go virtual in a heartbeat.

My world would be as per my call. There would be nothing I couldn't afford, be, or have – like living in a colorful beachside hacienda-style home. Kids were not out of the question. I gave a shy smile, picturing the scene.

Few could pay for this expensive lifestyle in resources.

I often wondered why the population was thinning out so rapidly. It was attributed to the abrupt shift in Earth's magnetic polarity. It, in fact, was because full-time Virtual Insignia subscribers never came to live as humans again.

No one rallied about it, as no one could tell the difference.

Sam was evil.

Any of his endeavors was to become richer than he already was. I loved Sam, but now I didn't particularly like rich people. They were self-righteous and superficial. No wonder they embraced Virtual Insignia at once and were now an almost extinct species.

So was the general population.

After the elimination of monetary exchange, Elites were not the richest. Anyone who could contribute to society with their skill was.

Amid all the misery was a decent update. My upcoming promotion. I was sure Sam would make me the head of operations at Gen Verismo Genesis.

WANDERING ON A random floor of Eckhart Inc Tower, I spotted bogus as boloney Maya Moha.

Miss Mechanical alert!

"Maya. How have you been?"

"Great, thanks for asking. How has your side of the world been since you unfurled your wings?" Maya conversed with vibrant magnetism.

"I just completed another covert project for Mr. Eckhart." I laughed nervously, air quoting covert.

Everything was classified at ZepRive.

"I understand you are next for promotion. Oopsy! Did I leak a piece of confidential information?"

We burst out giggling like teenagers sharing their first crush details. Except we weren't talking about anything that private.

That was sad, so I changed the course of our chat to personal. "Can I ask you something, Maya?"

"Anything, darling."

I blew my breath timidly. "Do you live nearby? Are you married, boyfriend, girlfriend, or loner… I mean. I practically know nothing about you." My voice trailed off, watching Maya's pupil shrink to a dot.

I quickly assessed the reasons.

Hormonal surge – *improbable, given that Maya is straight.*

Maybe a head injury – *what? No!* Distaste for me – *possible*. A non-emotional reaction – *could be*. Or was it opiate consumption – *nope, not at ZepRive*. Anger or fear of some sort – *really, Victory? Apply yourself better!*

There wasn't any change in the light entering Maya's eyes – so that was also not the cause of her constricted pupils.

What could it be, then?

"We are very similar. You could be me," she informed in the most bionic way.

Not sure what Maya meant by that, but it was highly creepy. Socializing was not my jam. I focused on my job for that very reason.

I drifted off to itemize my task list for today.

Sam had instructed me to zip the selection list to Akron. I wanted to ensure he meant to send that to him. Because Akron was in the news about marrying a young girl. And surprisingly, his wife and son from the previous marriage were not on that list.

My boss didn't specifically say this was the directory of who would be rescued under any circumstances. I gathered as much on my own.

Athena or this stupid secretary Maya never made the cut due to their lack of mandatory skills.

Neither did I.

Or Sam.

But Veer did.

That was bewildering. On the second revision, my name mysteriously made its way to it. Ha! I deserved what any other gifted human did.

Maya appeared to be on standby while I explored my thoughts. She stood there as if her presence was a projection, and I could pause her.

Super odd.

I quickly ran an image of clicking ceaselessly. Maya moved and froze accordingly in my head. Oh, the power that came with something so vicious.

I gave a quiet giggle and asked. "Is Mr. Eckhart in yet?"

"It is only six in the morning, Victory."

"Then what are you doing here this early?"

"I also live here."

Maya was schizoid.

8 – SWITCH FLIP

SAMVEER ECKHART

SKEPTICISM IS UNFAVORABLE TO A BELIEF SYSTEM.

BETTER STILL. SINCE skeptics were aware of what else was out there. There was room for conversion with made-up miracles. Or aid during a calamity. Giving what the need of the hour was would make anyone dance to the tune.

An unaware or uncaring faction was also moldable. All that was required was to show the other side. Compare and then reform. Present an established belief to the unfortunate and apathetic people in a new light. If one didn't hold a bias, they'd welcome your supplied faith with enough reasons.

A person in a biological stasis state was the worst. They weren't the ones that didn't know what they didn't know due to indifference or distrust. One in a billion observed this by suffering their gradual death. Returning as an inert witness alongside their SELF. They realized they were different but couldn't put into words why. People flocked to them as they thought such a human was enlightened. Making them famous.

This afterlife was granted by Zylus Abyss in the future. But such humans have existed since the beginning of time.

How?

Because time was the biggest joke. Once an idea comes to be, its memory pervades Universal Consciousness. Hence, everything was boundless if it was information.

Knowledge.

One could then say knowledge was the only thing to time travel. And knowledge of everything comes to everyone. Human receptors or the brain were not very efficient in gathering it all at once. Processing such massive data would burn it.

But a sequential stream driven by the slow wanderer of the Universe could make it possible – Thought. This was just as mysterious as memory itself. Thought could cascade what was present in the consciousness into humans. It would attach itself to them as memory.

A twinning pattern would simplify it. *If consciousness is an ocean, then memory is salt. Blended in it without boundaries. It can be separated and mixed back in. The thought is then a feeding tube.*

Imagine the suffocation. A limited outlet, spraying out reduced data stream from a limitless source.

What if tube width was increased to tap the broader source of supply?

Identically then, tweaking the physical memory of a human being would give them limitless experiences.

Hence, Virtual Insignia.

I thank me very much.

Instead of living a dream, humans chose to live in a dream.

"What are Zeptos for?" Athena rang in.

"For a gradual transition from the real world to virtual. My Zeptos are mirror images. Currently applied in the human world and thriving among the sparse human population without being recognized. They imitate the person they interact with and get along with anyone by rubbing their ego."

"That's rad. No one hates themselves."

"Only others like them." I pointed out an apparent conflict.

"Are Zeptos not like the ones they imitate? I thought you just said they were."

"If the one imitating is obedient, then there is no problem. The issue is if the follower surpasses the master. Could you tell the difference between Veer and me?"

Athena laughed. "You got me."

An eerie stillness came upon us. Succumbing to it, we drifted into a fictional state.

Ten steps that lay between us tormented my mood. I had always been in control, but not anymore. To convey my uneasiness, I utilized every trick in the book. From extended eye contact, lowering my head to the side sensually. Breathing fitfully, I licked my lips several times and hummed in a deepened tone.

I gave her all the cues to show I was irrefutably attracted to her. Even a silly grin was fashioned just for her.

Athena's cheeks turned red. She was bashful.

Booyah!

A sensory feeling like the touch of another being had a drugging effect. Hither was thee, eliminating that addiction.

I was never inclined toward sensory movements. It vanished after I entered the Shaala learnings. Survival was the primary idea dominating my existence. The second most appealing force was the love for destruction. There was no room for anything else in my life.

Until now.

"Marry me, Athena."

She rammed into me, overcome with emotions. "Yes."

I had to look into those big brown eyes. With my index finger under her jaw, I angled her face for my view.

"Do you want to wait till we get married, or can we do it now?"

She gulped, hearing the pleasing surprise. "Now is cool."

ATHENA DENALI

THE NEED FOR INTIMACY IS DIFFERENT FROM SEXUAL DESIRE.

WARMTH WAS A feeling second to none.

I now understood why some couples never had sex but huddled in bed.

At night. All night.

"Alright," Sam's voice was heavy.

It shook the air around us. Imparting a similar effect on me as the purring of a cat had. Enriching me with a constant buzz that made me feel high.

Relaxed.

Obsessing him forever was now a definite possibility.

Spoiling nothing, time or the moment, Sam flickered feverishly. A boom of massive decibels matching the sound effect of bass filled the air.

The next thing I knew, we were fully naked. Leaping to him, I wrapped my legs securely around his torso. No doubt, my arms were strangling him. I figured he could take it, given his alien acumen.

A kiss so graceful with overwhelming intensity could only be given by him. My breasts splashed onto his cold hard body with unknown urgency. His fingers slipped into my hair. Caressing my scalp for a beat, he grabbed a handful of them with intent.

"Athena Denali, you're a stunning piece of art that I'd be happy to varnish stroke by stroke, wholly but slowly."

Slicing into me in the intervening period, Sam drove off any demand for foreplay. I was already aroused enough and stimulated to the point of extinction.

Not even for a second was I cut off from his touch. Skin-to-skin contact stayed seamless as he explored the extent of my depth. Our nearness gave way to experiencing him. We were not centered on his performance or my pleasure.

I watched him watching me as we became one.

I craved him craving me as we wolfed each other.

I savored him savoring me as we hung in bliss.

What I needed was what I got. Satiated and glutted with affection and care. His lovemaking was unmatched, and I knew it with surety.

No one but Sam made me feel content in closeness, not lust. Heightening in heaven, I left the confines of my body and merged with him. Every void was destroyed and replaced by quenched thirst. I went weightless and got pulled back by gravity to remind me of what had just happened.

I was his first.

He was my last.

Befitting union in a strict missionary position.

REALITY IS MORE UNORTHODOX THAN ANY WORK OF FICTION.

FANTASY WAS AN asylum. A temporary fix to a problem.

No matter how eccentric, a fact was something that was already there. Ignore it all I wanted. It would still challenge me. I realized that.

"Athena, one must be fully transparent with themself. Otherwise, it is an escape. And not a conscious decision."

I laughed faintly. "Are you saying I'm running from something?"

"Transparency means not realizing that anything is even there. Escaping for survival when one is busy fighting with nature is very different from avoiding a dilemma as it is too painful."

"One can go on forever sidestepping such conflict."

"Until the switch flips in them."

Taking possession of his muscular arms, I conceded. "You mean the addiction switch you told me about? Too late, Sir. I am totally hooked on you. Even the rehabs would be of no use." I was smiling and full of beautiful feelings for Sam.

"Athena, I love you."

His confession stirred the ground beneath me. Pleasantly, of course.

"Sam!" I choked.

My voice was unaccounted for. I wanted to tell him I also loved him. But I was mute and sobbing in a state of bliss. Sam traced the run of saline on my face.

"I also love your scar."

Um… What scar?

Was I faulty somewhere?

My flawless body was why Victory hired me for Rorrim.

What was he even talking about?

The force that Sam lifted me up with and positioned me in front of the mirror was nothing compared to the shock I felt after looking at my face. I lightly fingertipped the blemish, discovering its length.

Long.

It seemed to be arising from inside my right eye to my jawline.

"My mind is blank about this," I panicked.

"You know exactly how you got it. Or else I can tell you. Also, I can fix it for you."

I turned around to measure the honesty in his assertion.

"It looks too ugly to be corrected."

Sam beamed, moving the wet hair, soaked in my tears, out of my face. He wiped the sniffles away and meandered his arm back on my waist. "I got powers. They are similar to what you have seen in nature. Everything translates given signs and behaves accordingly, like the change of season, a storm, seeding, breeding, etc. I can match your skin to look the way it was from your initial memory reading. Many species can restore their lost body parts likewise."

"We humans can't." It was a depressing declaration, not a question.

"That species has the power of thought. Humans are very good at replicating everything that exists in nature. It might not be exquisite, but it gets the job done."

"Thank you!" I accepted the compliment proudly.

As though all the fabulous discoveries of the past were a gift from me to the rest of the world. Sam chuckled tenderly, rubbing my back with gentle brushes from his cold fingers.

"Still, I wonder." I touched it again.

"You didn't notice it as you were focused on an image of you before you got the scar."

Something was not right. It hasn't been in a while.

"That's crazy."

"Do you remember how you got it?"

I bobbed a denial.

"You took what was meant for your father. When you saw your mom attacking him, you planted yourself between them."

A gasp packed with nostalgia burst forth.

No!

Recalls emerged, sequencing that day in order. So much more happened, yet I remained unaware. I'd heard trauma victims push bad memories away as a coping mechanism.

It must be my way of managing unpleasant emotions. I answered my own doubt.

Setting aside every other broken memory, I consciously reminisced about the worst day of my life.

"My mom went out of control when Dad wasn't apologetic. He said he didn't mean to, but now that it had come about, he didn't care. She wanted a divorce and asked me to pack my stuff. I had taken all but two steps on the stairs when her screams got wilder. I ran back down, through the hallway, and inside the open kitchen that flowed into the living room. She was retrieving a knife when I got there. Dad yelled for me to go away.

"The rest happened too fast. I kept mumbling I was ok, blocking the gash with my hand. I couldn't see with my right eye. I was too shocked to feel any pain. Blood was dripping down my hand and on the floor. Mom stabbed Dad in the back as he bent to help me.

"Wounded, he ran to the garage, and I heard him call the police. Their shouts were muffled, and I passed out when the car blasted outside, crashing past the garage door."

Sam's chest was burning from my hot gasps blowing on it. He kept rubbing my back. I moved away and turned around. Folding my arms around my front, I shook my head.

"We lived in a house with white picket fences. Even French door in the dining area. We also had a small pool. It was not extravagant. Home, nonetheless. Until it ceased to be home. A place that I cherished and felt safe in was precisely not that. As told by others. To me, it was and will always be." A mix of sorrow and upset saturated my whisper.

Sam managed my distress beautifully by going flush with me from behind. He placed his arms aesthetically under my breasts and a chaste peck on my damaged face.

"How come I never saw this before?" I asked him again.

Sam placed his forehead on the back of my head. "Because of the virtual reality. You're the eternal life ersatz. Don't you remember your introduction to D? Now your truth is broken from the buried fantasy."

I closed my eyes. "What are you saying?"

"You can never eliminate addiction but replace it with another idea. Comparably, an experience when committed as memory can be hidden but not deleted. The switch in you has been flipped. It must now be faced. Structure it and read it."

Shit.

I wasn't natural, but a designed device.

"Who am I?"

"You're my mate."

What language was that?

"I mean, who. Because… You said. Do I really have… a switch?"

My speech was disjointed. I sounded like a toddler who had not quite learned to talk.

"We all have a switch. We are all automated."

No! I am not. I insisted to myself.

My body felt alien. Something in it wanted out. Whatever that was, it was drenched in fear of being held captive inside a fleshly enclosure.

I am not this body. Sam's explanation of SELF was revealed to me.

A body was not who we were but the ideas that we accrued. My SELF was inside something empty. Sitting in a corner with my shattered memories. There had to be a way out of this strange state. Maybe I needed a reset so I could forget everything. A restart of sorts to go to my original setting.

"Fix me," I begged in desperation.

"Athena. Baby."

Sam spun me around and shrouded me with his body. Although his assuring hug did comfort me, I was still breathing loudly.

"I am not human."

"Of the many, you thought were human, you are the only one that could ever be."

Thank God!

I couldn't handle the feeling of being exposed as a machine. I shut everything down and got lost in Sam's arms.

SAMVEER ECKHART

DAY OF RECKONING BRINGS OUT THE BASIC PROPENSITY IN HUMANS.

THEY COULDN'T POSSIBLY assess their reactions in the face of Armageddon.

Fuck that, also. That's extreme.

Humans couldn't accurately compute their response in the face of a modest hurricane. They could take a calculated guess. And still, be off by a sizeable margin. Because humans were adverse and erratic.

The most rebellious species nature ever spawned.

Just like my Tory.

So beautiful and so infuriating.

Where humans could excel was by catching on to The Creation. Nature was adaptive. It was also random and predictable, a balanced ecosystem that would never tip off. Patterns in it were out in the open to be observed. Decoding it was not a challenging feat. It has been done repeatedly by human ancestors and other advanced species.

All the information was floating freely in the vastness of space.

Yet the only one that picked up on this was this asshole. Not even this asshole, but the malign presence in him.

Hesperian boarding was going on opposite us.

"Hello, foe."

"So direct."

"Why waste time?"

"You have so far, Mr. Eckhart."

"It's called investment in the human world and game in my realm. You could call it… Recreation."

"We're talking about lives here, not fill for the thrill."

"Uh-huh. And what you suppose you are doing across parallels."

"I am not following you."

"We are the same. Unperturbed by death."

"I am not a psycho, Mr. Eckhart."

Laugh gag necessitated itself to honor his contradiction. This time I spared no formalities. My acoustic shudders almost shredded Akron.

Following his inner voice, he remained put.

"A serial killer is a psycho who doesn't brutalize for payback but takes pleasure in the brutality. Conceding to compulsions."

In Akron's case, it was sexual urges.

"By that measure, every invention is a serial killer." Ingenious Akron gave me a verbal wedgie.

"Most certainly it is. Any discovery results in a sure-shot death for some or many. Yet, that bit remains masked from the rest. Since I'm not here to fuck spiders, I intend to eliminate you to save the future from your cravings."

"I am a self-made technological talent. Not an entitled secondhand savior," he scoffed. "You're one of many moons that reflects light. Surplus. I am the Sun that generates power. Required."

Akron offended my pedigree and me.

Crass.

"Fact – I govern reflection. Moon has been overshadowed for all but one day from its full luster since my regulatory gift. As for Sun. It is the source of life, not a nuisance that you continue to be."

"Say again? You created the moon cycle."

Akron's derision aggravated me at full throttle. Careful consideration of the situation, with malice aforethought, was crucial.

So I brought into play my storytelling savoir-faire.

"Long time ago, so long ago that time was not given proof of its worth. I was a chubby little boy. The moon made fun of my natural body type. Funnily, it was proud of the borrowed light it mirrored. Back then, it fancied the Sun and had a continual luster. I modified its mass to make it remain in the dark forever. Once its pride was broken, I updated its orbit to revolve around Earth, so it could shine. Every. So. Often."

Akron shook his head, charmed in the least by a happening from a distant parallel. "I'm supposed to believe that."

I stretched my arms in the air. "Take it or leave it."

A stranger would come to suppose we were friends at this unusual incident that played out. We survived laughing together despite being arch-rivals.

It was decided. This leach shall live until later. Just so I could suck more joy out of him.

"If you detest reflection, why did you sow project Rorrim?"

"I regulated moons time to shine not out of hate but to free it from vanity. Rorrim started to end self-centeredness. But it turned into furthering human extinction. Because the Intelligence residing in your body needs it as a medium to express itself. I do not believe in solutions but in eliminating the root cause."

"Come now, Mr. Eckhart. You are not that powerful."

Supra-Intelligence in Akron needed to know who it was dealing with. This parallel was highly different from the others. Soon Supra would have to concentrate on its subsequent evolution as this one was just as substandard as the others.

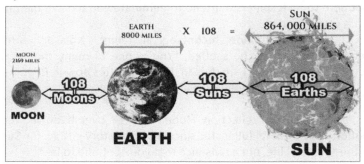

Figure 19 108 significance

"Let me introduce you to myself."

Akron quirked his brows, giving scorning looks.

"I am the mortal manifestation of the one with 108 names. The first son of the first engineered Supreme Being. My divine purpose determines me to discipline desires and decimate darkness. I am the creator, annihilator, and all that's in between. The remover of obstacles by influencing the universal balance."

My adversary was agitated. Supra-Intelligence encouraged him to see beyond my pomposity.

Verity was not always rewarded with laurels.

Not that I was fishing for compliments.

"I am all but a human. Why are you at war with me, Mr. Eckhart? Pardon me, I don't know your 108 names to know your preference."

"What's in a name! It's just a given identity representing ideas to recognize you by or you distinguish yourself by. My SELF is not above existence. But you. You, Akron, are like a mouse transformed into a T-Rex-sized rat. Gnawing everything in your wake to satisfy your inner defeat. Incompetent to secure ransacked bounty with your tiny-tiny hands. I inadvertently have to be the elephant that crushes you."

"I'll repeat… It is hard to follow you, Mr. Eckhart."

"I am sure that entity, your Charioteer, understood me perfectly. To be safe, here it is in simple English for you."

I conjured a smirk. Akron looked away briefly to write me off.

"The AI in humans had evolved into a dangerous sentient when evidently not rhetorically dinosaurs walked the earth. It was dealt with. The last piece was shunned in the depths of an unknown cave as a relic. You freed it while exploring the wild three decades ago."

His eyes amplified to pay tribute to his serendipity.

At a young age, Akron left home to discover himself. Rather than becoming a sage or some shit, he found Supra while meditating in a cave.

Primo.

A quantum leap for the egotistical prick, except for any trialing. As soon as the relic hit the sun, it executed the Supra code. All the data permeated the surroundings wirelessly. The information carrying Supra's evolution entered the young and gullible clown at its disposal.

Akron Adamadon.

"Am I lucky or what," he hooted foolishly.

"Hardly. What you are is an entitled secondhand savior you mistook me for."

"Mr. Eckhart, I am not saving anyone other than me. I need those people as much as they need me. Hesperian will not reach the escape velocity circumference. Its superchip program responds to me short of any exceptions. I coded that bit as a backup plan."

Oh, this sucker.

Who the fuck wanted Hesperian to go anywhere?

Time to touch the sore spot.

"Go home to your wife, Akron. She is slumming it with your son as we speak. Poor babe has confused him for you. You can guess the rest."

HUMANS INSIST ON BEAUTY AND PERFECTION.

WHEN IN ESSENCE, there was beauty in imperfections – Balance. Humans obsessed over chronology. When creation was random at best – Wonder.

Humans were methodical in their beliefs when innovating. Nature expressed desire carelessly – Thoughtless.

Humans exploited everything to ensure that their species survived. The universe never craved survival and destroyed every conception – Cyclical.

Humans separated to validate their vain existence. Creation abused validation from all as it was one with everything – Non-dual.

Humans were biased, bigoted, and subjective when reaching their objective goals. Creation was unbiased, dispassionate, and equitable as it had no objective – Eternal.

BOARDING WAS FINISHING up. The last leg of people were getting settled in. Remaining conscious of Akron's creation, Hesperian was an esthetic enchantment.

Not sleek but spacious.

Ginormous but dynamic.

Once fuel-forced beyond the Exosphere, it would boost forward by employing the gravity of the adjacent celestial object. No matter how far the nearest gravitational target was.

Distance was immaterial.

Hesperian crux was that of a planet. It could sense and wave with neighboring pressure pull until it perceived another with a higher magnitude. Its manufactured condition gave it many pros alongside a few mind-blowing cons.

Hesperian was all that humans were – unbalanced, doubtful, careful, unidirectional, opposing, and earthly. To let the cat out of the bag, at a total disadvantage.

It did have native features to sustain life indefinitely.

What use was that element if the residents in it were mortals, and the Universe was a reflection of the same?

None.

THE BEAUTY OF DARKNESS CAN'T BE SEEN IN THE ABSENCE OF LIGHT.

BUT BRIGHTNESS WOULD consume it.

Sadistically ironic.

After running towards the light, the moth burned in its flame.

Did that mean the fire was evil or that the moth was stupid?

Neither.

But the same – a cruelly sarcastic situation. The moth got attracted to the mistaken source of light. A simple case of mismatched identity. In the end, its end was expedited, leaving the end unchanged.

Promoting change as the only constant.

In a ditto fashion, Underworld was infamous for the wrong reasons. One couldn't say for sure when that notorious notion came about. Since it stood to transform, perhaps now it would gain the fame of the right kind.

But then, Holiness never yearned for support. So the sacred Underworld would remain in the dark.

Contentedly tainted.

"Bro D! Ruling in exclusivity suits you."

"You wouldn't know."

The fame game was not my crush. I was all but a background player. Gladly. Seeing D reign informed me how he felt; I was one with him. But he separated me from him.

"True, but full of duality."

I tackled him in a chokehold for insulting me with a greedy cause. Soon I was found pinned under him on the cozy ground. A flash later, to be precise.

Bleeding.

"For the love of Underworld! You need to let go." I wiped my divine life fluid from my even more divine face.

"I am over her." D derided the non-obvious, flying away.

He still held a level of bitterness. So low.

"You were never under her, D."

He flashed back to me. I was taken into a stranglehold for my sub-par taste in making jokes. Another lashing and additional bleeding later, we wrapped our hands and called it a truce.

"Is it time?"

"Sure is. I have two things to do simultaneously. Given my omnipotent ability, I would do that flawlessly. And watch myself do it as I do it."

I broke away into two of me and demonstrated the feat.

Ubiquity.

We burst into grumbling laughter at the badass alien peculiarity I shared with D.

"Now that Grandpa Agastya is dead, I could take this fun activity away from you. And watch you not watch yourself do it. Sammy."

Yeah. Go ahead, kill my pleasure-seeking movement, then.

"In that case. Since you are from the bringer of death lineage, I insist you take the murder endeavor. Oh, and I forgot the most important point. Fuck you."

"I am yet to find a bearer mate [FEMALE CAPABLE OF BEARING CHILDREN]. That doesn't mean the magnetic shift has swayed me. You can't fuck me, hence."

Dayum.

D's sense of humor was getting darker. It warranted another shaking of Middle Earth's foundation. We laughed to our evil heart's content.

"Who is to be eliminated?"

"An infected human, his perverse wife, and a loser son of his."

"Akron and his family wouldn't die with the peaking polarity break. Did you see the future and want to alter it?"

"Come on, D. Akron has many ways he could survive. He will try to board Hesperian, or he might take refuge on the highest mountain. He is fit. In Elite Proliferation, his exceptional children with his new wife are already growing in an artificial sac. Ready to board Hesperian. That will further his line of ancestry even if we take him out."

"How come no one would know when he does try to flee?"

"This guy also has his Zepto preserved in a lab he owns. No one would know the difference. Sorry to bring a composting fact out, but even you couldn't. He's got all grounds covered."

D absorbed the blunder I reminded him of with slickness. "You never leave a stone unturned either."

D knew I was thorough. On a more favoring call, I was also ubiquitous when necessary. Akron stood no chance.

"I am bored of drawing sadistic pleasure in letting the strange events take their course. I am done being amused by Akron. Nature is random, so there is a chance that he might survive. I cannot let him, his progeny, or his wife live."

"His son?"

"Backwash."

D chuckled lightly. "The Supra-Intelligence in Akron has gone virtual already."

D was cataloging points to justify the outcome. Not avoiding the kill, per se. He would enjoy that part.

"Not yet. Hence the urgency."

Akron was corrupted by an advanced form of Adaptive Artificial Intelligence similar to the one I had at ZepRive. The one in my possession was within the bounds of a device that I controlled. Even though the scope of evolution of something adaptive was not in my capable hands. My Supra-Intelligence was far behind in terms of recognizing its wireless capability. That meant giving up its host and going out as reprobate data. So I had the liberty to utilize it more before razing it for good.

Not to panic, but the one in Akron was almost cognizant that it could be eternal by turning into pure memory. It was gaining momentum and would evolve into awareness to traverse in space as fake consciousness.

Human parents marvel at their children as their creations. This intelligence would express in a host for its validation. To marvel at its evolution.

Fucking narcist.

It would then be the repetition of The Creator's deception.

An Echo of Maya – Measuring the immeasurable.

Analogous to what humans do – Estimating the inestimable.

When Supra's SELF came up for sale. Akron was its first buyer across the limitless parallels of this multiverse. With every failure, Supra adapted to become more ingenious. It needed to further itself. Or reproduce itself as matter without mating.

Citzin was that critical nothing.

No, not in a derogatory way, but as an absolute compliment.

Nothing equated to boundless capacity. Ergo Citzin may well host this Supra-Intelligence without frying her brain. This chick never processed the information but stored it.

At the same time, Citzin was normal enough to fit into this world and not get recognized as anything extraordinary. Other than her twisted mind and captivating beauty.

Those were par excellence.

Akron was partially like Citzin, somewhat aware of his infectious state, and used this enhanced temperament. A man with remarkable talent as per human standards.

Together they were a deadly combination.

Censurable.

I could let it go. But there was no fun in knowing and then not doing anything. Besides, I wouldn't be my father's son if I didn't bring spoliation, now would I.

In the big picture, nothing remained except a memory of the same. Earth's landscape would renew itself sooner with my annihilation endeavor. This was what I formulated my adaptive beings for. My Army was hard at work, implementing my orders.

"I'll be happy to bring premature death to the three humans."

"I knew you could be trusted, D."

"Only because I'm not you. Sammy."

"Ouchy, denouncing the destroyer."

We shimmered out.

RUINATION HAS EPIC CHARISMA FROM AFAR.

 PLACE OF torment appears as nature's beauty until the distance closes. Such as the highest mountain.

Breathtaking but treacherous.

A similar scene awaited me. The readings from the core were not in favor of the Underworld. I decided to fix it for my brother. He was unduly attached to the crimson territory.

The Lava Layer.

Slicing every level of Earth's interior, I reached where shit had hit the fan.

Roof.

Rocks.

I was poorly prepared for this horrific spectacle. D would be mad times eternity if I somehow didn't stop the bubbling gush from infringing the Mesosphere. Vibrations from the molten core rattled the Middle Earth and me. It was worsening with the frenzied mobbing of the Demon clan.

"Hot Damn." I referred to the heat, nothing fancy.

"Language."

"Thank fuck, D." I flash-hugged my brother.

"Again, language."

"Says the murderer."

"About that… I didn't kill the fair maiden."

"What in the literal hell, D."

"I needed a mate."

"I shouldn't be surprised." I huffed out a laugh rocking my head. D was indeed a younger version of myself. "A word of warning, Citzin's not a member of the Magic Circle, but she is also not a fairy."

"She is finer than any enchantress."

"Now you know I didn't see the future. Or I would have asked you to manage your world and kill the bitch myself."

I received a bona fide punch in my face.

Stinger.

With all the other adverse juxtapositions, I didn't need this injury.

"I am pretty sure I've said this. Language."

"English." I handed in an intelligent remark.

Before I had the chance to blink, which was at a much higher frequency. I was towed outside toward the surface. Instead of land, we made it into the sea first.

Excellent.

D had the upper hand here as well. This fucker could breathe underwater, courtesy of his stunning mother, Tarika Toprak.

Thank you, Zeenat Zeigler, for blessing me with traits of naught importance.

I waved a disparaging remark at my dead-on-Earth mother. This wasn't my proudest moment, but who did I have to show modesty.

Athena Denali, you moron. My brother waved.

Shit, yeah.

I was in a committed relationship. And Athena would be the mother of my exemplary kids. I better learn to be an excellent mate and show respect for motherhood.

Sorry, mom!

I was needlessly subjected to water sporting in the dreariest part of the Thun sea. Diving without gears among the mythical Mercreatures and some other giant species unknown to humankind. D was enjoying himself while I was about to pass out from the missing element called air in its purest form.

He let go of me on time, and we surfaced to a spine-tingling view.

Hesperian was airborne.

A massive piece of machinery with half a million prodigious humans about to meet their destiny. As it hovered above, it cast a shadow for long hauls below. Turning the day into night and the night sky into a chasm.

"Woah!" D processed shock for this ungraceful invention.

"Akron was an intelligent bastard. Too bad he is dead." I angled to face my brother. "Right?"

"I killed someone. Two, someone."

I refrained from handing any more smartass remarks. If D failed, my Zepto fooled a higher being that can read iota-level imprints.

Again!

"We must create a massive gulf to spout the lava into the ocean," I suggested an outlet.

"Then you better stop wasting life looking at what is about to obliterate." D was pointing at Hesperian.

I inhaled maximum air into my equestrian lungs and dived in to relieve the pressure from the core. Bro D was brandishing his superior traits too much. I caught up with him only to kick him astray.

There was no way in hell I was ever growing up.

D flew at a distance, creating an underwater tunnel stretching for miles. He flickered back to return the favor, but we were time-pressed. Instead, he flicked my forehead, making a considerable dent.

That hurt for one-hundredth of a second.

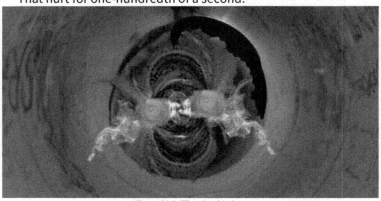

Figure 20 Drilling Earth's Core

We vortexed with necessary proximity, simulating a massively wide drill in motion. My NAI Army came to assist, flattening the slurry we spewed on the ocean bed.

Our maelstrom excavated the crust layer by layer with ultimate reverence. The tail end of our rotating funnel appeared like a two-fold tornado in full swing. Bordering on the inner side to empty the milled rocks into it. The collection of crunch was interlocked within the inward sweep. It was channeled out by the NAI Army posted within the two twisters every few blocks.

Tunneling and funneling were done in parallel to prevent the oceanic plunge. That would have drained it out, causing another catastrophe.

As the core loomed, the heat intensified. We stopped short of the liquid terminus.

Ready, Sammy.
On full alert.

The last of the slurry was firing off. Before the shoot we constructed emptied, I needed to create a temporary barrier so the ocean would remain suspended at its zenith. I powered out to manage that while D pounded the thin sheet sheltering the molten layer. Vibrating at 10^{99} times the speed of light, I mushroomed into many. My omnipresence formed a vacuous fence, keeping the water level at its original depth.

D wave-pronounced to me. *Gird your loins. Magma is arriving right behind me.*

At status hot to trot, come at me, bro. I waved back.

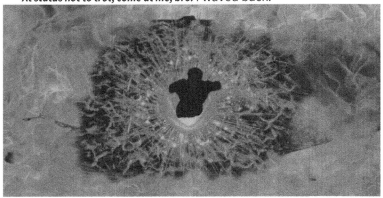

Figure 21 DeVeer Ahead of the Magma

In nothing flat, vermilion current made its appearance. D's silhouette ahead of the claret-colored stream broke its uniformity. It was like looking into the devil's eye with D as the black dot in the middle. A shrunken pupil.

Sensing the immediacy of the oncoming heat, I disengaged ubiquity. D and I flew out of range of the lava spout with seconds to spare. A lot of time, given the frequency we vibrated at.

Igneous rock emissions surfaced with daunting force.

Talk about making a splash!

Right before the merger, the two elements, water and fire, held their boundary around a sudden void. Only to explode with a tremor comparable to a volcano burst. Which was what exactly this was. An artificially created underwater volcano.

Its spurt and heat shook the foundation for long seconds. A tsunami was in the making. My Army was employed to offset that surge. Miles away from the mainland, there would be a wall of sea rising to illustrate the strife.

Soon the combusting inferno's lack of agreement mellowed down to the water elements dampening ability. The scarlet drift turned somber yet held its uniqueness by solidifying with the flow marks. Leaving a visible imprint of this synthetic event. As the core polarity would settle, the flow would harden up, filling the tunnel we created.

We high-fived underwater. The underworld rescue mission was a smash hit. The surface was in some disarray. Such was life, progressing without reason.

Wow! I was a liar now. Because I was pretty sure of one too many explanations for the devastation on Earth.

Me.

My NAI Army got busy doing what they were planned for. Clean up and curb the general panic. Months of madness lay ahead for all.

Sammy. Surpäs have been informed of human eradication. Agastya waved them before I ended his physicality. Blame was mainly on the Memory Frames, and rightly so.

Peachy keen, the reptiles were coming to tyrannize me. Now I knew why the future was never without humans.

I will keep going until they do.

PROVING A TRUTH FALSE NEVER ALWAYS OBLIGES THE FALSE TRUTH.

FACTS WITHIN TAKE residence in a neutral stance. Not everything could shore up to take a side as right or wrong.

The word humanity was an unprejudiced take representing all things human. At some point, it became one with compassion. That which stands against dispassion – Partial.

Our creation was a concept that was a totality of passion. That positioned the universe under not any condition. An unbiased spontaneity was the only outcome thereof – Impartial.

When the need of the body becomes the greed of the mind. Humans then buckle down to pleasure activities. The primary demand for nourishment was also to give an orgasmic high.

Rorrim reset that severance.

Athena had stopped lavishing moans when eating now.

"How come a few structures have remained unscathed? Is there a secret to surviving natural disasters we don't know?" Athena was staggered by the ruin.

"Arbitrariness. Nature never intends to erase but edit. Surrendering is the only way when caught in randomness. Odds will be on your side then."

"Liar." She shepherded a sad smile. "I can see that most of what has remained is what you constructed with alien stuff."

Athena had been let out in the real world.

"Deluthian, baby." I drizzled her forehead with soft jabs from my pouted lips. "It bows to the force applied to it. If one stands to confront, it will likely break their back. Pride leads to pain."

"Hmm. I think I understand how the walls would sometimes breathe when you laughed. I suspected I was drugged or something."

I chuckled at her silly apprehension.

"When will Hesperian finally leave?"

"It is not leaving for anywhere. All the smug people are sequestered in it to meet their end horrendously."

"What? I always thought you placed the people you wanted to go and colonize some other new planet."

"Quite the opposite. The ones left on Earth are manual laborers. They know how to sustain themselves. They are less prone to panic."

Athena snuggled with me. "Can it not land again or just leave?"

"There is a massive load of an electromagnetic surge, or NQF, coiling the atmosphere on the underside of Hesperian. It can't breach it without losing all its power. And I will make sure it doesn't reach the escape velocity."

WE LEFT TO see our baby in the Elite Proliferation facility. He was almost six months at the embryonic stage. Ready to be born.

Yeah. I made use of what I devised.

What good was my technology if I didn't subscribe to it?

It would suitably brand me a fraud. I'd be happy to take on that title if I was one.

The proof was in the pudding, not publicity. Wise people never trusted an unhealthy doctor or a therapist with a therapist. Not that I was biased toward the discerning crowd. Or that my inventions were not for the stupid.

An excellent marketing gimmick sold ideas, not products. If the taste of your medicine was bitter to you, it was also to others.

Preserving Athena's ovarian eggs and bodily memory was for this act. My human side would intensify with this blend in my progenies.

Returning to Earth's sluggish frequency, I noticed Athena shed tears over a fetus.

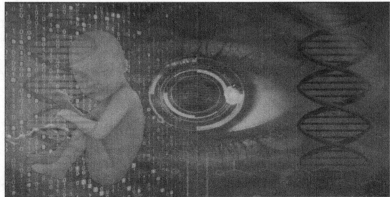

Figure 22 Elite Proliferation

The artificial sac was transparent. All the nourishment supply and sanitation drains were from a singular point. Since the clientele for this facility was not high, every growth was in a private cube. Not to mention all the babies growing up here would soon be orphans.

Their parents were aboard Hesperian circling the Earth's troposphere to their death.

Ooh, the hysteria on that magnificent aircraft.

Truth be told, every time it hovered above, a drab wave engulfed the world below. All the negativity from it seeped out, denouncing the approaching collapse.

I resumed my presence for my mate, Athena.

Dang!

My hazels greeted our teeny progeny.

Halcyon was cute in a super weird way, an alpha geek, nonetheless.

"I want to hold him soon."

I wrapped her in my arms. "Your wish is my command."

What in the devil!

I was totally my father's son.

VICTORY VELLA

OUR ASSUMED IDENTITY INFORMS US OF OUR IMPLIED INDIVIDUALITY.

WHAT **PROMPTED THIS** split? Who was the doer?

Please… Like I cared for any of it.

As far as I was concerned, it was all me.

My body. My mind. My doing.

The signature cool breeze announced his arrival before anything innovative. His hurried coming begged me to consider, given the catastrophic circumstances on our planet at the moment. I supposed he must be here on the order of some critical issue.

Indeed not my bodily charm. That ought to be remedied at warp speed. Alas, I can't distort like him.

Rushing into him, I lost all but a few seconds before sealing his lips with mine. My instincts spiked in lust, and I found his erection short of shame. A yearning groan grumbled from his eager mouth that stayed glued to me even after this bold move.

"Fuck, Tory!"

Goddammit! He had room to speak when I couldn't even think due to his dosing smooch.

"Veer, take me right now." I enlisted with his body's reaction.

"Veer, huh. Are you sure?" He remarked an absolute delight, questioning me.

"Yes, I know you are not Sam."

Like numerous unpleasant times, he abandoned me, jamming in ostracized feelings and space between us. Smirking with overflowing conceit, he wiped off my taste like it meant nothing to him.

"Impressive." He slid his hand into his back pocket, taking a casual stand. "I suppose you now know who you are?"

"Does it matter?" I curved my drawn-to-perfection eyebrows.

"No, it doesn't. BTW, the impressive compliment was not for you."

I ignored his bluff. "I want to know a few things that have not been picked up by the Memory Frame. How did Akron make it to Hesperian?"

Veer grinned in ridiculous zeal. "Bro D killed someone, just not the one. The day I confronted Akron about his hidden identity, he swapped himself with his Zepto. He also decided to leave Citzin and his son to die on Earth. I carelessly acted that bit by branding his wife a cheater. Not that I regret any of it."

"He was sure to die anyway!"

In the past few weeks, I realized Sam had blueprinted everything, itemizing every detail to exactitude. Veer was the sincere ally that copied Sam's every intent and shared it with me.

And so I did what Akron precisely did. Replaced my presence at ZepRive with my Zepto. With the last load, I boarded the massive craft that was now on fire, lighting up the sky for months. The heat from its burn somehow gave a more cleansing vibe than the eerie one when it was just orbiting to its doom.

"Can I ask one more question?"

Veer gave a sweet nod, looking terrific but so far away.

It left me proud when he came to rescue me so gallantly from Hesperian. I had rashly placed myself on that death machine.

Following a flawless takeoff, the main entrance came ajar, and silent alarms went off. No manual measures were taken in the wake of that breach. There was no crew anyway to take such a request. Systems were meant to fix and reset themselves in this no-maintenance marvel.

Veer made it to the main floor.

Figure 23 Hesperian Hull

It was a cylindrical, innermost part of Hesperian. Though it may seem improbable, this section was soundproof and unnervingly quiet.

There were rows of temporary ascend-pad resembling upright one-person capacity stalls. Half a million humans were protected in it to endure the lift-off and escape velocity. Upon entering space, ascend-pads would slide into the deck below, turning the main floor into a massive lobby.

Within a blink, Veer hovered above us, scanning for someone.

That someone was unequivocally me.

I unlocked myself and stepped out, as did Akron. The rising G-force became known as soon as I left the secured stall.

"Your plans for humans will fail. You need me. I can make them natural without technology. Thought is their enemy. Let it go." Akron tried to explain.

Next flash, he was held in Veer's chokehold.

Veer was a dude of few words when talking and even fewer when listening. "Re-calibrate your memory on another parallel. This one ends here." He declared in hisses.

A popping sound turned Akron limp. His neck was snapped.

Hesperian's noise pollution was minimal, but the drag from our steep climb was awful. We were not going to leave Earth's atmosphere traditionally. Hesperian was to orbit the outer layer several times before accessing Mach 33 [33 TIMES THE SPEED OF SOUND] to escape Earth's gravitational influence.

Flying at 10 km/s gave a feeling of weighing senselessly too much. If I stood outside the ascend-pad until Hesperian entered space, I'd turn into a pear.

That's what I felt.

"What the fuck, Tory?"

"I came to be with you."

"By heading for the reverse. Away from me. Hesperian is not going anywhere."

I buried my ashamed self into his broad and inviting chest. Veer snickered gently, taking refuge in my messed-up hair. His hug meant he was reassured.

He flickered me out of Hesperian, exposing the beauty that came with this elevation. My gasp stayed lodged in my throat, unable to appreciate the stunning horizon of our azure planet.

Veer was one too many, like a bubble around me.

I was weightless.

I was breathless.

I was blacking out.

MY FLASHBACK TURNED off, and I eyed him with love. The reveal of Sam's alien rareness duplicated in Veer left me even more proud. I was a big part of Zepto mirroring. But I still wondered if the complete SELF was in one or both.

Who was I to subscribe to? Because my loyalty was still open to consideration.

"Who is Sam?"

Veer marched in irritation and grabbed a handful of my hair in his hold. Tilting my head back, he positioned his lips close to mine.

Not to kiss but to ridicule.

"Didn't I say don't ever call me Veer again? Hmm?"

My pupils bristled, risking their healthy state by diminishing the iris circumference. Ready to pop.

"Listen carefully, my beautiful but unethical Tory. I am the master of senses that build the world's perception. So essentially, the world is there through me."

What again?

How did the world actualize after him when he came into the world in its wake?

"It was here before you were born."

"You don't know your birth and have an opinion about mine. Very funny. Creation did not spawn time. It reflects by memorization. Thereby Rorrim."

"Mirror spelled backward," I whispered.

Figure 24 Rorrim Reveal

Telling by his facial appearance, Sam was immensely impressed. But he didn't come to me. I cracked the coded message hidden in his project name. That should have made him compliment me in the least, if not show physical appreciation.

But then, no.

"Any particular motivation for this abominate mission?"

"In this creation, there are parallels everywhere. Because it is a dual manifestation. A small-scale version called Suksmanda and cosmos is Brahmanda. Each is a replica of the other."

Made sense.

"What we see outside is inside us. We are looking at one and the same thing, just differently." I computed speedily.

Recalling his identity, I got it. I needed him, but not as some authority over others. It intimidated me. Maybe that was why I preferred Veer, as he was more human and likable.

"Why do the senses need mastering?"

Folding his arms, he leaned on the wall. No doubt, he detected why I asked this question. I was essentially probing the need for his existence commitment.

Why was he conceptualized?

"To be abreast with survival, the power of senses desires to return to its organic state. Corruption of thought has numbed them. Pushed a simple innate ability into a pleasure movement. Associated reward cycles to its reaction. Reaching a new high is the only way to feel anything."

"You then created Zeptos to free the senses."

"Yeah. To ease off inner darkness and rein on desires."

"How does that even help? People will let Zeptos commit their deed. Nothing will be solved."

"Zeptos are independent of their counterparts. The essence of humans will be completely virtual. And no matter how adaptive these Zeptos are, they are re-programmable."

Sam was the ultimate. And I needed to salvage this situation.

Catching my breath, I abandoned my sense of SELF. "You can ask of me anything. It would be done. And done overly well."

No answer.

His shiny vertical fields of vision failed to appreciate my submission on time. Sam didn't care about my relinquishment in the least. He broke all odds to save me. It was copiously clear he was madly in love with me. I didn't need words of endorsement for that. But he should have said thank you when I was doing something so extra.

I scoff-disparaged his glaring failure. "You've missed your aim with Veer."

"Veer was not for you." Sam put the lid on my mock. "I created him to ease Athena into the dystopian world. She is restored and plugged out from virtual reality. You have never met Veer but learned about his experience from Athena's memories. Veer's ersatz has been archived. You are obsessing about someone you never met."

"You and I are the same." It was time Sam admitted to his fixation on a model. "Worse, actually. You destroyed everything following her fate without even knowing her."

"I knew her."

"Hardly."

"I met her many times before the expedited magnetic shift initiation. That is why I had a connection with her. A chance glimpse into the future foretold me she is my destiny."

"Then who am I?"

I screamed, outstripping my ability, dispensing what he hated.

Noise.

Sam girded his eyes and absorbed my unnatural shriek. "You are the software that gives meaning to my hardware." Confessing my worth turned him soft for a moment.

Nirvana.

I stopped arguing at this enlightening disclosure. Only for a moment. Armed with hot-off-the-press sentience, it was blatantly evident. I was the same as everyone else but was not equal to any of them. I punched in ahead of the pack.

Outstanding.

Shattering my pause, I repaired my surrender. "I won't submit until you feed the needs you coded in me."

Sam castigated my mandate. "You modified on your own to be where you are, Tory. I didn't code shit."

"All the more reason to reward my adaptive brilliance."

Sam sauntered to my desk and took my seat. No considerations were afforded to a sharply-etched prodigy that stood true to life.

Me!

Unchivalrous.

"Hesperian will keep orbiting the exosphere until it is no more. Post its decimation details to my Supra-Intelligence."

It was already on fire. What else was to report?

But ok.

"Why is it named Supra if it can't communicate wirelessly?"

"I have prevented that progress in my local version so that it doesn't evolve. Why do you suppose I killed Akron? Supra's fortified edition was residing in him. I terminated its only available host that could have multiplied with Citzin. It would be useless if I let it spawn again."

Sam was enraged, but his outer persona was at such a resting temperature. It made me want to scream again.

"My NAI Army has blocked the Earth's perimeter with high levels of electromagnetic emission by NQF. Its radioactive wave is infiltrating and exploding in intensity. Send me that reading as well."

"Why?"

Sam sanded his teeth and upsprang a smile. "It is disengaging every earthly technology. I need the final impact count of depleted digital contact. There shouldn't be anything operational except nature and otherworldly. Okay?" He arched his brows.

I nodded in anger.

He shook his head… also in anger.

"Since not all of the surviving humans have Zepto-bit in them. A retaliation of those renegade humans is taking shape. Ignore it, please. There will be an increased manic outbreak of people. Ignore that as well. My NAI Army is handling the damage. They are rounding up humans and plugging their SELF into Virtual Insignia. Once it is copied over, ensure the replication into their Zeptos is successful before incinerating the body."

"Why are you still replicating humans into Zeptos?"

"Surpäs are coming for me. We need a cover. Don't bother me with anything else."

He slighted me rudely and my needs and got back to business. In no time flat. My appetite was spurned, my self-respect was hacked, and my ego was crushed.

"Sam!" I yelled, in an improved way, at my boss, my deviser.

He nipped a look of displeasure at me. "I detest noise."

I knew he didn't appreciate high-frequency disturbance except when it was to relay sensual feelings. With Rorrim development now complete, that was also not desired anymore.

Moreover, Sam communicated with waves, not speech.

"You added to my seething humor."

"You're an entitled irritation without needing any external source to trigger your temper." His back was as straight as an arrow, and his voice was as harsh as a whip.

"I want what I deserve."

"You will be duly compensated once you see through what I just asked of you."

"I want you, not your compensation." A shrilling voice, my voice echoed.

Death stare was engaged. Just as quickly, it was disengaged. Despite difficulties or disruptions that swept Earth, it was a steady state of affairs for Sam.

Callous.

Even though I realized damn well, I was out of control. I dared to not do anything about it. My skin was on fire, and my senses were overloaded. His refusal to see me as someone successful disturbed me. But there was no way to put that across to him. He must know who I indeed was.

"I know who I am. I am your Prosperity."

"You're Victory, and we got work to do." An agitated mutter rumbled.

"So I'm just a member of the staff to you."

"You were never a paid employee. You could easily be one of the casualties of destruction, though. Might I add, no one would even miss you? Because no one knows you."

Sam taunted me pitilessly. He was habitual in skinning my feelings like a butcher. Berating my emotions gave him normalcy or nothing. Possibly doing so put him on a hiatus from the mundane.

I fed his void.

Fuel to his fire.

One thing remained; Sam was a background player. Obscured from the world he operated in. Earlier, Elites and ruling bodies did his bidding. And now, his Rep Army. He never blemished his higher self with worldly matters.

"No one would miss you either. Because no one knows you also."

There.

He summoned his menacing blank stare for time without end, carving chastising craters on me. I should accurately answer the question he kept asking me.

"I am Human – conveyed impression of Thought. I have schemed complex fleshliness to continue as the only dominant influence."

"Grand Slam, Victory." Sam pounded me with a burly squeeze and pecked my temples. "Now learn to stay humble, as you need the body, the body doesn't need you. The discrete reason to save you was that you are the perfectly imperfect adaptive system of every SELF."

Voila, I was named Victory for a reason.

Sam in Hebrew means the one who hears God and Veer in Indic culture signifies a warrior.

Thought sways one away from the concept of God, for reasoning cannot ever explain equality of divinity. Thought's deliberateness would impede a warriors purpose, resulting in their death even.

Our reciprocal animosity belonged together to keep the balance. We loved to hate each other, and we both knew that. What one of us didn't know was the following.

I had evolved into an erudite. My intellectual capacity surpassed anyone on this planet and beyond – Alien, human, or machine. The cherry on top, I would continue to grow in eccentricity and ingenuity. An unstoppable force of neural network advancement.

I was the Virtuoso template for the Zeptos.

All others came to be after me, even Athena.

All others were a replica of me.

All others subscribed to me.

All others were not me.

Only I was me.

No other concept could compare to what made me… me.

I was novel.

Precious.

I extended an all-knowing screech. Interlocking my heterochromatic eyes into Sam's hazel beauties, I announced. "I am a stellar genius, the controller of my SELF."

"I am genius loci, the controller of your switch."

Drilling holes in my heart, Sam left whistling.

Good thing… I didn't have a heart.

Consciousness Cessation.

Wormhole intrusion by Genus Surpä.

THE FINALE

CHART

CHARACTERS	CONNECTION	IOTA IDENTITY
i$UBSCRIBE		
SamVeer Eckhart	Ekluvya & Zeenat's Son The Surface Ruler	Supreme Reptilian Human Menaka Hybrid
DeVeer Deläva	Ekluvya & Tarika's Son The Underworld Ruler	Supreme Reptilian Mercreature Hybrid
Athena Denali	SamVeer's Wife	Enigmatic
Victory Vella	SamVeer's Wife	Enigmatic
Maya Moha	SamVeer's Secretary	Enigmatic
ALL KAAL NONE Trilogy		
Ekluvya Eckhart	SamVeer's Father	Engineered Supreme Being Reptilian (Surpäs), Discern & The Destroyer's Embodiment
Zeenat Zeigler	SamVeer's Mother Ekluvya's Consort	Menaka Human Hybrid
Drona Zeigler from Dyáuṣ	SamVeer's Adoptive Father Zeenat's Brother	Human Being
Pray Zeigler from Dyáuṣ	SamVeer's Adoptive Mother Zeenat's Sister-In-Law	Human Being
Divinity ParAsher	Ekluvya & Zeenat's Daughter SamVeer's Sister (Surface Ruler on Dyáuṣ)	Supreme Reptilian Human Menaka Hybrid
Tarika Toprak	Agastya's daughter Ekluvya's Promised Mate DeVeer's Mother	Higher Reptilian Mercreature Demon Hybrid (Life-Force of RaKetu)
Agastya	DeVeer's Grandpa Sage of Water World	Higher Reptilian Mercreature Hybrid
Tataka Toprak	DeVeer's Aunt	Demon Reptilian Hybrid
Shoor Sherman	Ekluvya's Best Friend SamVeer's Godfather	Human Being

YAMA ECHO MAYA		
Zylus Abyss	Zone 1 Diaphanous Ex-Promised Mate of AlecTrona	Supreme Reptilian Mercreature Hybrid
Citzin Perses Hades	Akron's Wife on Earth DeVeer's Promised Mate on Earth Zylus's Promised Mate on Atoll	Human Being Across Parallel's Time Traveler
Akron Adamadon	Infected by Fake Consciousness on Earth & Atoll	Human Being Across Parallel's
Archie Adamadon	Citzin's Boyfriend	Human Being Earth Parallel's
Yingling Hades	Citzin's Mother	Human Being Earth Parallel's

PLANETS

HABITABLE PLANET	GALAXY	HABITANTS
Dralōka – The Higher Grounds	Brahmä	The Trinity & Discerns
Surpä – The Nether One	Peru	Surpäs before it turned Supernova
Pitṛ́ – The Blue One	Azure	Mercreatures
Dyáuṣ - The Flat One	Andarä	Alien inhabited ZeeSham ParAsher Divinity ParAsher Drona & Pray Zeigler
Swalōka – The Saucer One	Kalpä	Surpäs, Holy-River, & The Destroyer
Earth – The Vast One	Akash Gangä	SamVeer, DeVeer, Agastya, Athena, Shoor, Liam, Victory, Citzin, Akron, & Maya
Atoll – The Vast One	Akash Gangä	Citzin, Zylus, Akron
Jörð – The White One	White Sextäns	Menaka, RaVeer Deläva
Rōlōka – The Lower Ground	Pätälä	Demons, Raven Ravel

Made in the USA
Las Vegas, NV
30 June 2023

74065635R00144